UGLY DOGS DON'T CRY

DD ARMSTRONG

JACARANDA

TWENTY
in 2020
Black Writers, British Voices

This edition first published in Great Britain 2020
Jacaranda Books Art Music Ltd
27 Old Gloucester Street,
London WC1N 3AX
www.jacarandabooksartmusic.co.uk

A CIP catalogue record for this book is available from the British
Library

ISBN: 9781913090272
eISBN: 9781913090470

Cover Design: Rodney Dive
Typeset by: Kamillah Brandes

Printed and bound by CPI Group (UK) Ltd, Croydon, CR0 4YY

This book is dedicated to the memory of
my late cousin Jermaine '*Jay-Jay*' Fisher
&
Mr Emmanuel Omokoledola Adenitire

Prologue

Kyle Jones despised being questioned by strangers. If he didn't know the person quizzing him, even the smallest of questions could feel like an interrogation. He wasn't suspicious by nature, but his spirit never took to having to explain himself. So any type of probing that wasn't to his liking could easily test his patience—especially if it came in a sequence:

"When last did you see the victim before the incident?"

"Why?"

"We're just trying to establish your movements beforehand."

"Why?

"Kyle your fingerprints were found on the murder weapon."

"What does that matter?"

As a child Kyle's mum had often told him, "Kyle, don't answer my question with a question, do you understand?"

He did. His mother's words were often filled with the oxymora of her Caribbean upbringing and the hypocritical nature of parents. She could be stern and demanding, and at times liked to call him a 'Human Why-ing Machine,' but there were still levels to who Kyle Jones was willing to share or distribute information with. Where he was from, answering a question wasn't always just answering a question. His older cousins had beat that into him from a young age. There were consequences to who you spoke with. A thin line in how much a person should convey, and questions were designed with one purpose. The difference between punishment and reward, stigma and accolade hinged on two factors—the agenda of the person asking, and how you answered.

So by instinct whenever questioned, a series of counterarguments ticked away in the back of Kyle's mind. *Who are you to question me? Have you earned the right to a sufficient answer? What do you gain from my answer? And where does answering you leave me?* If Kyle couldn't satisfy he own inquisition, he had an inherent mistrust for those who posed too many questions.

So when he was contacted by Mansfield and Thompson, one of the top legal firms in London, he was apprehensive. He knew that if he agreed to attend there was no turning back. His every word would be open to scrutiny and anything he said could be put down on file and possibly used against him.

Normally Kyle would've scoffed at that. He was too familiar with professionals from the legal justice system. They didn't scare him. He had been paraded in front of police officers, detectives, solicitors, barrister, QC's and hawk-faced judges that peered down at him just long enough for Kyle to meet their eyes and scowl back. He had spent hours in the dock, mouth dry and asking for water as legal wizards tried to dissect and pick holes in his testimony. Spinning their spells. He had listened as they berated and fiercely rebuked his account as a pack of lies. He'd studied the reaction of enchanted jury members as they heeded warnings of his personal vendettas. Too many times he had looked towards the public gallery where guards separated feuding families while in the midst a victim's mother cried, only to be consoled by those who sought retribution in the guise of justice.

Kyle wasn't scared of legal people and their umpteen questions. Why? Because he had studied the law himself. He'd studied it in a way that most of the people at Mansfield & Thompson would never understand or appreciate. So why did he feel so nervous?

Sitting in the waiting area suited and booted in a white shirt, tie, and navy suit, Kyle felt like a foreigner. He was an alien in the truest form. He looked around at the paralegals and barristers that buzzed around the office like bees in a hive. They were the types he'd seen all his life, on their way to work carrying the huge leather satchels and stacks of files in their hand. The type that didn't give people like him a second glance outside the courtroom or police stations unless it was to calculate whether they could reach the empty seat on the train before him. Even now he was still invisible to them. He watched as they worked in a hum akin to a war room, performing in a chaotic harmony, dodging archive boxes, passing folders and printing documents as though this were their natural order.

He sat in wonderment and asked himself, 'What am I doing here?'

He concluded this wasn't his world. No one looked like him, no one moved like him, and no one really wanted to see him....

Then one person caught his eye.

The moment he stepped in, his aura screamed at Kyle and

wooed his attention. The tall figure was an outsider. He leaned on the reception desk and with long spider-like fingers signed the logbook. His hood obscured his face like an assassin, or Death. His presence rattled Kyle, but as he came closer Kyle recognised something about his long limbs and thin frame. He recognized the heavy stride and bad man bop. Kyle recognized the roadman uniform of black hooded top, jogging bottoms, black gilet and Air Force Ones as though he had issued it himself from a JD Sports. As the man dropped and slouched into the seat opposite, Kyle knew he recognised everything about this man—but from the expression on both their faces, it was obvious neither of them actually knew each other.

For a moment the man eyed Kyle curiously, not seeming to know what to make of him in his navy suit. It was clear that Kyle must've been an anomaly to him, something strange that didn't belong. He frowned and his dry face was full of angst. He looked like he had just got up and this extra puzzle vexed his lack of sleep. He shifted in his seat, sizing Kyle up, then snorted. Restless, he checked his surroundings like Kyle had, then turned to the potted plant on the side table of magazines and gobbed in it. His green, phlegmy spit soaked the dark soil and he rubbed his thick, uncombed hair before picking up a GQ magazine. He flicked through, seeming uninterested in the pages, but instead using the magazine as a prop. He tossed it back down, and then looked up at Kyle, daring him to glare back. Kyle smirked and met his gaze, and the two outsiders entered into unspoken ritual that was invisible to the foreign world around them. Unbeknown to the hooded man, Kyle grinned because he knew they were polar opposites on the same spectrum. He could have broken the ice and reassured the man he was no threat to him, but that's not how the ritual goes. Instead he tilted his head and glared back, waiting for the man's next move. The longer they stared at each other, the more the man would have to say something or look away. The man looked away, but he wasn't done. He turned back again, leaning forward to sit on the edge of his chair.

"You good, bruv?" he said, escalating the ritual to the next stage.

Kyle face stayed placid. His grin didn't move and he replied, "More than."

His answer threw the man and Kyle watched him calculating his next move.

"What ends you from?"

Kyle chuckled to himself, but before he could answer the receptionist called his name. "Mr Jones? Mr Mansfield is ready to see you now."

At the sound of the prestigious barrister's name the man sat back and looked at Kyle, intrigued. Kyle stood up and fixed his the crease in his trousers. He looked at the man trying to work out the enigma in front him and said, "I'm from West, blood. But man are bigger than da ends, you get me?"

Outclassed, the man smiled. The ritual was over and Kyle gave him a cheeky wink before disappearing towards Mansfield's office.

Their brief encounter knocked the edge off Kyle's nerves and he felt more assured as he entered Mansfield's office. He found the QC sitting behind a large vintage ebony wood executive desk, reading a document. He wore a pair black of Ultra Goliath frames like Elliot Gould in *Ocean's 11*. Looking up at Kyle he smiled and offered him a seat. His deep voice rumbled in a baritone pitch that had the magnitude of thunder. Although he barely exercised it, Kyle was fully aware of Mansfield's vocal dexterity. His reputation preceded him. Barristers weren't just bestowed the honour of Queen's Counsel for length of service. Robert Mansfield had over 40 years of experience trying high profile cases. From defending IRA suspects, to prosecuting warlords in The Hague, fighting right wing racists and police corruption, 'Our man Bob', as the press nicknamed him, was a legal giant. Closing the document, the heavy-set man in his seventies removed his glasses. His thick white mane reminded Kyle of his old college principal, with the addition of a side parting. Without the thick frames the heavy bags under Mansfield's eyes were visible, and experience hung from the jowls around his cheeks. Leaning back, he rocked in his chair and studied Kyle. Raising a bushy eyebrow, he looked like a grizzly bear chewing a piece of bark as he gnawed the arm of his glasses.

"Kyle Jones, is it?"

"Yes, Sir."

"Nice to meet you, Mr Jones" he said taking a sip of water. He flicked through the paper once more. "This is a very bold paper young man. Did you write it yourself?"

For a nanosecond Kyle frowned. He didn't like that question, but before he could say something stupid his inner voice screamed *professionalism*. Masking his annoyance, he smiled politely and replied, "Unfortunately."

"Good, good," Mansfield said scratching his ear. "It's a well written piece with lots of ambition, lots of vigour. Your case study is well researched, very analytical."

Kyle went to thank Mansfield again, but the man held up a huge paw. "However, there is something that disturbs me about it." He paused to think. He licked his lip, tasting the air, and said, "I don't get a full sense of you. You've been smart and elegant with your arguments, but I want an insight into you. Tell me what made you want to practice law?"

As Mansfield posed the question, the pistons in Kyle's mind were already firing up his cognitive engine, and he wondered where answering would leave him.

Part I

Dear Summer

CHAPTER 1.1

So long as the Thames has flowed through London, it has always been a city of two faces—a sprawling metropolis of the haves and the have-nots, and a municipality of dreams and broken promises. When the Romans built the city's first bridge they turned London into a nexus of trade and drew a line for all to follow. Those who can afford it may settle here, and those who cannot may learn to aspire. And so London's population has always grown with aspirations and exasperation for most of the time with very little toleration of those who live on the wrong side of the line. Underneath the tenements of Beer Street and Gin Lane, you'll find the remnants of Saxons, Vikings, Normans and Moors that testify to the dreams of the poor and London's first melting pots. A time when cultural diversity meant paki or wog and signs told the Irish they were on the level of dogs. The city has always invited the influx of dreamers, from Caribbean shores to apartheid lands, and bullet ridden states with Eastern blocs. The common wealth of London has been entrenched and enriched by every wave of immigrant. By those who made their homes in the slums and squalor of Brixton and Ladbroke Grove, creating communities and raising the value of property, only to be duped by gentrification. London weighting has never meant that Londoner's are waiting or weighing their options and so in these pocket communities where credit is universal, there is a commodity on dreams.

Less than a mile away from the looming figure of Grenfell Tower, past the ivory apartments of Kensington, Notting Hill and the trappings of the Westfield shopping centre, the sun began to dip over the burgundy bricks of White City estate. Lapping up the last days of summer, Kyle made his way home from playing football in Wormholt Park. Nearby, the sound of police sirens screeched in the air. As the sirens drew closer, two teenage boys on a stolen moped roared pass Kyle. The passenger held up two fingers to the pursuing police car and yelled, tapping on the rider's helmet,

"Oi blud! Bust left, bust left!!"

Masterfully, the rider dipped the red scooter, did a U turn, then whizzed into the estate. By the time police were able to maneuverer their car and give chase it was obvious to Kyle they had no chance of catching Custard and Crazy Ish as they disappeared into the maze of blocks.

Laughing, Kyle passed the dingy row of shops on Bloemfontein Road that sat opposite the new Sainsbury's Local and a modern set of new-builds. They had replaced the once focal Janet Adegoke swimming pools and were another sign of London's duality and class divide which created a simmering tension from residents of the old estate as they witnessed the council's promises of redevelopment manifest into a transfer of resources.

Kyle had lived on the White City estate all his life and

at sixteen he had begun to realise that no matter whether the council called it redevelopment or regeneration nothing ever really changed; they just rehoused and evicted people, that's all. He remembered on his last day of school his form tutor Mr Tulloch had said to him, "Kyle your mind is the most powerful thing you possess. If you have the power to change how you think, you have the power change your whole life." He pondered how many people in his estate still possessed their minds, because they seemed powerless to change anything.

Entering the labyrinth of low-rise blocks, Kyle listened as the sirens faded away. For a moment the estate felt still and the aroma of somebody's laundry filled the air. Making his way down Australia Road the sun blared in his eye and he shaded his brow. Squinting, he saw a familiar figure in the distance and smiled. Instantly he recognised the tall frame and lethargic bop as the person strolled ahead. The signature blue rucksack that sat between his broad shoulders was a dead giveaway as he slowly rocked from side to side with every step.

"Yo!" Kyle yelled after the tall figure. Jogging to catch up, he called another two times before the figure turned around. Although his face barely moved, Kyle recognised the slight curve at the side of the young man's mouth and labelled it a smile. It was accompanied by the slightest of head nods as he waited.

"Yo Siddy, wha gwan?" Kyle said, holding out his fist.

"Nothing," the tall teenager said, shrugging his shoulders. He bumped Kyle's fist with his huge hand and gnarly knuckles. Peering past Kyle, he checked the rest of the street and said, "I just picked up some new supplies."

He spoke with a soft and sombre voice that was characterised by a slight slur, and Kyle could tell he had something on his mind. Sideeq Gustav had stopped being a big talker by the age of twelve and life had made him somewhat melancholy. The smooth brown scar that wound from above his left eyebrow past his temple and across his left ear in a snake-like fashion told a sinister story. It made the glass eye that sat between its tail easy to misconstrue, and left his cinnamon brown face a constant enigma. At times it could look dark and restless, yet completely void of any expression. Yet the more you looked at it, the more it invited you to ask. His placid demeanour made him even harder to read. Kyle knew exactly why. Unlike most of his friends, Sideeq had become a deep thinker long before his time and preferred to wrestle with his own thoughts. If he welcomed your opinion he would let you know when he was ready and not before. With this in mind, Kyle decided not to probe. Instead he fell into step with the solemn giant.

Standing at 6'3, Sideeq dwarfed Kyle's 5'6 stature and some would never believe Kyle was the older of the two. Physically they were complete opposites. One was built like a tree trunk with powerful arms and long legs. While the other was thin and slender and appeared light enough to blow away in the wind. From a far they looked like a duo from a classic Steinbeck novel. They walked in a comfortable silence until Kyle asked, "Did your mum cook?"

Head straight, Sideeq completely ignored him. Kyle, looking at the scar by Sideeq's ear, shook his head. He stuck his foot between Sideeq's legs and tripped him up. As his friend stumbled,

Kyle moved toward Sideeq's right side so he could be seen by Sideeq's good eye. He spoke slowly.

"I said, did your mum cook?"

"Hmmm," Sideeq murmured. He reached into his pocket and brought out a beige coloured hearing aid, fitting it in his left ear. "She cooked oxtail."

"What, enough for me?" Kyle grinned with a glutton's glare.

"No, enough for me." Sideeq cut his eye.

"So what, you saying I can't get a plate?"

"Bruv, whatever you get is between you and my mum—after I've dished my plate."

"Rah, Sid!" Kyle took a step back and put a hand on his chest, pretending to be offended. "Are really gonna begrudge me a plate?"

"I ain't begrudge shit." Sideeq tried not to entertain Kyle with smirk. "I'm just saying."

"Nah, you are, bruv," Kyle started to play act, when a text message beeped on his phone. "Nah, I can't believe this, G," he said, taking his phone out. "I thought you were my guy—"

Kyle stopped mid-sentence and Sideeq watched him as his eyes scanned over the text again. "Oh shit!" Kyle covered his mouth in shock.

"What is it?" Sideeq asked, but Kyle held up a finger silencing him then started to text back. As he replied, a big grin blazed across his face.

"Yo, what's going on?" Sideeq asked again.

"Oi, come, come! We gotta go to your yard now, man, now!"

Kyle bounced in the air and started pulling Sideeq's arm. He was already half way down the road before Sideeq even moved.

"Oi cmon Sid man, Monte said he just sent Touch One and Sharkey G my track to play on Reload."

Chapter 1.2

DJ Touch One's set was in full flow as Sideeq locked his Bluetooth speaker onto ReloadFM. From downstairs Kyle could hear the electronic sounds and gritty Grime beats playing as he impatiently peered into the microwave. Counting down the seconds on the LED display he watched his plate of oxtail rice and peas, macaroni pie and steam vegetables heat up. Reaching into the fridge he grabbed a can of strawberry Nurishment and filled a tall glass before taking a sip. Inspecting the salad Sideeq's mum had made, he checked the timer, calculating whether he had enough time to dish a side plate. Grabbing a colourful metal tray decorated with West Indian flags and some cutlery, he darted to the microwave as the timer hit zero and eagerly popped open the door, sliding the piping hot food on to his tray. Rushing upstairs, he followed the coarse rhythms and break-beats to Sideeq's bedroom and planted himself in the middle of the bed.

Carefully balancing the tray, he kicked off his shoes and shuffled until his back was against the wall, and rested his drink on the bedside cabinet. Looking up, he studied the artwork on Sideeq's walls. They were like a living art exhibition, covered in an array of sketches, ink drawings, graffiti letters, stencils and prints.

You could always tell when Sideeq had found a new artist because their influence would soon find their way upon his wall. Whether it was renowned artists like Monet, Van Gogh or Picasso, or contemporary street art like Shepard Fairey, Osgemeos, Swoon or C215, Sideeq would mimic the style and slowly merge it into his own. At the bottom he would tag the pieces with the moniker DE-1, which was short for *'Deaf-Eye One'*.

Kyle wasn't necessarily fond of the tag and preferred to call him Black Banksy, until Sideeq told him, "I don't need to be the black version of any artist when I can be DE-1—or de one, as in thee one." The double meaning behind the name had flown over Kyle's head at first, but once he understood, he never called Sideeq Black Banksy again.

Stripping the meat off some oxtail, he studied the new pieces of artwork. They were a collection of A2-sized portrait pictures that were laid out in five panels to make one panoramic piece. They were drawn in pencil and shaded in watercolour tones of grey with splashes of diluted red. Sideeq had then outlined the detail in black markers, which added to the scene he was trying to capture. The panels depicted a view of Shepherds Bush Market from the train tracks above as the train wound pass. Each panel was framed by what Kyle realised was the train doors and windows along with the heads and shoulders of passengers. The concept was amazing, and on any other day Kyle would be jumping around excitedly praising Sideeq's brilliance—however, not today.

Today was one of those days when the luxury of sitting within Sideeq's living exhibition had a darker privilege. His artwork could be so brutally honest that it had the ability to transport you from the confines of his bedroom right into the depth of his mind. Here you got a clear insight into his thoughts and witnessed the unspoken manifest itself to life.

Chewing his food, Kyle eyed the middle panel. Swallowing, he noted the scribbled detail of the market stalls with their pots and pans, fabric, haberdashery, fish, meat, fruit and veg all on sale. He could imagine himself amongst the hustle and bustle of the market. Sideeq had captured it well. However, what troubled Kyle was the depiction of the young black boys in the market. There was a group of four boys running through the centre of the stalls. It was hard to tell their exact age, but they were in a red school uniform with red striped ties, blazers and jumpers and black rucksacks or jackets. With their long limbs, Kyle gathered they were teenagers. The pack seemed to be in pursuit of another two boys. These two were smaller and one boy had managed to make it on to the fourth panel. They wore a darker toned uniform of black and grey shades and their red rucksacks looked huge on their tiny backs. These two seemed younger and Kyle thought he saw fear in their eyes, but Sideeq's pen work, as always, left it open for interpretation.

"Is that Bush market?" Kyle asked, reaching for his drink.

Sideeq, who was putting away his supplies, looked up for a moment to register the question, but didn't bother to answer, although he had his hearing aid in.

"Whose style is that you've incorporated?" Kyle quizzed. "I ain't never seen you draw a cityscape that deep."

"It's a mix."

"Of who?"

"Deathburger and Stephen Wiltshire."

"Who's that?"

"Artists, innit" Sideeq grunted.

"Durr, I know that."

"Well, what else you want me say?" Sideeq replied

"Nothing, bruv, nothing," Kyle said, shaking his head.

He looked at Sideeq, thinking *sometimes this guy can be such a paigon*. Shovelling a fork full of rice and peas into his mouth, he decided to change the subject. He was still excited about his earlier text and eager to hear his song on the radio.

"Oi, bruv I beg you text the station again, Touch One needs to hurry up and play my tune."

"In a minute."

"Why can't you do it now?"

"Coz I said in a minute."

Kyle frowned. It was unlike Sideeq to not share his enthusiasm. He knew how much being played on radio meant to Kyle; that was an understatement. They had often talked about both becoming emcees as young boys in the back of class or on the long way home from school. Together they had aspired to be two of the best emcees in London, up there with the likes of Dizzee Rascal, Wiley, and Kano. Getting played on pirate stations and then mainstream was always the first step in their master plan, and although Sideeq's passion had slightly changed, Kyle thought his best friend would be happy for him. Instead, he was pottering around in a mood. Kyle watched Sideeq as he sat down at his desk. He took out a bunch of thick nibbed marker pens, then

DD ARMSTRONG

wiped off an old pair of Nike Air Forces for customizing. He began studying the shoes against his sketch pad before drawing on the side of the sole.

Kyle sniggered to himself. Wiping the gravy off his fingers, he decided it was time to rattle Sideeq's cage.

"So what you saying big man, you don't want text the station for me, no?"

"I said I'd do it in a minute."

"Cool, that's cool, say no more. In a minute, yeah? That's calm, innit," Kyle said nodding on the bed. He knew how to play this game. He was a master at it and pushed his piece a little further.

"Bruv, it's only true say I'm eating that I'm asking, you know. Otherwise I would do it myself. It's no big ting innit, but if it was me, I woulda just sent text the one time, no long ting. It's not gonna hurt man to send it, but minor."

"So why don't you put down the food and send it then!" Sideeq slammed down his pen.

"Rah, what you shouting for, bruv?"

"Coz it's like y-y-you don't hearrr," Sideeq fumed. The angrier he got the more pronounced the stutter in his speech became. "You just keep going on and on."

"Going on about what?" Kyle played dumb. "All I asked was for you to send a text. You ain't gotta get vex y'know. You're gwarnin' like you don't wanna hear the tune."

"B-b-b-blud, I gotta b-b-bigger things on my mind than your friggin' t-t-tune."

And there it was. That's what Kyle was waiting to hear and

25

Sideeq knew it. They both fell silent, looking at each other as the MC on the radio's lyrics filled the room.

Sideeq was the first to drop his gaze, and turned back to customize his old trainers.

"So what's on your mind?" Kyle asked.

"Just leave it, bro"

"Bruv." Kyle put his tray to the aside and perched on the side of bed. "You might as well speak up, coz you know I ain't going nowhere till I know what's going on."

Sideeq swivelled his chair round to face Kyle, but he couldn't look Kyle in his face. His broad shoulders were slumped and he seemed defeated, before he had even begun to share. He was nervous and played with the markers in his hand. Patiently Kyle waited while he composed himself.

"Take your time, bruv."

Sideeq let out a huge sigh then looked up. Kyle could see the anguish in his one good eye.

"My mum said the probation service called here the other day." Sideeq paused.

"And?" Kyle said impatiently.

"They said that Nana is up for parole."

"What?" Kyle sat up, not believing his ears. "Are you serious?" From the look on Sideeq's face it was no joke. "But that don't make no sense. His still got another four years."

Sideeq shook his head. "They reduced his sentence to seven and a half on appeal."

"When?" Kyle scowled, hearing this information for the first time.

"Last year." Sideeq dropped his head. He knew Kyle would question why he hadn't said anything so continued speaking, "Which means he's severed almost three quarters of his sentence, and he's eligible for parole on good behaviour."

"Nah!" Kyle hopped off the bed shaking his head. Furious, he started pacing up and down. "Nah man! I ain't having this. This is some bull-fraff."

Kyle was about to start ranting, then he stopped, looking at Sideeq sitting silently in his chair. His face was covered in a veil of turmoil and angst as tension visibly powered along his jawline. Kyle turned towards the panel pictures on the wall. It all started to make sense. Realising that he was hijacking Sideeq's moment to share, he simmered down and took a seat on the edge of the bed. He lowered the volume on the Bluetooth speaker.

"Bruv are cool? How'd you feel about all dis?"

"I don't know," Sideeq shrugged. "It's a madness innit." Sideeq let out a deep sigh. He ran his palms over his face and looked up, covering his mouth as though he was going to pray.

"They said that he wrote a letter to me." Sideeq chuckled at the irony. "They said I don't have to accept it, but it's their duty to let me know."

"Eff that." Kyle scowled. "You don't need my man's letter, he's just tryna get parole."

"Yeah I know." Sideeq nodded and inhaled, closing his eyes. He continued to nod as though he was assuring himself, before exhaling. It was a silent cry and Kyle heard it. Leaning forward he tapped Sideeq on the knee. Opening his mismatched eyes, Sideeq turned to Kyle.

"Listen, bro." Kyle spoke softly. "You ain't no little 12 year old no more y'know. Trust me, no one can't do you anything again. Don't let the devil try tell you otherwise. You're good out here, bruv, swear down, y'get me."

Sideeq turned to smile through the pain, but his head dropped.

"Nah, bruv!" Kyle slapped Sid's leg, taking a coarser tone. "What's wrong with you? Hold your head up high! High, high, high, high, high!"

Energised, Kyle leap to his feet. "Come man." He tried hoisting Sideeq up.

"Oi K, I beg you 'llow me, man," Sideeq tried to protest, but it was too late. Kyle had already seen a smirk breaking through.

"Nah get up, bruv! What you trying to tell me? Man's 6'3 and can't hold his head up high?"

Reluctantly Sideeq stood up, towering over Kyle, who was now animatedly jumping around him like a pup welcoming home its master. He sprung on to the bed, almost puttting his foot in his plate, and spun Sideeq round so he was facing the window. Then he leaned in so he could put his arm around Sideeq's shoulder.

"Alright bruv, your head's held high. Tell me, what can you see?"

Siddeq shook his head. "Oi Wheeler, I'm not doing this."

"No cmon, bruv! Just do it, do it. "

"Blud this dumb, my window faces the A40."

"So what?"

"Blud it's a motorway."

"Ok, ok, well pretend we're looking out my window, innit. Humour me. What, you can't do that for me?"

Sideeq sighed, realising it was useless resisting. He tried not to laugh at the big grin on Kyle's face. Clearing his throat he began to speak in his deep voice, reciting the words as though he had said them a thousand times before.

"You see when I look out my window, I see bare man; bare man out there that look like me. Man that go school or don't go school. Man that go college or don't go to college. Man that go to work…"

"Or just sell work," Kyle joined in with delight.

"Oi K, why don't you just say it? You know the lyric better than me."

"No, no, you carry on bruv, I like when you say it."

Again Sideeq shook his head and continued. This time he added a touch more energy.

"Man that go to work or just sell work. Man that do trap or Man that do wraps, Man that kick ball or Man who risk it all. To sit up in a cell, without no bail, while other man talk and other man tell." Soon Sideeq was fully emceeing, with Kyle playing hype man. "Those Man aren't like me or my family tree…"

"KJ Wheeler wid the Hype SG!" Kyle screamed their old skool MC names.

"Gonna have a label gonna have cash, gonna have wife with a big phat gash, gonna do clothing, gonna do art, gonna do music that comes from the heart. You're gonna know my name, gonna know my dream, coz bare Man can look like but could never be!"

"Brap! Brap! Brap!" Kyle jumped off the bed on to Sideeq's

back, and when Sideeq finally got him off the two sat back, laughing.

"You're crazy. I don't know why you love those bars so much."

"Bruv, you don't get it, do you?" Kyle said, picking up his tray. He resumed his original position on the bed and started eating again. "I don't wanna be like no other man out there."

Sideeq frowned, "What d'you mean?"

"Bruv, listen to me. My uncle use to say to me, if a man ever wants to be successful in life he needs to have a vision, he needs to have a dream and needs to surround himself with likeminded people. You're the first man I know who ever had a dream and sold that to me, y'know. "

Kyle could see that Sideeq felt choked with pride. His friend rubbed his forehead, blushing. Seizing a moment for grandeur, Kyle gulped down what was left of his drink, then wiped his mouth.

"Bruv, you're the reason why we're not like other people. Between what you do and what I do, there's not one man that's gonna be able to chat to us. None. All we gotta do is stay on job."

For the rest of the evening the two friends talked about their visions and plans, and inside Sideeq's bedroom they found a safe haven for West London dreams. That night Touch One never played Kyle's song, but they were both sure his time would come. Tomorrow was their first day of college, and a mob of opportunities awaited.

Chapter 1.3

The first day of college was always a symbolic event for most students in West London and at Cardinal Manning Sixth Form College it had become a rite of passage. It was a day that welcomed change and social metamorphosis, opening the doors of opportunity for its new cohort. It gifted those who had struggled or been bullied in secondary school the chance to shed their past labels and a forge a new identity.

On this day that quiet plain Jane girl that had worked diligently for four years to get good grades—the one who had sat in the front of the class and had paper balls thrown at her when the teacher wasn't looking, or was constantly overlooked and belittled because her intelligence threatened others—on this day, that girl came armed with a summer's worth of YouTube tutorials, make-up from MAC and a contoured face, a fresh 'You-Go-Girl-outfit' from Pretty Little Thing, and a 'nobody puts baby in the corner'-slash-Sasha Fierce attitude that would make Queen Bey proud. She turned up and 'tunn'up' to turn heads and when she strutted her stuff, those who wondered who she was thought she looked a bit like…

"What's her name? You know, the one from Ms Powell's class.

The one who use to think she was too good for everyone?"

"Who, the Mute?"

"Yes that's her! Mute."

"That's not Mute!"

You damn right that's not Mute. The same way little Kyron shot up six inches, and his acne had cleared up. Or how Dusty Jayvon cut his filthy plaits and removed his durag to reveal his new Ceasar waves. Now he was working part-time in Ladbroke Grove Sainsbury's, he walked with a new swag after replacing his busted Air Force Ones and upgrading them to 95's. His new name was 'Is that you yeah?' And how about Skinny Chantel, who had finally filled out and the bee stings on her chest had swollen into a D-cup bra with no space for tissue or fillets?

Yes, on this day the adolescent jungle was alive, as teenage snakes, lions and wildebeest migrated through the college gates and assembled on to the courtyard like flocks of animals at a watering hole. Here Darwin's theory of survival of the fittest was due to be tested, as betas and omegas chose to redefine and rebrand themselves and their groupings in an attempt to move up the social ladder. It was the last chance to take a stab at popularity and status as they transitioned from kidulthood to adulthood. The window wouldn't come again until university or employment, and in that time many would fall prey. In this climate of apex youth and peer pressure predators, Kyle and Sideeq made their way to college.

When the friends arrived the college was heaving with anxious and excited students, either standing in their corners or running up to those they hadn't seen all summer or since last week. Kyle, who had a fresh trim and new slim cut Zara track-suit, looked around beaming. His eyes seemed to dart everywhere trying to take it all in, and he nodded at those he deemed suitable as future affiliates. Sideeq, who carried his huge A1 leather art portfolio under his arm, wore a light grey Nike hoodie, denim jeans and signature blue rucksack, and remained more reserved.

Finding a quiet spot not too far from the gate, he pulled on his hood, covering his hearing aid.

This didn't escape Kyle's attention, and he asked, "You cool?"

"Hmm." Sideeq nodded. "Just taking it all in."

He put down his folder, still observing his surroundings. The building looked different in the daylight. When he had attended the open evening with Kyle and his mother last October, the grounds' lighting had illuminated the central block and made it glow like a butter-kissed temple of education and excellence. It made the college easy to fall in love with in comparison to some of the others he had visited. That first impression was blasted upon his psyche, along with his mother's smile. That night, Valerie Gustav had turned to her son and said, "I'm very proud of you, Siddy. If you come here you will be the first in our family to go to college. Imagine that! On the same road me and your Aunt Janet use to go school."

A curve in Sideeq lip appeared as he studied the college landscape. The modern buttery-beige stone building was situated in the centre of St Charles Square in Ladbroke Grove, and if you looked past the central block with its stone steps, four pillars and stained glass window, you could see the building was divided into various wings, along with its annexes and a recently added red cubed extension. Once an old all boys' school, the refurbished main building still sat adjacent to Sion Manning all girls' secondary. The high school had now become a feeder school for the sixth form and throughout many a semester it wasn't abnormal to hear gaggles of young girls calling at college boys from the other side of the wall.

Sideeq remembered his mum telling him she had attended Sion Manning in her teens. It was where she had met his godmother, Janet. The two school girls had become inseparable. It was the same place Janet had met his godfather, Linton, after the girls had intervened and stopped Linton from beating up one of the Cardinal Manning boys. Sideeq's mother didn't tell many stories and those that she did usually involved his godmother. He realised their bond wasn't too different from Kyle's and his own, and pondered some of the events which would have made them lifelong friends. His mind had begun wandering on to his older brother, when he noticed a smiling face in the crowd.

A freckled faced white boy with shaggy mousy brown hair and a whisked moustache stood smoking the last of his morning spliff. Figuring Kyle and Sideeq had picked up the scent, he gave a friendly nod in their direction.

"Yes, yes, what you man saying," he said, stepping closer.

He was accompanied by an aging brindle-coated bull terrier with a white snout and podgy stomach. The dog, who looked like he'd been in the dog wars, had a torn ear, cataract in one eye, and walked with a limp. It was obvious it had seen better days and together the two looked like a ghetto version of Shaggy and Scooby Doo.

"What's happening?" The boy said holding out his fist to Kyle. "You're K.J. innit?"

"Yeah," Kyle said, dubiously touching fist. The boy had 'beg friend' written all over him.

"Yeah, yeah I thought as much," The boy nodded his head excitedly. "You use to play left wing for Burlington Danes. Bit heavy with the first touch, but nippy. I played against you in the cup. 3-2 quarter final against Hurlingham. You proper skanked us, scored a last minute tap in from offside."

"Nah man," Kyle laughed. "I was onside all day."

"Mate if you were on side then I'm black and the line-o must be colour blind, too."

Both Kyle and Sideeq pulled a face at the boy's joke, which caused the dog to bark.

"Rizla!" the boy hushed the dog. "Don't worry about him, bruv he won't bite. He just likes to make up a little noise when's ready."

The boy held out a welcoming fist to Sideeq. "I'm Danny, geez, what's your name?"

Sideeq stared at Danny's outstretched fist and answered, "Sid," leaving Danny's hand hanging.

"Nice, nice." Danny nodded like bobble-head toy. "What you saying, Sid? I remember your boat from the open evening." He stepped forward and fist bumped Sideeq's pocketed hand. "You bless?"

Straight faced, Sideeq looked at Kyle, who chuckled and gave Sid a look that said *play nice the with white boy, he's harmless*. "I'm good." Sideeq replied.

Clearly knowing that Danny wasn't gonna get anymore out of Sideeq, Kyle bent down to stroke Rizla. "Oi bruv, how comes you brought your dog to college?"

"I only live round the corner." Danny pointed to the top of the road. "I had a couple dog walks to do before we start, so I thought I'd let the ol' boy stretch his leg. His got arthritis in his back two, morning walk does him good."

"OK, so you're a dog walker yeah? You must make a little P, still?"

"Yeah, not bad—twenty pound a dog, a day."

"Rah, like that, yeah? Bruv you might have to bring me in."

As Danny and Kyle began to chat about the dog walking business, the sound of a moped ripped through the air and a boy on a black Gilera moped whizzed by. Immediately there was a stir in the jungle, and it was plain to see that an alpha had arrived. Onlookers stopped what they were doing and watched him as he parked up. Dressed in a green bomber jacket, black hoodie, black jeans and black, Jordan Vs, the alpha took off his shark-motif helmet. He was a tall slim boy with dark skin, smooth fade and a neatly shaped moustache. Flicking his wrist, he set the alarm on his moped and put the keys in his pocket. In that small motion Kyle clocked the silver Rolex on the teenagers arm as he stepped towards the college. Looking up the road, he caught eyes with the group and smiled.

"Wha gwan, Dan!" He saluted the white boy.

"Yes, yes, Kof," Danny hailed back to the onlookers' surprise.

"Rah, is that…"

"Sharkey G," Danny finished Kyle's sentence. "Prince of

ReloadFM. His Uncle's Yogi and Smallz own the station."

"But I thought Touch One owned it?"

"Don't be silly, he just runs it. He's like the face. Yogi and Smallz are the real owners, you know what mean? But the less said is better." Danny winked and zipped his mouth.

"Yeah, yeah, course." Kyle agreed. "So how d'you know Sharkey then?"

"Me? Me and Sharkz was at academy together, till QPR kicked him out. He musta fly-kicked some kid from Charlton Athletic in the chest. It was a proper Goku from Dragonball Z style kick." Danny tried re-enacting the scene.

"Every time our striker got the ball their centre half kept making monkey chants and hacking him down. Well coz the ref didn't say nothing, Sharkey run up to dude at half time and fly-kicked him in the chest. I'm mean proper both feet POW! Well then, when the Charlton boys came to ruck, Sharkey was well up for it and pinged the first one flat on the nose. He went straight down, lights out." Danny started laughing. "Uncles or no uncles, Sharkey's proper handy, he knows how to look after himself, if you know what I mean? He don't let nobody take the piss, but he's a proper cool guy. One time…"

Danny was about to rant on, but Rizla had decided he'd heard enough and started barking. "Ok, ok." Danny patted the dog on the head. The dog barked again then peered up at Sideeq and Kyle. Tilting his head and twitching his brow, it looked as though the dog was trying to roll his eyes.

"Listen," Danny said, giving Rizla a treat. "I better go and drop this one off before induction starts." He held a fist to Kyle.

"I'll meet up in class. You're doing music production, right?"

"Yeah." Kyle touched his fist, mystified. "How did you know that?"

"I hear a little bit'a this, I hear a little bit'a that." Danny winked. "It helps."

"Stop' bullshitting, man" Kyle said working it out. "You saw my name on the induction list."

"Now that would be telling," Danny said. He turned to Sideeq, holding out his fist. "Sid, it was nice to meet you, mate. I look forward to seeing some of your artwork, geezr."

"Bless, bro," Sideeq said. The ice was broken and this time he didn't hesitate to bump his with Danny's.

As Danny and Rizla disappeared up the road, Kyle and Sideeq headed inside.

"Oi, I like my man," Kyle said, steering past the throng of people.

"Hmmm," Sideeq agreed. "He's cool. A bit chatty patty though."

Kyle laughed.

Danny definitely seemed like he could talk for England.

CHAPTER 1.4

In life, there are some people's names you never forget, or where you were when you first heard them. It doesn't matter whether you were introduced to them, or if their name cropped up in someone's wild adventure, or another person's gossip. These names manage to lodge themselves on your psyche and whenever someone speaks that name, they leave a mental impression. Some of these names make a firm statement, while others become Chinese whispers, easily associated with tragedy or laughter depending on how you received them. Several names you don't speak too loud in certain circles, and others automatically open doors. There are names you're happy to be associated with, while others are so cringe worthy or difficult to pronounce they warrant a nickname, making you ask, 'Cor blimey what was your mum smoking when she came up with that one?'

There were spiritual names that move you or give insight into a person's heritage and names when you looked at the owner's face you said, "Yes that name suits you to a tee." Then finally, there were some names that could change your life in an instance and came with a special disclaimer.

Mr Ghodstinat was not one of those latter types of name. It

belonged to Sideeq's new art teacher, a short olive-skinned man of Persian descent, with a prominent nose that sat between his light Havana brown coloured round framed glasses. His neatly groomed beard complimented his artsy look of granddad shirt, rolled up chinos and long hair that was tied in a loose man bun with the sides shaved.

Greeting the class, he spoke with a camp, diluted Italian and Persian accent.

"Hey guyyyyss welcome, welcome, it's a pleasure to meet you all. My name is Mr Ghodstinat." He rolled his tongue to pronounce his name, elaborately gargling the G and H together in a manner only common to Farsi speakers.

"Some of you may remember me from your interviews, others this is maybe our first time meeting. Don't worry if you can't pronounce my name, it took my wife three years to get it right. So if it's too much of a mouthful, please feel free to call me Mister G."

Mr Ghodstinat made a rap style pose with two gun fingers eager to show *'he was about that life'* to the group's dismay and silent screams.

"So normally, guys, what most teachers would dooooo, is go around the rum and have everybody say their name and one thing about themselves. Luckily for you guyyys, Mister G isn't a normal teacher. So what I'm gonna do is put you into pairs and in your pairs, I want you to introduce yourselves and look through each other's portfolio. Then I want you to select one piece of the other's art that you like and I want to speak about it so you can present it to the class."

Immediately, Mr Ghodstinat started pairing people together. "You can you go with you." He pointed at a chubby white girl with long dark hair and a slim Flipino boy with singles braids.

"And can I have you—" He pointed at Sideeq with his outstretched finger. "And you." He ushered over Sideeq's partner. Wearing a navy blue Nike tracksuit, the black boy stood up and stepped closer. For some reason Sideeq thought there was something strange about his bop. The boy had a slender frame and stood around 5'7 with a slim face, brown eyes and a curly high-top haircut and fade.

"Yo, what you saying? I'm Swank."

The boy greeted Sideeq, slapping his hand leaning in for half a hug. Sideeq dipped his shoulder low to embrace Swank. As they held hands he was surprised at how soft and small Swank's hand was. He frowned and took another look at the boy. He had an oval face and brown skin that lacked all facial hair around the chin and jawline. For a good moment Sideeq studied Swank's androgynous features, thinking *his skin's too smooth for a teenage boy*.

Recognising the expression of bewilderment on Sideeq's face Swank chuckled and said, "What, fam ain't you got a name?"

"Yeah, yeah, it's Sid, Sid."

"OK Sid what, you gonna show me your portfolio den?"

"Yeah, course."

Sideeq tried to play it cool. He was surprised at how husky Swank's voice was for a girl. Giving her a second look over he began to see a bit of shape in her hip and the slightest hint of cleavage in her chest.

After ten minutes the class began to present each other's work. As each member spoke Sideeq eyed them and their partner. Mind ticking, he wondered whether their outer appearance was represented in their work or whether the art took on a new persona. Sometimes the two could be on two different ends of a spectrum.

Having been asked to remove his hood, Sideeq also slipped off his hearing aid. He didn't like speaking in front of people, especially a group of unknowns. He knew automatically they would be looking at his dead eye and scar pondering a myriad of questions. Wearing his hearing aid would just add to the curious eyes. When they were looking at each other portfolio's, Swank had originally chosen a self-portrait he had drawn, but Sideeq had asked her to choose another, stating the picture would raise too many questions.

"Say no more," Swank had agreed. She had her own understanding about people asking too many questions, and opted to choose another piece.

"The reason why I chose this piece was because of the composition and facial expressions of the two brothers. I liked the way the older brother, who looks about eleven, is holding his baby brother in his lap. And although you can't see his mouth, the rest of his face seems to just be proud of his baby brother, or maybe the idea of being big brother."

"Oh yesss, I can definitely see that, Charmaine."

"Swank. Call me Swank, Mister G."

"Oh sorry, Swank," Mr Ghodstinat corrected himself. "And what about the younger brother's expression?"

"Well, true he's a baby, sir, he looks a bit lose a bit bewildered as to what's going on. You know how babies have that look, like everyone around them is mad."

A little chuckle of agreement went around the room, and Swank continued. "But I think it's the contrast of the baby's innocence and the older brother's joy or pride that drew me to this picture. It's almost like you can imagine their bond and ting, and the older brother relishing the idea of being a protector or guide for his younger brother."

"Yasss that, is sso true. That is an amazing interpretation Swank, and of course a wonderrrfool pitch'ure, Sideeq. Wonderfool. Soooo Sideeq, let's see what you have chosen."

Swank took her seat and handed the floor over to Sideeq, who held up a large screen print on distressed Kente cloth. He cleared his throat and composed himself. He knew that when he got nervous he slurred, stammered or mispronounced his words, especially without his hearing aid.

"I chose this one be-be-be—" Anxious, Sideeq took a moment and closed his eyes. When he opened them, the whole class was watching him waiting and he thought, *Eff you people you don't know me*. Using his angst, he started again. "I chose this piece because automatically I was drawn to its symbolism and political statement. The concept of the young militia boy with the gun in his hand conjures up ideas of conflict and war in Africa. But I think Swank makes a bigger statement by putting it on distressed Kente, which I think represents a deeper message of Africa's history. And, and, and—"

Suddenly Sideeq started to stutter and then went silent. He stood in a strange state of wonderment and Mr Ghodstinat and the rest of the class were looking at him, bewildered, when there was a knock on the door. Everyone turned to see an attractive mixed race girl with dark brown hair and highlights standing in the doorway. Her hair was pulled back into a ponytail and she wore a red bomber jacket, Jack Wills grey sweater and black leggings that showed her toned thighs. Her fingernails were red and matched her red and white OG Air Max 1s. Biting her rouged-coloured lip, she smiled seductively at Sideeq, grabbing his attention.

"Yess how can I help you?" Mr Ghodstinat asked.

"Sorry to interrupt, but I'm a bit lost. Do you know where Room C12 is?"

"Yes darling, you want the performing arts room. It's just a few doors down to your left, before you get to the stairs."

"Oh, thank you," she said in a demure manner. She waved at everyone as she backed out of the door, then turned to address Sideeq. "I like your picture."

Before Sideeq could reply, the girl had disappeared and he stood dumbfounded looking at the space she had vacated.

When he had finished presenting Sideeq sat back down. Swank leaned in and said, "Wow, what happened to you? Da lightie catch tongue?"

"No, no, don't try it," Sideeq replied, trying not to laugh.

"Fam, my girl had you weak. Mouth all drooling and ting. I swear you must be one big lightie lover"

"Nah, man," Sideeq sat with a smirk on his face, pretending that he was listening to the next presentation. "I've seen that girl somewhere before. Her face looked familiar."

"Yeah, that Nerissa, she lives round the back of Emlyn Gardens."

"Oh OK. You know her?"

"Yeah," Swank said with a dubious look. "She use' to go my school. But I wouldn't go chasing that if I was you. That's Gobbler's girl."

"Who's Gobbler?" Sideeq asked with a frown.

CHAPTER 1.5

From the dark Victorian street gangs of Forty Elephants and Wild Boys to the infamous high profile cases of the Richardsons and Krays in the sixties, London has always had a love affair with bandits and gangsters. In fact crime, poverty and young boys asking for more have existed in London centuries before today's media reports of escalating knife crime and postcode wars. And with every generation and spike in crime you'll find hundreds of Artful Dodgers or Bill Sikes'. The twist is that with over 200 active gangs in London and at least 45 in the West London area alone, it was getting harder to find the Olivers. Officially, by UK law, it only took two or more young people gathered in public to be identified as a gang. So by the time Kyle, Sideeq, Danny and Swank met up outside college, they could be afforded such a title by police.

While the others students had flocked to explore the cafeteria for lunch, the newly-formed gang decided to follow Danny, who offered to introduce them to some local cuisine. Collecting Rizla, they headed up the road to the famous George's Chip Shop. A family-run business, it was situated on the cross section of Goldbourne Road and Portobello Road and had been serving traditional fish and chips and kebabs to locals for decades. The shop had become a staple of the community and rumour had it, if you lived in less than a half mile radius of the chip shop and ate from anywhere else, you were cursed to eating soggy chips and poorly-battered fish for seven years. Other folklore hailed George's as the originators of burger sauce on chips, which had slowly filtered out to the echelons of London and beyond.

Treating everyone, Danny ordered a round of kebab rolls and chips, and a saveloy for Rizla.

"That's £12.60 with drinks," the Cypriot-looking woman with icy green eyes said from behind the counter. Danny took out a twenty-pound note and paid her.

"How's you mum, Dan?" The woman said cashing up Danny's money.

"No too bad, Maz."

"Good, good, and what about, Mr Rizla the old drum and bass dog?"

Rizla, who was waiting outside, barked at the sound of his name.

"Yes I'm talking about you!" The woman laughed. She handed Danny back his change and dished out the orders. "You gonna gives us a song and dance then?" She continued to speak to dog. Rizla barked at her again then started to howl, rocking from side to side to everybody's amusement as Danny played an old Jungle tune called *Bonanza Kid* by Firefox on his phone. Danny told him, "Go boy, do the Hot Paw skank." To which Rizla started shaking his head and hopping from side to side lifting up his feet like he was standing on hot coals. When he was finished he let out another howl and sat down, tired. Tongue hanging out and tail wagging Rizla, barked at Maz.

"Yes, OK." She smiled at the dog. "I'll add an extra nugget in for you."

On the way back Rizla wolfed down his saveloy and nugget, and when Danny refused to share his kebab roll the dog took a liking to Sideeq, who supplied him plenty of kebab meat and chips on the sly. For all that Rizla lost in looks he made up in smarts. As he trotted alongside the group it was easy to see why Danny brought him out at any opportunity. Quietly he trailed at the back with Sideeq as the others debated.

"So what's the difference between Jungle and Drum & Bass?" Swank asked.

"Drum & Bass is more moody," Danny replied with a mouthful of chips. "More darker, than jungle. It's got more of techno-ish vibe. Jungle is more dub and ragga samples."

"OK. So which one came first?"

"Drum & Bass."

"No, bruv," Kyle interjected. "Jungle came first."

"Are you sure?" Danny gave a Kyle a scrutinizing looking.

"Course am. I grew up on old skool Kool FM and AWOL tapes."

"Yeah me too," Danny said trying to remain on par. "My sister's boyfriend taught me how to mix on his Technics 1200 and vinyl. He told me that Goldie and General Levy invented Drum & Bass and Jungle."

"Bruv, if your sister's boyfriend told you that, he's a

wasteman."

"Oi K, I beg you don't try par off my people like that, mate," Danny tried protest as the others started to laugh.

"Nah, bruv, it's true." Kyle remained adamant. "I ain't saying them man weren't pioneers, but to say they invented it is like saying So Solid invented House & Garage. Bun that."

"OK fine, whatever." Danny rolled his eyes. "So if they're not the inventors how'd Drum & Bass come round?"

"Evolution innit," Kyle took a bite of his kebab roll and decided to give the group a quick history lesson. "Look, lemme break it down. The way music evolved over here in the UK is like this.

"First you had dancehall and soul in the 60's. Then in the 70's and 80's you got reggae, lover's rock, roots, ska and a bit of disco. In the mid to late 80's, happy hardcore and techno started to come through, then in the 90's you got ragga and bashment. That's when Jungle came in and then later drama and bass."

"So when did garage come in?" Swank asked.

"That came in around late 90's-early 2000s on a House ting; and then you got all the So Solid, Master of Ceremonies and Heartless Crew vibe, which turned in UKG ting and then outta that came Grime, and now there's Trap and this new ting called Drill."

"Rah," Swank looked at Kyle impressed. "How comes you know so much, fam?"

"I'm a micman innit, that's man's job." Kyle boasted. "Every DJ, MC and producer suppose' to know their history, otherwise they're weak," he said, smiling in Danny's direction.

"Mate, you tryna call me weak?"

"Nah, Dan, but you might need a bit more schooling." Kyle grinned. "Don't worry it's only the first day of college, you got plenty time to catch up."

"Mate, don't think just b'coz I'm a white boy I don't know how to make beats. I'll murder you on production."

"Oi, Dan, don't let the burger sauce go to your head, bruv."

The mood was light-hearted and banter was in free flow as Kyle and Danny took cheap shots at each other, then a voice yelled, "Swank!"

The group turned to see a small gang of boys congregating by a parked black Volkswagen Golf. They were all dressed in variations of black, like it was a uniform, and a tall Moroccan boy with a thin moustache wearing a black Trapstar cap and tracksuit waved her over. "Yo whagwan?"

For a moment Swank seemed apprehensive. She smiled dubiously before calling back, "Yo, what you saying, Hass?"

The broad smile on her face lasted for all of two seconds, and in an instant her whole demeanour changed. It was obvious she was trying to keep it moving and she stepped ahead of Danny and Kyle trying to make a subtle beeline towards the gates. However, Hassan called again, this time beckoning her over.

"Yo Swank, come akh."

Swank stopped. It was clear she was in two minds when Hassan stepped to the side and the driver's door swung open. A short, stocky young man with muscular arms and mahogany brown skinned stepped out of the car. He too was dressed from head to toe in black and wore a black Nike glove on his right hand. His powerful chest dominated his frame and his neck was thick as Mike Tyson's. His weighty jaw had a slight under-bite and governed his facial features like Desperate Dan from The Dandy comics. His tough hair was cut in a rough high-top with fade. Leaning up against the car he screwed up his face and took a long draw on the spliff that hung from his lip. Exhaling, his nose flared like a dragon breathing smoke, and he watched Swank with such a baneful look that she was compelled to walk over to the gang. As she greeted Hassan and the shorter guy, the others decided to wait.

"Oi, oi, man dem, don't look too hard, yeah?" Danny said, warning Kyle and Sideeq. "But you see that short dude over there, that's Gobbler."

"Who?" Sideeq asked hearing the name for a second time that day.

"His one of those Powis Square yoots, innit," Kyle said recognizing the name.

"Yeah, that's him," Danny turned his back so he could gossip. "Mate, he's bad news, proper bad news. I wouldn't mess around with him. I've heard one or two stories that didn't bode well for anyone that did, if you know what I mean."

"Yeah, yeah I've heard that still," Kyle said sceptically.

Concerned, the three boys watched Gobbler's conversation with Swank through side-glances.

"Listen…" Danny pretended to chew on a chip to mask his mouth. "All I'm saying is tuck your chain in, hide your phone. Coz if that dude wants something of yours, he's gonna try take it. You do know why they call him Gobbler don't you? He's frigging known for jackin', man. Straight gobbling them up, no questions asked. If you see him put his arm around a man that's it. Foregone conclusion they're getting jacked. You see that glove on his right hand?"

Both Sideeq and Kyle looked at Gobbler's glove as he smoked his spliff and pointed demandingly at Swank while speaking. Whatever he was saying, Swank was agreeing eagerly nodding and trying to reassure him.

"Mate," Danny continued. "I've been told that his gun-finger glove, and whenever he's got that glove on he's got his nine on him."

"Maybe you shouldn't listen everything you hear." Kyle scoffed. He eyed Gobbler taking an instant dislike to the boy. Ever since Nana's attack on Sideeq, he questioned any story of about these so called bad men. He considered most to be overrated bullies and they carried no weight with him. However he wasn't stupid, he knew better than to draw any unwanted attention. Finally Gobbler let Swank return to the group.

"Yo, you alright?" Kyle asked Swank, who looked a bit sheepish.

"Yeah, yeah, I'm good, fam. Come we go inside, quick."

Kyle was about to lead the way when Danny said, "Wait, I can't go inside with Rizla. I beg you man don't me leave out here."

Immediately each one them knew the exact implication of what may happen if they left Danny to walk back up the road on his own. It wasn't a moment for indecisiveness. Like a lion stalking its prey, Gobbler had already seen them hesitate and tapped Hassan, stepping forward.

"Oi, Eminem," he hailed Danny. "Justin Bieber. Come 'ere bro."

Danny's heart visibly sank as Gobbler walked towards him. Like a wolf smelling the scent of blood, Gobbler licked his lips as he came closer. "What you saying brudda, you gotta a cigarette?"

Danny seemed to wonder if it was a trick question. If he said yes then Gobbler might take the cigarette and leave him alone. However, that would mean anytime Gobbler saw him he had a reason to stop and approach Danny. On the other hand, if he said no then Gobbler could find a reason to pat him down. Still carrying sixty pounds worth of dog walking money on him from earlier that day, Danny decided to give Gobbler a cigarette.

"Yeah, yeah course." He slipped a cigarette out of the box and handed it to Gobbler.

"Nice one, Bieber," Gobbler smiled. "You don't mind if I take two do you?"

Gobbler took the box out Danny's hand. Taking another cigarette, he checked the box for any weed. Fixing the first cigarette behind his ear he took a second and offered another one to Hassan before giving Danny the box back.

"You're from Grove, innit," he probed. Nervously, Danny nodded his head so fast you would've thought his neck was made from rubber.

"Yeah, yeah, I seen you about with your dog."

Gobbler looked down at Rizla, who had moved to sit between the young thug and his owner.

"Friggin' ting looks like an oversized rat, blud. How can walk with that? You need to get yourself a real dog, blud. This dog is *dead*."

Hassan laughed. "Rah 'llow my man's dog, ahk."

"What y'mean, look how it's ear all chewed off and ting. The dog looks like it's got rabies and shit. Listen to me big man, do yourself a favour, go put that dog down. Save yourself some money on dog food. That dog can't help you no more. I'll tell you what, if you want I'll do it for you. I won't even charge you."

Knowing Danny wasn't going to defend his dog, Hassan pulled Gobbler away laughing. "Oi my nigga, stop dissin' my man's dog like that, leave him alone."

"Eff that." Gobbler brushed Hassan to the side. He turned his attention to Kyle and Sideeq. "Where you man from?"

Hassan shook his head. "Oi Gobbz I beg you, it's my first day of college ahk. I beg you don't keep up no drama."

"What drama you talking about, blud?" Gobbler smiled deviously. "I'm just talkin' to the man dem." Gobbler turned to Kyle. "What, blud, you got a problem with me asking you what endz you from?"

Kyle looked Gobbler in the eye. He wanted him to know he wasn't intimidated. "No, not at all. I'm from City."

"City, yeah?"

"Yeah."

"OK, my gee, say no more," Gobbler chuckled.

He admired Kyle's bravado, but clearly knew if he had to he could fold Kyle over with one punch. Therefore, his eyes shift passed Kyle to the silent giant at the back—Sideeq. He took a moment to size Sideeq up, perhaps calculating what type of punch it would take to knock him out. "What about you,

Cyclops. Where you from with your one eye?"

Sideeq, who had been distracted by something, turned to look at Gobbler. He stared through the troublemaker and his face stayed indifferent. There was a pause, and Kyle realised Sideeq wasn't wearing his hearing aid.

"He's from city too."

"Blud, I dint ask you?" Gobbler stuck two gun-fingers in Kyle's face. He moved them slowly to point at Sideeq. "I asked him. Let my man speak for himself. What, he ain't got a tongue of his own?"

"He's got one, but liked I said, he's from City, I'm from City, we're all from West. What's the problem here?"

"There's no problem, ahk." Hassan pulled Gobbler back. "But next time man's speaking to your boy, tell him to speak up. Man's tryna be hospitable out here."

"Furthermore," Gobbler said, mean mugging Sideeq, "you man better know this ain't W12, y'nah. This is LG, 10-11 Powis Square, rudeboy." Gobbler threw up his gang signs. "You man are guests right 'bout now, you better remember that."

"Gobbz, Gobbz." Hassan threw his arm around Gobbler. "Allow the gang signs, G, they don't bang postcodes man. 'Llow it."

"Allow what?" a voice said from over Hassan and Gobbler's shoulder. Everyone turned to see Sharkey approaching with his helmet in his hand. He must have seen the exchange from a distance and came over to investigate. "You man alright, Dan?"

"Yeah, yeah cushty, Sharkz," Danny replied gingerly. He was still weary about upsetting Gobbler. Sharkey, on the other hand, wasn't. Stepping past both Gobbler and Hassan, he put a hand on Kyle's shoulder. "You good, bro?"

"Yeah, I'm blessed." Kyle pretended to greet Sharkey liked he'd known him for eons. Gobbler eyed them suspiciously and waited for his own acknowledgement, which Sharkey was clearly aware of.

"What's happening Gobbz, Hass?"

"Yes, yes Mr. Sharkey G?" Gobbler responded. "I'm good, you?"

"I'm alive brother, I'm tryna be like you out here."

Gobbler sniggered at what he knew was a backhanded compliment. "Nah blud, I'm tryna be like you."

Although they'd never had any drama, Gobbler had a simmering dislike for Sharkey, but for now he had to respect the levels.

"So what you know these dudes, Sharkz?"

"Yeah dem man are in my class. Why?"

Gobbler screwed up his face. He wasn't happy with Sharkey's affiliation, and his eye lay firmly on Sideeq.

"Blud, you and Swank better talk to your people unless you wan' them to get violated. The next time I speak to dem, they better open up their mouth. Especially my man." He pointed at Sideeq. "Otherwise I'll poke out his other eye."

Gobbler made a stabbing motion which made Hassan laugh, "Astaghfirullah!"

He put his arm around Gobbler and walked him back to the car, leaving the friends with a clear warning. When he was out of earshot, Sharkey turned to Sideeq and reached out his hand.

"You cool big man?"

He shook Sideeq's huge paw with a welcoming smile. "Don't let Gobbler get to you, y'know. My man's a dickhead."

"I'm not," Sideeq said sounding slightly subdued.

"Good." Sharkey smiled at two girls passing by. "Coz Gobbler's just one of those guys who's always got something to prove. He's got a shortman complex."

"It's true," Swank smirked. "He don't like no one over 5'2."

"I don't care," Kyle said, unimpressed. His protective side had leaped to the forefront. "That don't give him the right to come and start trouble with Sid, I don't care what postcode we're in. If he tries it again, I'm involved."

"K, hold it down mate, he ain't gone yet," Danny said checking to see if Gobbler and his goons were watching.

"Eff that," Kyle fumed. "If he tries it again, Siddy, knock him out. Straight knock him out."

"And live where?" Danny said sceptically. "Nah mate, if it was me, I'd give him wide berth. You don't need twenty Grove man running up in your house on some gang ting. Eff that for laugh."

The debate continued, going back and forth until Sharkey decided to join the others as they followed Danny to take Rizla home. Heading up the street, Sideeq remained quieter than usual. His head was filled with questions. He pondered why bullies liked to home in on him, and what he would do if he actually had to fight Gobbler. He wasn't in year seven anymore, and he had no intentions of running from anyone again.

Part II

The Come Up

CHAPTER 2.1

In the golden light between late afternoon and early evening, Kyle and Sideeq walked the long way home. Over last fortnight they had found their feet at college and were slowly settling into their new routines. Strolling down St Mark's road in deep conversation, they cut through Kensington Memorial Park disturbing a group pensioners bowling on the green. An old man in his bowling whites and federator hat cursed at them, "Oi you two, can't you flipping read?" He pointed to a white sign with black lettering. "This part of the park is for members only."

Breaking their conversation, the pair looked at the sour-faced man with his turkey-like neck and ignored him. Turning on to Barbly Road they passed the Pavillion pub opposite their old secondary school, then crossed the busy Scrubs Lane on to Ducane Road. They head towards the iron bridge that was a stone's throw away from Hammersmith Hospital and the high walls of Wormwood Scrubs prison. As they entered the estate, Sideeq looked at his watch. Somehow Kyle had turned a twenty-minute walk into an hour by frequently stopping to elaborate on a certain part of his story or to send a text mid-conversation. As always, Sideeq had attentively listened to Kyle as he explained how Sharkey had offered to help get him on to Reload FM. Then he made a quick call to DJ Touch One and said he was sending over a track and wanted to bring an artist on the show.

The call didn't last longer than two minutes apparently, and according to Kyle, the most Sharkey said to the DJ was, "Touch, listen to me family. All I gotta say is dude is fire." Five minutes later, Touch One called back and Sharkey turned to Kyle and said, "You free next Sunday?"

In his excitement Kyle had practically retold the story six times by the time they got to Sideeq's house. Each time he gave extra emphasis to how big a move this could be for them. Finally, as he crashed down onto Sideeq's bed, he sat patiently waiting for Sideeq to respond.

With his one good eye, Sideeq took a long hard look at the dodgy stickman drawing and lettering Kyle had scribbled on a piece of paper. Turning it sideways he grinned and said, "K, you need to describe what you want me to design again, because this drawing ain't making no sense to me."

"Bruv, I beg you stop mocking the ting, man," Kyle snatched the paper back. "You know what I want. Stop trying to make man feel like some prick out here."

"Why you catching feeling?" Sideeq said with a smirk.

It wasn't often Sideeq had Kyle on the back foot, and he relished the moment.

"Oh whatever, bruv, are you gonna do the ting or not?"

"Course I am, bro." Sideeq gestured for Kyle to hand over the sketch. "Just leave it with me and I'll see what I can do."

"Please, bruv, I beg you. This logo has gotta be sick. You

know dem ones when man first see it, they have to just say that looks 'ard. Not hard I mean like proper *'ard.*"

"Yes man," Sideeq rolled his eyes. "I said I got you. Don't you trust me now?"

"I do," Kyle stressed. "But I need everything to look solid, bruv like proper."

There was a steely look in Kyle's eye as he spoke that Sideeq had seen a thousand times. It happened whenever he got a step closer to his dream. He had this tendency to go into overdrive and he became obsessed. Everything had to be done immediately and with a certain precision, and it often fell on Sideeq's shoulder to explain to Kyle that there was a fine balance between quality and speed. People who usually wanted both either had the money to pay, or generally had to sacrifice one. Today he had decided to indulge Kyle in his industrious dreaming.

"I'm telling you, bro, this it." Kyle stabbed at the air with a pointed finger. "Do you know how many followers I could get after I go on that show?"

Kyle slid his phone over to Sideeq to look. "Touch One has got over a hundred fifty thousand followers. If man could push at least ten percent of that to my IG account, that's like fifteen thousand new peepz."

Sideeq hand back the phone. "So you gonna get him to play that track you and Sharkey made in class the other day?"

"Nah, Sharkz said to wait till it's mixed and mastered, then he'll get Touch to drop it like an exclusive, for Reload."

"So you finally moving, yeah?"

"No." Kyle grinned. "*We're* finally moving. That's why I need you to get everything ready for my socials." He jumped off the bed and started walking around. It was the only way to control his energy.

"I need everything. Logos, artwork. I want it to look like a proper marketing campaign, proper profesh', so when I tell people to go check my Insta or YouTube it's on."

"OK, say no more." Sideeq took out his pad. Finding a fresh page he reached for a pencil and took another look at Kyle's diagram before sketching. "Have you thought about what you gonna do about a video?"

"Hmmm, yeah…" Kyle stopped pacing. He fingered one of Sideeq's graphic novels from of the self and flicked through the pages. "I was thinking about asking that breh Marcus if he could shoot a couple hood ones for me. Or even a couple quick freeestyles. I heard he's shooting some bits for GRM Daily and Road Reportz."

"That could be a good look," Sideeq agreed. "You should ask Sharkey if Touch One will let you film when you go on his show. You could post that up too."

"For real, that's a bangin' idea, brudda."

"I know." Sideeq smirked. "That's why I told you."

"Whatever." Kyle shook his head. "So what's going on with you?"

"What y'mean?"

"Bruv, did you set up your DE-1 accounts?"

"Nah not yet." Sideeq looked up from sketching and shrugged his shoulders.

"Bruv, that's what I mean about you." Kyle put the graphic

novel back. "You're not taking this thing serious, man. I thought we were suppose' to both be in this thing together. Everything we do, suppose' to help push the other man's ting."

"I know, I hear that," Sideeq said with a coy look on his face.

"So why you stalling?"

"I ain't stalling. I just ain't got round to setting them up, that's all. Don't worry, I'll do it," Sideeq said, trying to fob Kyle off. However, Kyle wasn't ready to let the matter go so easily.

"Bruv, what's wrong with you, man. Don't you get it? I can't bus' unless you bus' you know. When people look at my tings, I want them to recognise that's a Deafeye One design. If I go to certain shows or make lil viral vids, I wanna be rocking a hoodie or t-shirt designed by you. Look." Kyle snatched away his diagram and held it up. "It's not like anyone gonna wear anything I design," he said making Sideeq laugh. "Nah man, don't laugh bruv, I'm serious."

"Alright alright, cool." Sideeq raised his hands and signalled for Kyle to calm down. "I get what you're saying, but I'm not inna all the social media ting, checking for likes, seeing whose following you etcetera, etcetera. That's bare time consuming."

"Bruv, it's a minor. All you got do is take a couple of pics of whatever you're working on and a buss a little caption underneath. Why you gwanin like you can't do that?"

"Fine," Sideeq conceded. He tossed Kyle his phone. "If it's that easy, you set it up. I'll take the pictures and post up them. But, he warned, "I don't wanna hear you telling me anything about what I can and can't post."

"Bruv," Kyle said, grinning as he unlocked the phone. "I

swear you're like a proper vibe killer when you're ready. You know that's why you need me in your life."

"Whoa, whoa, slow your roll a bit bro, you're the one who's begging me for designs. So I think it's the other way round."

"Maybe, but that's the trade-off, bruv."

As Kyle began loading a list of social media apps on to Sideeq's phone, Sideeq finished sketching a design for Kyle's logo. He scanned the drawing into his computer and started to manipulate the picture. After five minutes busying away in silence, Kyle asked, "Bruv, do you know why Japanese people are so successful?"

Turning away from the computer screen, Sideeq frowned, wondering where Kyle was going to go with this theme. "No, but I'm sure you're gonna tell me."

"It's because they don't dream."

"What?" Sideeq sat up at the lunacy he was hearing. "What y'mean they don't dream?"

"They don't. Swear down, bruv," Kyle said adamantly. "I read it online. In their language they ain't got no word for dream. They use this word called '*Yume*' instead. It means to have a mysterious vision while asleep, or hope and aspiration."

"Kyle, that's the same thing."

"No it's not, man. It's different"

"How?" Sideeq laughed. He refused to accept Kyle's nonsense. "You just said that they have a vision while they're asleep." He repeated the words again, making quotation marks in the air with his fingers. "I think there's a big clue there, bro. How's that's not the same as a dream?"

"Because it's not."

"Oh my days." Sideeq threw his hands up in the air. "Oi, K, you been standing around Danny too long? The fumes are getting to your head."

"Shut up, man."

"I can't believe man actually said Japanese people don't dream."

"Bruv." Kyle punched Sideeq in the arm. "Lemme finish before you start dubbing the ting."

"Fine." Sideeq held up his arm, laughing. "Speak your madness."

"Look," Kyle explained. "Check it. The Japanese don't believe in having dreams. To them it's strictly a vision, or aspiration, whether that's at night or not. So in Japan when a vision or a yume comes to you, they say you gotta act on it so that it comes to fruition."

"What if it's a bad vision?" Sideeq asked, trying to catch Kyle out.

"Durr, then you act against it."

"OK, so what if you're not sure if its good or bad?"

Kyle cut his eye at Sideeq. "Bruv, why you trying to annoy me?"

"I'm not," Sideeq smirked. "Finish what you was saying."

"So, as I was saying. In Japan they don't have dreams they aspirations they have to act on or against. Which means they don't stand around daydreaming. They have a set vision and they go about chasing, *or,*" he added some extra emphasis on this last word, "change it if it's a bad one."

Rubbing his mouth, Sideeq took a moment to ponder the concept. "So what you saying we need to move like Japanese people?"

"Yes." Kyle smiled, finally reaching his point. "And that's why you need me."

"Pardon?" Sideeq laughed.

"You heard me." Kyle handed him back his phone. "Bruv, lets be real. You're a proper a dreamer out here, but me? I'm a visionary. I keep us focused; always moving closer to our yume."

"Wowwww is that what you think?"

"Bruh, that's what I *know*."

"OK." Sideeq laughed shaking his head. "Well lemme tell you what *I* think. I think you're the dreamer, but sometimes you get so carried away with chasing your dreams or whatever that you need someone to bring you back to reality. And that is why *you* need *me*."

"Mmm, maybe." Kyle shrugged his shoulders and grinned. He sat down on the edge of Sideeq's bed with a mischievous look in his eye. "Bruv, I bet you this. If you bang out some t-shirt designs, I guarantee three months from now, we'll have the first range of our own clothing line. What you say?" He held out his hand, ready strike a deal. Sideeq eyed him for a moment. He could tell Kyle was eager for him to accept the challenge. He knew his friend always worked better when there was a wager involved, but there was one thing he wanted to know.

"How you gonna get the money?"

"Don't worry about that. I'm a visionary, I'll find a way." Kyle grinned. His eyes began to scan the room. "If you're ready to put in the work then were all good."

"Fine," Sideeq shook his hand. "Three months, no long ting."

"Easy!" Kyle jumped his feet, beaming. He began rubbing his hands and said, "So let's get to the first order of business then. What you doing with those trainers?"

Feeling like he had been set up, Sideeq looked at his collection of hand-painted customised trainers and then wearily back at Kyle. "Why?"

Smiling Kyle replied. "Lesson number one in business—supply and demand, bro. We need create some demand."

Sideeq frowned. He didn't like the sound of that.

CHAPTER 2.2

The hair stood up on the back of Kyle's neck as he sat in the studio at Reload FM. The station was based in an empty office space in back of Sharkey's uncles' record shop in Ladbroke Grove which they had renovated a few years back into a make-shift radio booth. The black and red room had been completely soundproofed and kitted out with some state-of-the-art broadcast equipment. It was a big contrast to the station's humble pirate radio beginnings hidden in a rickety old portacabin at the back of the scrapyard behind Latimer Road, where DJs did their best with two mics, mixer, amp, and a pair of 1210 Technics. Reload had survived numerous police raids and outlasted any sabotage from rival pirate stations to finally become a thriving legitimate community-based station, and a rite of passage for any West London MC.

Smiling, Kyle watched the round-faced black man on the other side of the desk. Touch One was a burly man in his late twenties who had a thinly lined beard that linked to his goatee. The scars of teenage acne lined his temples and he sported razor cut lines in his eyebrow. He fixed the navy-blue fitted Yankee cap on his head then raised the levels on Kyle's mic. Sliding the fader, he loaded a Grime instrumental and introduced Kyle.

"London, I got something special for you. Now you know I've been playing his tune, 'Wheel up Specialist', all week, it's a big one. So I had to get the man up here to see what's he's got. So with no further delays, I beg man, KJ Wheeler drop a little fire on dem."

Kyle gripped the cans of his headphones. Listening to the rhythm of the 140 bpm beat touching his ears, he closed his eyes. Miraculously, like a lyrical alchemist, he began to transform energy from the electronic sounds into verbal bars of gold. Feverishly he leaned forward, hovering over the mic. Savagely he bombarded the instrument with a slew of words, raining down on its pop-guard with an artillery of punchlines and metaphors. Devouring every break, he seized the moment with a battalion of fire, and masterfully he combined a sequence of intricately-structured wordplay that even the greatest of wordsmiths would have to salute. He was determined to control the airwaves. He could have gone on rhyming forever, but Touch One, overwhelmed with excitement, pulled up the track.

"Hold on, hold on, hold on!" He pressed the button on the mixing deck to drop some pre-recorded exploding bombs and air siren sound effects. "Hold on London!" he yelled, throwing down his headphones and tossing his cap in the air. He held his chubby cheeks in astonishment.

"Reload, Sharkey G! Are you hearing this?" He stood up and reached over the decks to touch fists with Kyle. Excited, he continued to bounce around the small soundproof room with its sponge-lined walls, his pot belly jiggling, and hit the sound effects button one more time.

"No swigging away! London! LONDON! I had to pull up that track coz I don't think you know. We just found a new king. Seriously, KJ Wheeler is in the HOUSE!"

Kyle laughed and shouted, "You dun' know already!"

"No seriously, KJ we have to salute dem bars. We do. Please Mr, Sharkey G. talk to me."

"Boy, family, what can I say?" Sharkey leaned back in a chair with a smug grin. "I told you, innit? Tell the truth, Touch, I told you." He waged his finger.

"No you, did, you definitely did." Touch One wiped his sweaty brow and loosened his top to cool down. "You told me he was gonna be fire, so I give gotta credit where credit is due."

"OK den, say no more family." Sharkey laughed. It was clear the two had plenty synergy. Rearranging the microphone levels, Touch One turned back to Kyle. "So, KJ talk to us. Tell us a little about yourself. Where you from?"

"Boy, there's not much to say y'know, Touch," Kyle replied, trying to play bashful. "I'm just a West London boy that loves music. You get it me, G?"

"OK, so tell us about that. We've heard *'Wheel-Up Specialist'* What's next? What else can we expect?"

Kyle swivelled from side to side in his chair, "Erm well right about now I'm gonna be working with Sharkey on a six-track EP called *'The Wheel Up Chronicles part 1.'* So look out for that. That's definitely gonna be fire when it lands. And make sure you follow my Insta, @ KJ underscore Wheeler. That's wheeler with a e-r. "

"What about if anyone wants to hear some more of your music now?"

"Oh yeah, they can check out my Soundcloud, I got a couple freestyles and mixes on that. Again, they can find that @ KJ_Wheeler. Oh yes, Touch!" Kyle jumped up and leaned right into the microphone. "Before I say anything more, can just shout out my partner-in-crime Big Sid, aka DE-1 the Deafeye, on the camera."

He pointed to Sideeq, who sat in the corner filming the whole show on a small grey JVC camcorder. Sideeq tried not to smile and kept his hand steady as Kyle gave him a big up.

"Yes, what you saying camera man?" Touch One joked. "Big yourself up for real."

Sideeq chuckled, giving Touch One a thumbs-up and raised an eyebrow at Kyle, who continued to speak.

"Touch, lemme tell you about this guy. He is an amazing artist—no, *phenomenal*. He's like the black Banksy out here, I swear down."

"OK that's a big accolade right there." Touch One looked over at Sideeq, impressed.

"Yeah, he's sick. Proper sick," Kyle went into sales mode and began plugging. "Me and him just set up our own graphic design and customising company. So if there's anyone out there looking for artwork or custom trainers, please go check out his work on Insta. You can find him @deafeyed_1."

"Wow," Touch One sat back in his chair. "That's a big move, brother. Sharkey told me he was bring on an emcee not an entrepreneur. You sound like you got your finger in a few pies."

Kyle smiled. "Boy sometimes, Touch, you gotta know the difference between a dream and a vision."

Chapter 2.3

The sun had already given up on a late cloudy autumn afternoon. The skies began to rattle with thunder, and rain beat fiercely against Sideeq's classroom window. From his desk he sat like a one-eyed sentry, watching the boys from the college football team race across the courtyard to the awaiting mini bus. With their rucksacks on their backs they looked like a group of scuttling beetles trying to stay dry as the PE tutor, Mr Dick, ushered them to hurry up. From his high viewpoint Sideeq managed to observe most of the students' comings and goings throughout the day. He had a thing for people watching, especially from a safe distance. He liked to read the different types of body language; particularly those heading to and from the common room, which was situated to the far left of the yard.

On many occasions he would find himself plodding away with his artwork, and then by chance look up at the precise moment a spritely suitor tried to approach on a young lady. It was like a sixth sense. Instinct just told him when to look up, and yep, more often than not there was another horny adolescent trying to make their move. Studying, Sideeq took note. There were a few different styles of courtship and wooing, for each suitor and female. Firstly there were the Callers and Chasers. These were the guys that fell into the pursuer category. Usually they would wait for a female to cross the courtyard on her own or maybe with one other friend. Then, stepping out of the common room, they would call out to the female asking her to wait, in an attempt to invite her to indulge in polite or intimate chat. If she stopped completely it was generally a good sign of high interest. However, if the female acknowledged the call yet carried on walking, the caller now had to pluck up the courage and chase. If he didn't, the courtship was usually doomed no matter how many attempts he made.

In the past few weeks Sideeq had noticed that the best Caller-Chasers were the '*Armthrowers.*' The Armthrowers were the suitors who did the call and chase all in one swift move. They had managed to perfect their style into one smooth motion. Wailing out the girl's name they would move toward their potential mate with a certain vigour, descending upon the female—or females— with a swooping arm around the shoulder. Some were even bold enough to use the arm technique to lure a female away from her companion. Sideeq noted that the boisterous and bantering nature of most armthrowers created a specific effect in females that induced them to laugh. This ability to produce the dopamine associated with humour allowed armthrowers, even when spurned, to return for numerous attempts at courtship. The armthrowers' only flaw was that sometimes their displays could be so colourful that their pursuits aroused attention. This could make females very wary, especially if an Armthrower was seen to be wooing a significant number of conquests.

The next category was the Positioner. These adolescents conveniently positioned themselves in prime locations to maximise their ability to approach a female. They frequently posted themselves in entrance or exit areas, posing while waiting for a female to pass. When she did, they would quickly pull her arm or pass her a compliment to court attention. Positioners, social predators, could be easily found by the common room doors, the college gates or anywhere a heavy flow of people were due to pass. Sideeq had noted that both Chaser-Callers and Positioners would often be accompanied by a third category of suitor, the Wingman. The Wingmen were adaptable fellows. They never really set the pursuit off, but offered support by courting the target female's companion. This gave the first suitor enough time to lure his conquest, and also gave the Wingman a chance to create an opportunity of his own.

Every day seemed like a lesson in teenage anthropology for Sideeq as he watched his fellow students. These intricate courting patterns were all part of the teenage mating rituals he was still yet to partake in. What intrigued him most were the girls' responses. There were those who outright shut a boy down and others who slowly came around to a boy's advances. He would study the interactions, logging the slightest of touches or a hint of flirtatious smile. Secretly he wondered what some boys said to warrant the right response, then pondered whether he could do the same.

Reflecting, he noticed a group of girls huddled under an umbrella. They were making their way to the common room when a gust of wind blew the umbrella inside out, making the girls scream in unison. As they scampered inside Sideeq realised there was one last category of suitor in the teenage mating pool. That group was the 'Apexers,' and they were very different from the other categories for one specific reason. An Apexer did not pursue—he was *pursued*. Whether he was a Hot boy, Top boy, Roadman, Intellectual, Sports Jock or just the cool guy, the small number of Apexers at Cardinal Manning drew girls towards *them*. For whatever reason, the girls had deemed them desirable, and acted according to their desires. Immediately, Sharkey came to Sideeq's mind. He had seen how Sharkey's presence created a stir. Girls would whisper and giggle in their groups. Others would wander over to make doting small talk, while Sharkey played oblivious to attention. Some girls had even reversed the roles when it came to Sharkey. Sideeq called them the Hi-Girls, Huggers and Linkers. At the same time, Sideeq had found himself in awe of Sharkey. He had a silent charisma that didn't command respect but allowed a person to openly offer it. Sideeq wondered what it was like to be Sharkey. Everyone loved Sharkey.

Then he wondered what it was like just to be normal.

Peering down, he spotted Danny and Kyle sprinting across the courtyard with Rizla in toe. As they got to the common room doors, Kyle slipped while trying to slow down. He almost lost his footing. Luckily, Danny caught him and the three disappeared through the white doors.

Things were changing. Ever since Sharkey had taken Kyle to ReloadFM, Sideeq had noticed how people were beginning to respond to Kyle—especially the girls. A month ago he was an average positioner or at best a reluctant chaser. Now he seemed to have been promoted to an apex wingman, courtesy of Sharkey.

For a moment Sideeq felt a pang of anxiety. Deep down inside he realised that Kyle had always strived to be an Apexer, and he contemplated where that would leave him. Looking at his reflection in the window, Sideeq sighed. Sometimes he could barely look a girl in the eye, let alone talk to one. Who the hell was going to be interested in him with his deaf ear and one eye?

In deep thought, he watched the rain run down the window when the 3 o'clock pips sounded.

"Yo, what you doing?" Swank said, tapping him on the arm. "You coming?"

Snapping out of his trance, Sideeq looked around the class. Most of the other students had already packed away their equipment and were rushing to leave. "Nah, I'm gonna kick back and jam for a bit," Sideeq said, brooding. "If you see Kyle, tell him he don't need to wait around for me. He can leave when he wants."

"Rah, so what, you're not hitting gym with us den?"

"I dunno." Sideeq shrugged. "I might do. I'll see how I feel in a bit. What time you lot going?"

"In about an hour, bruh." Swank tapped her watch. "Why what you saying? You know it's leg day today, right? I thought you loved leg day."

"Yeah, yeah, I do," Sideeq said, trying to muster a smile. "But I think I'm gonna stay and bang out a few bits for this next module." He pointed at his artwork.

"OK say no more, my G." Swank threw her rucksack on. "If you change your mind I'll be downstairs with the man dem. If not, tomorrow."

Touching fists with Sideeq, she gave him a quick half hug

and headed to the door.

"Oi Mister G," she said, grabbing Mr Ghodstinat's attention. "Look after my boy, y'know. Certain heads told me you be hooking people up with da good brushes and ting when no ones about. Oi, make that happen."

"Err, I don't know what you are talking about, Swank," Mr Ghodstinat replied, waving his hand dismissively. "But maybe if you stayed behind more often then you would get some of the good stuff."

"Oh it's like that yeah, sir?" Swank pretended to smoke an imaginary joint. "Puff, puff give, puff, puff give. Say no more my G."

"I will puff you a slap, if you don't hand in your next assignment in on time."

"Rah, sir, are you allowed to say that?"

"No, but I don't care. Swank you are a good artist, but you are lazy, and that is why I will see you tomorrow." Mr Ghodstinat playfully pushed Swank through the door.

"Rah did you see that, Sid? This Persian don try move to me on a mad ting, fam! Nah, nah, I'm not having it, it's beef Mister G, it's beef."

Sideeq sat laughing as Mr Ghodstinat blocked the doorframe with his body, trying to keep Swank out. "Sideeq! Tell your friend to stop. I can't do this every day. She's very exhausting."

When Swank finally gave up harassing Mr Ghodstinat, she headed downstairs. Moments later, Sideeq watched her jog across the yard to common room with her hood up, and wondered where she fit into Cardinal Manning's dating pool. Up until now, a lot like himself, Swank had been quite aloof about her sexual preference and dating experiences.

Sideeq was about to create a new category for the likes of them when he got distracted by Nerissa, in red bomber jacket dashing through the rain towards his block. She used a huge textbook to cover her head, which Sideeq thought couldn't have been her best option. He questioned why she didn't have her red-and-white polka dotted umbrella today and watched her darting run till she vanished inside. He hadn't forgotten the first day of college, when she had wandered into his class lost. There was something about the way she smiled at him. It was as though for the smallest of moments she seemed to stare at him. Not at his dead eye or the scar that ran from his cheek to his ear. She actually stared at *him*. He remembered the way she waved before leaving, as though she would've happily stayed to hear him speak more. Even the way she quickly said, "I like your picture" felt like a fleeting attempt to make some sort of small connection.

"*Nonsense,*" he heard his inner voice say. "*You're desperate. You'll take anything and make it mean something. How many times has she spoke to you since that day?*"

"None."

"*Well then.*" The voice scolded him.

"Yeah, but what about the time when she smiled at me, when I was heading to the gym that time?"

"*What time? Bruv, you're reaching, brudda. Behave. Even if she did, that was properly on a polite ting. C'mon, how many people do you think she smiles at every day on a polite ting? Do you think you're the only one?*"

Sideeq wanted to tell the voice yes, why not him, but the more he thought about it the more absurd it seemed.

"*Look, bruv stop thinking,*" the voice said. "*It's a nice idea, but it ain't gonna happen.*"

"Why? What makes you thing I can't draw a girl like that?"

"*Bruv, hear what I'm saying, coz in my heart of hearts I would love for you to be able to move a gyal like that up. But you know why it ain't gonna happen?*"

"Why? Just because of my scars?"

"*Nah, bro, it's not none of that. It's coz you're an Omega, bro. That makes you different.*"

Mixing his paints Sideeq, sat listening to his inner thoughts as the voice detailed the last category in the teenage dating pool.

"*There are levels to this ting, bro. You don't go punching above your weight. Whatever playing field she's on and you're on, it's not the same. Are you forgetting who her boyfriend is?*"

Sideeq didn't answer as an image of Gobbler intruded his mind. He waited.

"*Yeah, that's right,*" the voice gloated. "*Even if she weren't with him, you know the real reason you can't have a girl like Nerissa? It's because you're not an Apexer. Bruv, you're not even a pursuer. If you was, you would go out there and find a way to move her up, but you won't. You know why? Because you're an Omega. You're one of those people that have to come last. Life don't want you to win, life wants you to take the scraps. Don't worry, it's not your fault. That's just the way it is. There ain't no shame in that. There's plenty of Omegas out there. You, my brother, just need to understand, to play your position and realise that certain things and certain people aren't for you.*"

Testing his brush strokes, Sideeq sat in deep contemplation. As the sky darkened outside, he found himself stuck in his chair for the next half an hour. Paralysed by dark thoughts, he questioned how they could be so bleak. It was true. You only had to look at his face to see that misfortune had touched his life. Yet Sideeq internally refused to accept that he couldn't position his way out of hardship when an Instagram notification flashed up on his screen. For a moment he stared at message. It read '*@Sanusithe1st has started following you*'. Checking out his new follower, it slowly he started to dawn on him why Kyle had been so obsessed with chasing Yumes and not dreams. If three thousand four hundred and sixty four people were willing to follow Deafeye_1 in two weeks, they were willing to follow any vision Sideeq set for himself. If Kyle could become an Apexer, why couldn't he? He just needed to crush the Omega within.

CHAPTER 2.4

"Two shots."

Knowing he was about to lose again, Kyle studied the remaining coloured balls and eight ball as Danny chalked his cue. With the widest of grins, Danny blew a puff of blue dust off the nib of his cue and circled the pool table. Slowly he checked out his angles, crouching at the edge of the table the looking up for Kyle's reaction. Smiling, he peered across the green canvas then doubled back to check his other option. Mischievously, he groaned and rubbed the whiskers on his chin, feigning to be in a great dilemma in an attempt to wind Kyle up.

"Hmmm, which one you think, Swank?" he said, pointing at his two options. "This one, or that one off the cushion?"

Before Swank could answer, Kyle held up his hand in protest.

"Nah, what you doing, bruv? You can't ask her what shot to play?"

"Why not?" Danny smirked.

"Whaddya mean? Man ain't playing doubles out here, bruv. Play your shots."

"Rahhh it's like that then, donnie?" Swank said, laughing along with Danny.

"Yes it is." Kyle held up his hand to hush Swank. Gritting his teeth, he pushed up his face as Danny began chalking his cue again. "Bruv, how much chalk do you need? Play your shot?"

"Woooo, what you getting all touchy for, mate? It's just a game."

"Fine. Play your shot."

Strolling around the table one last time to taunt Kyle, Danny leaned over and lined up the white ball. Striking it with the skill of a seasoned pro, Danny hit the white off the bottom cushion so it doubled back and potted his last stripped ball. Then it gently caressed the eight-ball so it sat over the corner pocket. Grinning, he tapped the designated pocket with his cue. Setting up the shot, he whistled and Rizla jumped up and hit the cue with his paw, sinking the ball. Fuming, Kyle threw down his cue and slumped into his chair, sulking as those nearby laughed at the sight of Rizla taking the shot. Danny handed his cue to the next set of players waiting to get on the table.

"Good game, good game," Danny said, approaching Kyle with an outstretched hand.

"Move, man." Kyle slapped his hand away. "What you tryna embarrass me out here for?"

"Oh c'mon mate, don't be a spoil sport. I done seen you creaming off bare man at Pound-up."

"Fo' real, my G," Swank agreed. "You gotta take the highs with the lows."

"That's right!" Danny spuded Swank with his fist. "Now lemme check one them blueys you got hiding in your purse. Unless you wanna go double or quits?"

"Nah, forget that," Kyle said, taking out his wallet. Begrudgingly, he slipped Danny a five-pound note. "So what you saying Dan, ain't you got no more dog walking for me?"

"Mate," Danny laughed. "Not unless you're happy picking up dog shit."

"Nah man, I'm not on that. The last time you made me pick it up it was all warm and ting."

"Err, that's nasty," Swank said, pulling a face.

"Maybe." Danny stuck the five-pound note in his sock with the rest of his money. "But at twenty pound a dog, it's part of the job."

Kyle sat mulling over more ways to make money while Danny outlaid to Swank the nuances of poopa-scooping verses the plastic-bag-and-hand technique. In all honesty, Kyle knew no matter how lucrative dog walking might be, it wasn't for him. Neither was hustling people at pound up and cards during lunch break. If he was going to get his and Sideeq's clothing line and record label up and running, he need a proper cash injection.

Taking out his phone, he began scrolling through the time-line on his Instagram for some inspiration, then decided to switch to the @Deafeye_1 account he had set up for Sideeq. At almost four thousand followers he was surprised to see how busy it was, and he grinned at his own genius. After studying the other catalogue of street artist Sideeq had given him, and the current pioneers of the UK art scene, Kyle had quickly devised a three-step guerrilla marketing plan for Sid's online profile.

They began by taking shots of all Sid's portraits of popular rappers, Grime musicians and sketches of his Deafeye character.

Every day they would post a series of images in the same post. One of the music artist, the original picture Sideeq had drawn, and one of Deafeye character. Then they would tag the musician to the post so they could tap into the musicians following. From the amount of likes and followers they were raking up, it was beginning to win. Sideeq had initially cringed at the strategy as trying to ride other people's coat tails. However, Kyle was able to convince him that a lot of the best street artists had paid tributes to iconic musicians or activists, and that had made their work recognisable. This brought them to phase two, which was to highlight Sid's own work. Using what little cash they had, they printed some Deafeye_1 stickers and stuck them up in prominent tube stations and tourist destinations around London, taking pictures to post. When they ran out of stickers, Sideeq created a stencil which they used to spray paint the DE1 logo. On one trip through Chinatown, Sideeq came across a stall selling small potion bottles with cork lids. Placed inside each was a parchment of Chinese writing and a proverb. Immediately, Kyle had an idea that if they photocopied one or two pictures of Sideeq's, they could leave them around town for people to find. The bottles were cheap, but from the shortcomings of his own account Kyle had already realised that the third phase had to be about how they could monetise Sideeq's profile. Having already posted pictures of the upcycled trainer art, Kyle used his dog-walking money to buy two pairs of white Air Forces. He then had Sideeq take photos of the trainers at different stages. When Sideeq finished, he had him post them with a caption that read 'NEW COMMISSION!!! For Customised Trainers or Crep/Jay Art, inbox for prices.'

Kyle was convinced they could make some good money from customising or upcycling trainers with Sideeq's art. He figured all they needed was a few decent commissions and they could invest in creating some prints and posters to sell. Contemplating his next move, Kyle wondered whether he should have put some of his money down on more studio time instead of two pairs of Air Force Ones. Peering around the common room, he started to scan people's trainers when Olly, a mixed race boy with freckles and dark Afro hair, walked in wearing sunglasses. Kyle watched him curiously as Olly looked around sheepishly. With his long strides he stepped towards the snack bar and ordered a hot chocolate from Betty, the old St Lucian woman behind the counter.. Frowning Kyle asked, "Why's my man wearing sunglass when it's pelting down outside?"

"What, didn't you hear?" Danny asked.

"Hear what?"

Danny looked at Swank, who looked back at him. It was clear she had heard. She nodded her head, gesturing for Danny to fill Kyle in. Scanning the common room for prying ears, Danny drew his chair closer to gossip.

"Mate, he got smacked by the Goblin Prince."

"Who?"

"He means Gobbler." Swank rolled her eyes at Danny's dramatics.

"So why didn't you just say that?" Kyle snapped.

"Mate, get it right I'm not saying nothing. That guy is like Voldemort to me—he whose name shall not be spoken. I'm not giving him any reason to come after me. Sharkey ain't gonna be there all the time."

Danny took out a Mars bar. He chomped on half and gave the other half to Rizla. "I heard he proper battered Olly, like full on stomped him out."

Checking Olly wasn't watching, Danny made a stamping motion with his feet. "Wallahi, swear down. You should've seen when Ms Drake told him to take off his glasses in registration. He looked like Kung-Fu Panda without the kung-fu."

"Nah, you eff-ery." Swank tried not to laugh. She playfully punched Danny in the leg, but his mouth was on a roll.

"I'm telling you, I heard Gobble-gobble-boil-and-trouble took his phone, dough, and dro off him. Bang out of order. I don't care what anyone says, I'd fight a man for my dro."

"Fam, stop." Swank took another swing at Danny's leg. This time he swivelled to avoid the blow. "You're mocking my guy's life right now."

Kyle watched Olly as he paid for his hot chocolate and left. He noticed the boy walked with a slight limp. "So what he punch up Olly for?"

"Boyyy," Danny rubbed his chin. "I heard it was coz Olly got caught watching his girl. I think he tried to move to her."

Kyle sat up in disbelief. "Olly?"

"Yep, that's what I heard. Silly move really, unless you're looking for a quick way to get violated."

Swank looked unconvinced and shook her head. "You sure it wasn't the other way round?" she said.

"What'd you mean?" Danny stopped to think about the possibility.

"Fam, I use to go school with that girl. Trust me, they use to call her Narcissistic Nerissa coz she loves attention."

"What, you saying she's a hoe?"

"I ain't saying none of that." Swank wagged her finger. "All I'm saying is, man dem need to watch themselves around her, innit. She likes to watch man and get their attention. But when you got a man like Gobbler, dem antics can get man hurt."

"Yeah, like Olly."

"No, not just Olly." Swank paused realising she may have divulged too much. From the way Kyle knotted his eyebrows it was obvious that he'd picked up on it. Kissing her teeth, Swank sighed and decided to lay down a disclaimer.

"Look I ain't talking no one's business, but the other day me and Sideeq were coming from the gym and I saw her there watching, watching him, like she was tryna get his attention. It might be nothing, but who knows with that girl."

Without a word Kyle, acknowledged the information with a grimace, while Danny asked, "What makes you think she was watching him? She might've been watching you."

"Watching me for what?" Swank got her back up. She stood and picked up her backpack. "Don't get it twisted, fam, I don't get down like that. Me and her already had drama before so she could never be watching me?"

"Drama, yeah?" Danny smiled and nudged Kyle with a wink. "What kinda drama?"

"It's nothing. Just old history, innit." Swank put her backpack on and fixed the straps. She turned to Kyle. "Trust me my G, that girl is eager, and this is the second time I seen her watching Siddy.

True he's a lightie lover, I just thought I better tell you to look out for him, that's all."

"Cool, say no more." Kyle stood up and touched fists with Swank.

Danny waited until Swank left, then turned to Kyle and asked, "Oi bruv, do you think Swank bats for the other team or swings both ways?"

It was a good question, but Kyle thought he wasn't the one to ask. Instead, looking at his phone, his eyes lit up when he discovered @Sanusithe1st had started following Sideeq Instagram.

CHAPTER 2.5

Sideeq didn't hear her knock, but by chance turned around and saw her standing in the doorway. When Nerissa smiled at him it was almost like déjà vu. Her presence threw him back to the first day of college, only this time the room was empty. Out of instinct he didn't smile back. Instead the two remained silent, glaring at each other. Neither of them knew what to say. They just looked one at another, content in staring. Mesmerised, Sideeq studied her smile. She wasn't wearing her ruby lipstick today, and her damp hair had been brushed into wavy curls that dropped to her shoulders. Her bow-shaped lips were coated with a touch of gloss and shimmered ever so slightly in the light. It made her face looked more natural, and he noticed the smallest of scars on her chin. In their shared silence she continued to look him in the eye, and bit her lip seductively as her smile widened. Her brown eyes travelled the length of the room and fixed on Sideeq as she waited for a reaction. Taking a step closer she leaned forward, arching her right leg and pushing out her chest while clinging to the doorframe.

"I said sorry to interrupt you, but is it possible that I can borrow a prop?"

It took Sideeq a moment to register the question, then composing himself he asked, "What kinda prop?"

His tone remained as flat as the expression on his face. Giggling, Nerissa seemed to find his reserve intriguing. She shrugged, inviting herself in. "I'm not exactly sure."

She did a small twirl as she peered around the room and skipped two steps towards him. "Just something that looks like it could come to life."

Puzzled, Sideeq frowned at her answer, which prompted her to explain.

"I have to create a theatrical apostrophe for my drama class."

Again Sideeq looked at her, baffled, but managed to string two words together. "What's that?"

"Oh, it's kinda like a monologue, but when somebody is talking to an object or somebody that's not there."

"Hmm." Sideeq grunted an acknowledgement.

Laying down his brush, he slipped out of his chair and took a step to his right so he wasn't blindsided by Nerissa's approach. He turned to face her and became conscious of his scar. He thought about putting his hood up, but didn't want to draw her attention to it and for the first moment since she'd entered the room, he dropped his gaze. She was now close enough for him to smell her perfume. Its sweet violet scent made him blush and he was overwhelmed by her proximity.

Feeling uncomfortable, he shifted his feet awkwardly and took another side-step away from his desk to create distance. His heart was racing, but he hoped Nerissa couldn't tell. He scowled around the room. His nerves were active. He felt both a hint of anger, yet a sturdy flurry of excitement. He didn't like being caught off guard. Clenching his jaw, he cursed Mr Ghodstinat under his breath. Why the man had to be a serial coffee fiend was beyond him. Of all the times to run off and get a caffeine fix, he chose now. This was his department, his room, he should be the one to deal with this.

Damn, Sideeq thought. After all the time he'd been spent thinking about being good enough for Nerissa, he never once thought about what he would actually say to her. Somehow in his mind, they would just speak—they would connect and that would be enough. Now he felt under pressure. Sideeq loathed the idea of being on the spot. He kept telling himself *Sid don't be an Omega, don't be an overthink this* when his eyes finally fell on a statue of a porcelain dog. It was about the size of a small cat and was shoved in a corner of random objects they used for still life drawings. It had a purple and green paisley patterned scarf wrapped around its neck. Sideeq pulled it off the shelf and handed it to Nerissa. "What about this?"

Removing the scarf, Nerissa examined the dog. It was a beagle with brown droopy ears and a white muzzle and paws. Sideeq didn't know much about dogs, but he guessed from the inquisitive look on its raised head, the statue was modelled on a pup. Nerissa held the statue at eye level then stroked its black-coated saddleback.

"Awww, this so cute," she said, wiping some dust off its snout. "The expression on his face is perfect."

Sideeq grinned. Something about the statue reminded him of Rizla.

"Oh my gosh, are you sure I can take it?"

"Hmm, why not?" Sideeq said sitting back down. "I won't tell if you won't."

"Really?" Nerissa smiled. Following Sideeq, she hopped on the table opposite him, taking a seat. She placed the statue beside her and began to stroke its head as though it were real. "Are you used to keeping secrets?" she asked, titling her head seductively and biting her lip.

"No," Sideeq chuckled. He was finally beginning to relax and asked himself *what would Kyle or Sharkey say right about now?* "Not with strangers anyway."

"Ah, but you do keep secrets?"

"I don't have no secrets to keep."

Kicking her legs back and forth, Nerissa twisted her mouth, smirking. "Really? I'm sure you must have at least one secret." She paused. "Oh wow sorry. Here I am asking you about secrets and I haven't even asked your name. Oh wow, how rude is that? Sorry." She stressed the word.

Sideeq looked at her. He was still fascinated by her presence. She seemed like a ball of energy and he wondered whether she was nervous or if this was just her natural disposition.

"Oh my days, sorry," she apologised again. "My name's Nerissa, what's yours?"

"My name?" Sideeq hesitated, as though the one his mother had given wasn't enough.

"Yeah, your name." Nerissa stared at him, waiting.

Thinking fast, Sideeq turned his back. Taking a pencil he scribbled on a sheet of paper, tore it off and folded it. Turning back he told Nerissa, "Hold out your hand." Nerissa smiled as he reached out. He put the folded paper in her hand and gently closed it. His hand looked huge in comparison to hers. Standing back, Sideeq watched Nerissa rush to open the paper. Scanning his handwriting, her eyes lit up.

"Sideeq."

"Sshh." Sideeq put a finger to his lip. "That's classified information. Call it a secret between me and you."

Nerissa laughed. "OK that was smooth, very smooth, but I'm sure you're name's written in the register, so I guess that's not too much of a secret."

Sideeq shrugged. "I don't know what you want me to say, then. Like I said, I ain't got no secrets."

Again Nerissa smirked, as though she couldn't stop smiling. "I don't believe you. Everybody's got one."

Sideeq mimicked her smile, and shook his head. He wanted to say, 'yeah I really fancy you,' but thought that would sound so corny. As far as he was concerned, he was on a roll and *weren't gonna say anything that sounded Omega-ish*. Grinning, he said, "Nope not me. I'm squeaky clean."

"Oh shut up nobody's squeaky clean."

"I am."

"So you're trying to tell me there's no secret girl, or a big stash of money under the bed?"

"Have you seen under my bed?" Sideeq joked. "That's the last place you're gonna find any money."

"Oh OK." Nerissa slid off the table. She took a step over to his desk and placed her hand on his shoulder. "I noticed you didn't say nothing about those secret girls though."

Her touch excited Sideeq, and he wondered how he could touch her back. The thought of touching her sent his mind into overdrive and he immediately become nervous again. Blushing, he looked down at his painting and said, "Not much to say, they ran off with the money, innit."

"Wow," Nerissa smiled. "You got an answer for everything."

Luckily for Sideeq, she seemed to have misconstrued his shyness for bravado, and stood trying to calculate her next move. "Who's that?" she asked, pointing to the sketch Sideeq had on the table. Looking up, Sideeq reached for the drawing.

"That's my niece," he said, passing it to her.

Nerissa examined the picture of the little girl. "How old's she?"

"Four."

"What's her name?"

"Amara-Renee."

"She looks gorgeous. Do you have anymore?"

"No, just the one."

"No, not nieces." Nerissa laughed, thumping him on the shoulder. "I meant drawings?"

"Oh."

Sideeq got up and walked over to a large wooden chest of draws. Reaching inside, he pulled out his leather portfolio and lay it on the central table. He fished out a handful of pencil and ink sketches and passed them to Nerissa to look at. Nerissa appeared mesmerised by the detail in his cross-hatching and shading, and fell silent, marvelling at his work. All the pictures centred on women and children in his family. She picked up a sketch of a woman holding his niece on her hip, then a second drawing with the same woman, only this time younger. She stood in an identical pose, holding a little boy. The woman smiled at the toddler's chubby cheeks and cornrow braids, grinning as he dribbled down the front of his grey Spiderman sweater.

"Is this, you and your mum?"

"Nah," Sideeq shook his head. "That's my older brother."

"Awww, Sideeq, these pictures are beautiful."

"Hmm, they're alright," Sideeq said, cringing. He wasn't use to being complimented by girls. Rubbing the back of his neck, he took a seat back down at his desk.

"Are you crazy?" Nerissa followed him again. "These are amazing."

Holding the pictures in her hand, she used the opportunity to get close to him and positioned herself virtually between his open legs. Sideeq shifted back a touch, and Nerissa smiled as his leg brushed against her hip. For a moment he looked her over, before a miniature curve appeared at the side of his mouth.

"Your mum must really be proud of you. I wish I had somebody to draw a picture of me."

"Hmm." Sideeq's brow knit, thinking about the first part of her statement. For a moment he looked out towards the rainy window, lost in his own thought.

"Would *you* draw a picture of me?"

"Huh?" Sideeq turned to look at her, and it seemed the questioning expression on his face made Nerissa step back. Shying away, she put the first picture down.

"You don't have to if you don't want." She bit her lip again, but this time like she was in trouble. "I just thought that maybe I could pose for you or something. I don't know. Like a whatcha-ma-call-it…" In an instant Nerissa eyes lit up again as the word entered her mind. "Like a muse."

Sideeq dropped his head, chuckling. His huge shoulders bounced up and down.

"Like a muse, yeah?"

"Yes!" Nerissa said, thumping him again. "Why you laughing? Are trying to say I can't be a muse?"

"No," Sideeq grin. "But you came in here looking for a prop. And now you wanna leave being a muse?"

Nerissa gasped. Speechless she stood for a second with her mouth open as though she couldn't believe how rude he was—but she seemed to like it. Smiling, she hit him again and the two began to laugh as he tried to protect himself.

"Yo."

The voice came from behind them, and they both froze like they had been caught stealing. Startled, Nerissa immediately backed away from Sideeq as they turned to see Kyle standing in the doorway. He watched them with a disapproving look on his face.

"Wha gwan?" He nodded towards Sideeq. "What's all the jokes?"

"Nothing," Sideeq said, avoiding Kyle's glare. He looked at Nerissa, who looked back at him. She looked nervous and he smiled at her vulnerability.

"We were just talking. Nerissa, this is my best friend, Kyle."

Playing shy, Nerissa smiled politely and waved at Kyle. "Hi."

"Yeah, hi," Kyle grunted. He virtually ignored her and looked straight at Sideeq. "Talking about what?"

"Nothing much. Just stuff," Sideeq replied.

"What stuff?"

"Err, none of your business," Nerissa interjected. She didn't like Kyle's manners. "It's not a crime for two people to talk."

"Yeah?" Kyle raised an eyebrow. "That depends whose talking. You never heard of conspiracy?"

"Pardon?"

"You're excused."

Flabbergasted, Nerissa put down the drawing. "Do you have a problem with me?"

"No. Why should I?" Kyle gave her a fake grin.

"Look I don't know what your friend's problem is, Sideeq, I but didn't come here for any trouble." She picked up the statue and wrapped it in the purple scarf. "Thanks for the prop, yeah? I'll see you around."

Nerissa cut her eye at Kyle as she was leaving. She felt like telling Kyle to go jump off a cliff but decided there was more dignity in keeping it moving. Sideeq, however, was ready to explode. He had waited so long to speak to Nerissa, and Kyle just walked in and ruined everything.

"Y-y-yo what was that all about, K? Did you have to speak to her like that?"

"Me?" Kyle held up a hand, cutting Sideeq off. He ran to the door and checked the corridor to make sure Nerissa was out of ear shot.

"I'm doing you favour, bruv. What you doing talking to her? That girl's poison. Didn't you hear what happened to Olly?"

"What?"

Calming Sideeq down, Kyle began to explain what the others had told him down in the common room. Then he waited for Sideeq to pack up his stuff and the two head down to the gym to meet Swank.

"Bruv, you know me. I would never intentionally disrespect you like that. You know I love you, no funny man ting. But when I saw you with that chick, I just thought *this girl is friggin' dangerous.*"

Apologising, Kyle explained that he hadn't actually come upstairs to warn him, but tell him about Sanusi the1st.

"What about him?"

"Have you not checked your Insta? Sanusi the 1st the is the guy that runs Art Meets Culture."

Chapter 2.6

When Sideeq got home, he couldn't stop thinking about Nerissa. Lying back on his bed, he kicked off his trainers and began to mull over the day's events. In the privacy of his room he could barely contain his excitement, and put his hands behind his head with the biggest of grins. Talking to a girl was all new to him, and he relished his achievement like a striker bagging hat trick on his debut.

Replaying their conversation in his head, he envisioned the smile on Nerissa's face and then memorised, logged it and stored for safe-keeping. That one belonged to him and no could steal it. He knew if anyone were privy to his thoughts they would call him besotted, but for once he really didn't care. He kept trying to guess what Nerissa thought of him and whether they would get another chance to speak. He knew she hadn't been best pleased when she left, and in hindsight he wondered whether he should have done more to pull Kyle up. He wasn't in favour of how his friend had treated her, but couldn't dismiss what the others had told him.

Sitting up, he looked at the framed photograph of his older brother on his desk. He missed him. If there was ever a time he could do with some brotherly advice, it was definitely now. Studying his brother's face, Sideeq's mood momentarily took a dip. Feeling overwhelmed by the void of his brother, the rapture in his spirit felt wrong. These were the moments they were supposed to be able to share. What would his brother have said about Nerissa? "*Is that you yeah, Siddy? Go on lil bro. Go shoot your shot,*" or "*Sideeq, you got some good friends around you. Don't let no girl fool up your head. Listen to your bredrin.*"

Sideeq felt conflicted. The closest person he had to a brother now was Kyle, and he knew what it was like when Kyle didn't like someone. The word *territorial* was an understatement. He would become very stubborn and ignorant when that person's name was mentioned, and it took a lot to win him over. But what had Nerissa really done wrong? How could they blame her for what Gobbler did? Nerissa didn't have any control over his actions. No more than she had control over whether Olly was watching her or not. She wasn't even there when it happened. It was understandable why Kyle would have his concerns, but to call her poison seemed unfair. Sideeq sniggered. His mum had always told him, 'don't expect people to be fair; fare is something you pay to get on the bus'. For a split second, Sideeq wondered if there was another reason Kyle had taken a dislike to her. His mum also liked to say, 'The devil makes it easy to despise the things you can't have, rather than loathe the part of you that yearns for it.'

Scoffing at the idea of Kyle wanting Nerissa, Sideeq dismissed the notion and got up to get something to eat. Heading downstairs, he poked his head round the living room door where his mum sat watching a quiz show.

"You alright, mum?"

"Yeah, you?"

"Hmm."

"How was college?"

"Not too bad," Sideeq said with a small smirk on his face. "It was OK."

Valerie looked at him curiously as he clung to the doorframe. The miniature smile on his face lasted for too long, and he looked at her and back at the TV far too many times to really be interested in what was on the screen.

"Just OK?" she asked with her own little grin. Trading another impish smirk, Sideeq nodded his head trying not laugh. "Yeah. Just OK."

"Hmm, OK." Valerie pouted and pushed up her mouth in the way only black mothers did. What Sideeq didn't understand that like most mothers, Valerie had studied her son for his whole life. She had witnessed his first breath to his first fall and was so in tune with his natural behaviour that the slightest of change in nuance always registered. Also similar to most mothers, nine months of carrying him, then labour, plus the tribulations of motherhood had made her virtual a psychic. And even though after a certain age, mothers found it harder to deduce the reason for their children's mood swings, their instinct and intuition could always detect any shift in pattern nevertheless.

Valerie continued to watch her son with a probing eye. "You hungry?"

"Hmm, what's for dinner?"

"That's not what I asked you?"

Sideeq chuckled, playing along. "Yes, mum. What's for dinner?"

"Brown stew. Come."

Valerie got up and went to the kitchen. Grabbing a plate, she dished out some food, watching him with every spoonful. "So, you're not going to tell me what's going on?"

Sideeq looked at his mum. "What you talking about? There's nothing going on." He managed not to smirk, however mischief was clearly written all over his face. His mother gave him a stern look that in yesteryear would have had him confessing every little transgression and misdemeanour.

"Oh, some art curator-slash-promoter guy called Sanusi the 1ˢᵗ started following me and Kyle on Instagram. He runs some event called Art Meets Culture."

"What's that?"

"It's this night where they have this art exhibition and music showcase all in rolled into one, so that emerging urban and street artists can display their work alongside up-and-coming home-grown rappers and musicians, to get some of their names out there and get some exposure."

"OK, well that sounds good. You gonna enter?"

"Yeah, probably. Kyle reckons it will be heavy for us to get showcased at the same venue."

"Yes, but what do *you* reckon?" Valerie asked, pouring gravy over Sideeq's food. She showed him the plate to make sure it was enough. Sideeq nodded.

"Yeah, I think that'll be cool."

"Alright then, and what do you get if you win?"

"Nothing." Sideeq pointed at a plate of fried plantain. "It's not a competition mum, it's more for recognition."

"So you don't win nothing?" Valerie added four slices to his plate.

"Nah, but I might be able to sell one or two pieces or maybe get a commission."

"Ohhh, that will be nice," his mum reasoned, grasping the concept. "So other than that, everything else is OK?" Valerie quizzed. She was still determined to get more out of him, and waved the ladel in the air as she spoke. "There's nothing going on? You're cool, college is cool, everything is just cool?"

"Yeah." Sideeq stood by the sink with his arms crossed. "That's it."

Valerie smiled as he managed to maintain his ruse. "OK, Mr Cool, you carry on with your cool runnings then. Mr College-was-OK."

She put a tray under the plate and handed it to him. Taking the tray, Sideeq grabbed some cutlery and leaned in, kissing his mum on the cheek.

"Thanks, mum."

"Move from me," Valerie slapped Sideeq on the back as a big grin spread across his face. "That's why I can't stand you. You're really going to stand there in my face boy and tell me nothing ain't going on?"

"Yeah." Sideeq looked at her, pretending be lost. "There's nothing going on. I'm squeaky clean mum I don't have no secrets to keep."

"Hmm, whatever." Valerie smiled as he left the kitchen.

"Just you bring down all those mouldy glasses you got collecting upstairs. They look like a bloody science experiment. And make sure you wash them—you ain't got no slave round here."

Heading upstairs Sideeq settled down in front of his TV. He selected a tutorial on YouTube and began filling up his belly. Chewing his food, his mind drifted back to Nerissa again. He wondered whether she could cook? When he was finished wolfing down his food, he gathered up his plate and the stack of empty glasses. They swayed on his tray like the leaning tower of Pisa. Tip-toeing down the stairs, he placed his dishes gently in the sink and was about to sneak back up when his mum called out, "Siddy when you're finished washing them, bring my handbag in here, please."

Groaning, Sideeq ran the tap and dealt with the dishes. Drying his hands, he fetched his mother's handbag off the side table in the passageway and went to see what she wanted.

Thanking him, Valerie started looking through the bag and said, "Siddy, sit down please, son. There's something I want to talk to you about."

Taking a seat on the arm of the chair, Sideeq detected the apprehension in his mum's voice. She sighed, fishing out a brown envelope. Immediately, Sideeq recognised the red automated mail stamp on it and braced himself.

"Son, the probation service sent this letter today, from *that* boy's solicitors."

There was an awesome sting in Valerie's use of the word '*that*' and Sideeq couldn't help but note that his mother still refused to use Nana's name. Even as she spoke it was evident that the mere thought of him stirred a fury inside. Throughout the whole ordeal, she always referred to him as 'that boy'. Whether she used an adjective in that middle—'that *dutty, stink, wicked, evil, callous, ugly, baboon faced* boy', in their house he would forever be '*that boy*'.

Nana's letter was a stark reminder that in the same year her life had been destroyed by the perpetrators of knife *and* gun violence. As she buried her first born with his face still contorted from the pain of his murder. The second sat with his face and ear bandaged up like an injured solider in a war movie. Valerie would never forgive the likes of Nana (and the unknown men who killed her eldest), and his face was synonymous with her grief.

Taking deep breaths, Valerie composed herself. "The probation service sent a document, saying they've enclosed a handwritten letter from him. To tell you the truth, son, my first thought was to burn it. I dint even want to touch the letter, but I realised it's your letter, and there may be something in there you want to read." Valerie handed the envelope to Sideeq. "You don't have to read it now, son. You don't haffe read it *at all*. If you want I can hold it for you, or you can put it down 'til you're ready. But the main thing is you have it now. What you do with it is your decision."

Part III

The Secrets Beneath the Scars

CHAPTER 3.1

Did you ever wonder why London's morning commuters are the strangest creatures the world has ever seen? It's not because they come in an array of shapes and sizes. Nor is it because of the sheer savagery they may show when trying to board a teeming carriage. Nor is it because of the way they swarm Underground staff, jeering with a mob mentality at the first sign of any delay. No—the reason London's morning commuters are the strangest creatures is because of their innate ability to collectively ignore each other, while still occupying the same space. You can go to any tube station from Monday to Friday, between the hours of 7am and 9am and you'll find them standing there, performing the oddest of rituals. Watch. You will notice the same people arrive at the same platform at roughly the same time. One by one they will look up at the yellow digits on the LED display board, checking the time of the next train. Then they will look around at generally the same faces they have been seeing every day for weeks, months and sometimes years, then completely dismiss one another, paying more attention to the new poster that had been hung over night.

If you're lucky once in a blue moon you may see two who

raise an eyebrow at one another as a sign of acknowledgement. If you do, then you've been blessed. However, what is even stranger is that those who are in charge of London's transport have cultivated and endorsed this daily routine for over a century. They now provide travellers free newspapers and supplements, and hang posters above seats in the aim to avoid one thing—eye contact. It was the key to the commuters' success. The only reason that commuters were able to endure being packed in like sardines on the Central line, or breathe through the stench of that one traveller who was prone to heavy sweating no matter how much deodorant he used. Please, no eye contact. The less commuters had to look one another in the face, the less they had to connect with the person standing beside or opposite them. With smart phones or broadsheets, they could shield themselves from the eyes of the next man, never having to recognise their own woes in laden stares of others. With earphones installed, they could close their eyes and travel in peace or find the headspace to be consumed by contemplation. And so, in a sea of myriad bodies, morning-time travels could sometimes be the loneliest place in the world for London's commuters.

There were only two stops on the Hammersmith & City line between Wood Lane and Ladbroke Grove, but it was enough for Sideeq to get lost in his own thoughts. Standing by the carriage doors with his hood up, he peered at the concrete scenery. The train gently rocked from side to side as it snaked behind Westfield's mega shopping centre. The green football pitches by the Westway flyover were empty as the train continued to crawl through to the council estates of Latimer Road. The streets below were lined with cars in bumper-to-bumper traffic like a set of toy cars ready for play. As the train came towards Ladbroke Grove station, Kyle took a picture of Sideeq peering out of the window.

"Oi, this picture looks 'ard." Kyle smiled as they exited the train on to the platform. Heading down the stairs he said, "Look," passing Sideeq his phone. Sideeq checked the image. It was a subtle picture. Kyle had managed to capture his side profile. His head was at an angle and his hood covered the majority of his face. He looked like a hooded super hero, and there was a certain air of mystery in the pose. Above his head was a Deafeye 1 sticker slapped on a poster.

"Hmm, yeah that's cool," Sideeq said with a sombre tone. His eyes barely looked at the screen before he passed the phone back.

Taking in Sideeq's demeanour, Kyle decide to leave him in peace. It was obvious something was playing on his mind. As they walked up the road towards college, Kyle could sense the restlessness within Sideeq. He took it as a clear sign something was up when he saw Sideeq slip off his hearing aid and slot it in his pocket. Kyle hadn't failed to notice his friend had been in the darkest of moods for the past few days, but hoped he would snap out of it. Unlike most people, Sideeq rarely lashed out at people when he was troubled. He simply disengaged with the world, then chimed back in when he was ready.

As they approached the college, Kyle saw Sharkey parking up. Securing the wheel lock on his bike, he fixed his backpack and greeted them.

"Wha gwan, K? Wha gwan Sid?" he said, holding out his

gloved fist.

"Yes, yes, bruv." Kyle bumped his fist, but Sideeq totally ignored him. Baffled, Sharkey looked at Kyle as Sideeq carried on walking. Knowing Sharkey had approached on Sideeq's blind side, Kyle shook his head and stuck out a foot, tripping Sideeq. Breaking out of his stride, Sideeq turned to look at him, then seemed surprised to see Sharkey walk alongside them.

"Wha gwan, Sid?" Sharkey said, extending his fist again.

Sideeq murmured something incoherent and touched his fist, which obviously puzzled Sharkey even more. As they entered the gates, Sideeq turned to them and said, "I'll catch you man later."

"Later."

"Bless."

Kyle and Sharkey watched as Sideeq walked off. They both studied the towering giant as he stepped through the crowd. With his hood up he looked like a phantom—only he appeared to be the one who was haunted.

"Yo, K. Everything alright with Sid, yeah?"

"Yeah, why?"

"I don't know, he just seems a little off lately?"

"How d'you mean?" Kyle played dumb. He was glad he wasn't the only one who noticed it, but wanted to hear Sharkey's view.

"You know, quiet. I mean, I know he don't talk too much, but come like he's been ah bit quieter den normal."

"Nah, that's just Sid," Kyle said opening the door. They headed down the corridor towards the music block. "He gets like that once in a while. He's one those dudes who needs space to himself from time to time. You know how it goes. He'll be alright."

"Yeah, I hope so," Sharkey replied. "I like Sideeq, he's a cool breh. I got time for him. You man got a funny little relationship and ting."

"What tryna say, bruv?" Kyle demanded, defensively. "Man ain't on no fruity business, you know?"

"Whoa," Sharkey laughed. "How did you get all the way over there, bro?"

"Coz man try say we got a funny relationship."

"I dint mean like that, stop reaching."

"Yeah, but I'm just saying, innit." Kyle made sure to stress his point. "Man don't do fruity."

"OK, I hear dat." Sharkey laughed. He held his hands up, surrendering. "All I was saying was I like the way you man roll. The way you look out for each other. You can tell you man are tight."

"Oh." Kyle felt satisfied with Sharkey's explanation.

"How long you lot been bredrins?

"Since primary school."

"Figures," Sharkey said as they entered the class. "Was he always so quiet?"

"Not even." Kyle twist up his face. A memory of a younger Sideeq emceeing on stage at the school talent showed flashed into his mind. He remembered how in awe of Sideeq he had been, watching his friend tear up the mic. Sideeq's delivery was so amazing that afterwards, Kyle begged Sideeq to teach him how to rhyme. Taking a seat in the classroom, the memory brought a smile to Kyle's face. "Siddy use to be savage on the mic."

"Sideeq?" Sharkey coiled back, shocked.

When Kyle saw the surprise on Sharkey's face, it slowly dawned on him. People like Sharkey may never know that version of Sideeq, the one that wasn't plagued by his scars. "Yeah," he replied solemnly. "That was before."

Kyle stopped. He wanted to say more, but wondered if it was right. He looked towards Sharkey, whose calm demeanour invited trust.

"It's a long story."

"Mmm," Sharkey said, switching on his computer. He neither encouraged nor discouraged Kyle from speaking. Instead he sat nonchalant with no need to pry. Kyle sense he could confide in him, and began by saying,

"To tell you truth, bruv, it's all a madness." Kyle remembered the events well. "It all happened when we were in year 7…"

Five Years Earlier…

It was late April, and spring was in full bloom. The end of school pips at Burlington Danes had already sounded. The blossom tree behind the black gates waved pollen with cherry pink petals in the breeze as Kyle waited anxiously. He looked up the driveway to see Sideeq casually strolling out. When he arrived he wore a silly grin on his face, knowing he was late.

"Where've you been?" Kyle said annoyed. Sideeq knew he was in a rush.

"Nowhere. Where's Phonics and Kiss?" Sideeq asked, mentioning the other two of their four-man crew.

"They got detention, but I got their money. Come, let's go."

Kyle tried to speed Sideeq up. Most of their friends would still be mingling by the football pitch and he didn't want anyone to find out about his secret mission. He was still sour about being humiliated in an emcee battle between their Grime crew 5SG (aka 5ive Star Generals) and the rival crew in their year, Ice Squad. Since the emergence of Grime, anyone who could string two lyrics together was an MC and everyone wanted to clash. After a heated debate over the Wiley vs Kano clash on the *Lord of The Mics* DVD, Kyle got into a battle with Ice Squad's top mic man, Icey-3. The others had told Kyle to let Sideeq battle him, but Kyle refused and was subsequently humiliated when he choked his lines.

Avoiding the migration to the bus stop, Kyle and Sideeq hot-footed-it to Shepherd's Bush Market—jogging down Du Cane Road, across the iron bridge, through White City and down Loftus Road. Kyle dragged Sideeq on a mission to *Global Sport*. Global was a popular clothing shop in Shepherds Bush Market known for selling a variety of designer labels, custom sportswear, DVDs, and mixtapes. More importantly they sold the widest selection of fitted caps in West London, a staple of any Grime artist's uniform at the time.

Masterminding his revenge, Kyle had ordered identical Georgetown camouflage New Era caps with an embroidery G on the front. Collecting £30 from each member, he was eager to pick up the hats before he lost his deposit. He had arranged another battle with Ice Squad for Friday dinnertime and couldn't wait for 5SG come to the battle wearing their uniformed camouflage caps and bandannas. Kyle knew it wasn't going to matter what came out of their rivals mouths once they arrived in the canteen. That battle was going to be won on sheer presence. He had been practicing and writing new bars for days now—he knew he could kill Icey, but he wanted a landslide victory. For that he needed them all to make a striking impact.

Had he known what fate had planned in store for he might not have been so persistent...

When they arrived at Global, the two friends quickly found themselves stood in the furthest corner from the fitted caps. On edge, they pretended to look at some Akademiks tracksuits while four boys in Ashbird High burgundy school jumpers and blazers stood by the caps. Both Kyle and Sideeq knew it wasn't a good time to be wearing Burlington navy blue.

Ashbird High was a ten-minute walk from Burlington Danes. And like most neighboring schools, they regularly declared war on each other. The latest war had begun when a group of Ashbird boys came down to Burlington looking for Big Des in year 11. Apparently, Desmond had banged Ricky George's girl. Ricky being the top boy at Ashbird, that warranted a reprisal. Yet someone had forgotten to tell Ricky that Dessie Daniels was the strongest boy in year 11 and the best fighter in Burlington. As they tried to rush him, Desmond plummeted his fist into Ricky's face and then turned to his friend. The second boy fell to the floor as Jason Pincze fly kicked him in the back. Quickly the rest of the year 11 boys joined in. Fleeing with no pride, the Ashbird boys ran down Du Cane Road with half the school chasing them. The other half tried recording it all on their phones. Since then, a Burlington girl had her hair set a light on the bus, an Ashbird boy had been stripped of his clothes and made to walk home, and there had been two mass Burlington vs. Ashbird fights in the park behind the BBC.

Kyle had no idea his friend would be the next casualty of war.

"Go and buy the hats and let's go," Sideeq whispered.

"No," Kyle said. He didn't want the Ashbird boys to see him buy the hats. "They'll try and rob us outside. Either we wait or we go and come back. What do you wanna do?" he asked from the side of his mouth.

"I don't know," Sideeq answered nervously.

He didn't mind fighting year 8 boys, but these boys were older than that. He'd seen the tall dark skin one playing football against year 10 at Barn Elms. He couldn't forget the boy. His skin was as black as midnight, with large pimples that oozed pus from his face. They were like mini pink volcanoes waiting to erupt. The boy had scored a hat trick and been sent off in the second half. Sideeq remembered cheering as the boy made his way to the changing rooms. Now he was sure the boy remembered him.

Sniggering, the boy cut his eye and pointed in their direction. The other Ashbird boys laughed and started rubbing their hands together. Cutting off the exit, the boys approached Sideeq and Kyle.

"Oi, what year you in?" Pimple-Face asked.

Sid and Kyle looked at each other, not knowing whether to

answer.

"I said, what year you in?"

"Year 7." Sideeq flinched as the boy raised his hand to rub his nose.

"Rah, you see that, Nana?" One of the boy's friends laughed.

"Oi, these yoots are moist." Nana—the pimple-faced boy—smiled. "What you getting shook for, I ain't gonna hurt you."

"But I might," his friend said, grabbing Sideeq by the collar. He was a short mixed race boy with a protruding forehead and a gap in his teeth.

Nana took hold of Sideeq from the boy. "What you got for me?" He gestured with an open hand.

"Nothing."

"Don't lie," Nana growled. He stood on Sideeq's foot, tightening his grip and ramming his fist under Sideeq's throat. "I said, what you got for me?"

"Nothing I swear, I haven't got anything." Sideeq pleaded. He was frightened. Kyle remembered how he'd looked at him for help, but Kyle stared nervously at the floor when Nana began to pat Sideeq down. Shamefully, Kyle remembered he had thought *better you than me* and guiltily sighed a breath of relief as Nana asked, "What's this?"

He pulled out Sideeq's phone. Kyle hoped they'd be happy with that and not bother to search him.

"Nah allow it, please." Sideeq tried grabbing the phone back. "That's my mum's." Struggling, he caught the attention of the manager.

"Oi what you lot doing?"

"They're trying to take my phone!" Sideeq cried.

Instantly, Nana let him go. He tried to pretend they were playing, putting his arm round Sideeq. "Nah, it's OK big man, he's my friend."

"Oi, leave the yoot alone," the man said, stepping around the counter.

It was then Kyle had seen his moment of opportunity. With the Ashbird boys distracted, he pulled Sideeq's arm and bolted for the door. Instinctively, Sideeq ran behind him. Sprinting through the market, they raced towards Uxbridge Road with the older boys giving chase.

Dashing people out the way, Kyle yelled, "GET OUT THE WAY!!! GET OUT THE WAY!!"

Shoppers and stallholders they cursed him as they whizzed by. Kyle's heart pounded in his chest, but he dare not look back. He heard one of the Ashbird boys shouting, "WATCH WHEN I CATCH YOU, I'M GONNA BORE YOU UP!"

Kyle glanced over his shoulder. He could see Sideeq half a stride behind him. In the reflection of a shop window, he saw the mixed raced boy and Nana in hot pursuit. Something metal flashed in his hand and Nana yelled, "Oi, stop or I'll shank you!"

As Kyle ran on to the Uxbridge Road, he darted through the oncoming traffic to the other side with no thought for his own safety. Smiling he looked back for Sideeq—who'd attempted to follow, however wasn't so lucky. Kyle saw him hesitate as a blue Ford Fiesta neared. Then from nowhere, Nana booted Sideeq in his side. The force sent him to the ground, bringing a woman down with him. He hit the road hard and the skin peeled from his hands like tyres landing on a runway. But Sideeq still tried to get to his feet. His legs kept pumping, but Nana threw a blow to the face. It stopped Sideeq dead in his tracks. The punch was devastating. Kyle literally saw the pain explode across Sideeq's face. Sideeq's scream was deafening as he collapsed to floor, holding his eye. Kyle would never forget the sound of Sideeq high-pitched wailing as he looked on, powerless—too frightened to stop the Ashbird boys from stomping his friend.

In between the barrage of blows, Sideeq tried to protect his eye. That's when Nana swooped down at Sideeq three times with a stabbing motion. Then he stepped back and gave Sideeq one last boot to the side of the head. Kyle saw the glee on Nana's face as he turned and looked directly at Kyle before running off.

As the other boys fled, Sideeq laid totally flat on his back. A crowd quickly started to form, and a large Asian man in a turban pushed his way through. Calling for someone to get an ambulance, he ordered people to stand back and give Sideeq air. Kyle could barely see his way back across the road as tears streamed down his face. Between the bustling bodies, he could see Sideeq's bloody face. The left side was torn with a gaping gash, and what was left of his eye had ballooned shut. Horrified, Kyle stood staring as the Asian man removed Sideeq's school tie. He wrapped it around Sideeq's leg and tied a knot to stop the bleeding. A dark skinned Rasta man with a thick beard and dreadlocks tucked into a black woollen knitted hat came running out of a nearby stall with some towels. He passed them to a black woman in her thirties, who knelt down and cradled Sideeq's head. She pressed the towels against Sideeq's face while the Asian man bellowed in his thick accent, "Please, please we need more! They stabbed him in da back too—"

"Stabbed who in the back?" Danny said interrupting.

Both Kyle and Sharkey had been so engrossed in Kyle's story, they didn't notice Danny arrived late. He was still wearing his dog walking gear and had six homemade leads slung across him.

"No one," Sharkey replied. His tone was absolute, yet lacked malice. Danny knew not to ask anymore.

"Cool, no worries, you ain't got to tell me when I'm not wanted."

Taking off his rucksack and leads, Danny took a seat opposite Sharkey. Switching on his computer, he grabbed a pair of headphones and began loading up the composing he had been working on.

Turning back to Kyle, Sharkey said in a reassuring voice, "We'll speak later."

Kyle knew that Sharkey was shrewd enough to understand that everything he had said was strictly between them. Reaching for his own set of headphones, he caught his reflection in the monitor screen and dropped his gaze. He couldn't bare the eye contact with his own guilt. He his thoughts were caressed by shame and wondered whether there was anything else he could have done that day. Perhaps if he hadn't been in such a hurry, Sideeq's whole life may have been different.

Clicking the mouse in his hand, he closed his eyes and let the beat soothe his mind. Somehow he would make it up to Sideeq. Someday.

CHAPTER 3.2

At lunch, Sideeq knew he wasn't in the mood to go downstairs to meet the others, so instead asked Mr Ghodstinat if he were able to stay in the art room.

"Of course you can, Sideeq," Mr Ghodstinat obliged. "You're welcome. It's no problem to me, but don't you think you should eat something? A growing boy like you? You're so big with all those muscles. You need lots of fuel, no?"

"I'm not hungry today, sir." Sideeq mustered a smile.

"Well, maybe that is true, but you haven't had much of an appetite for the last few days. Is everything alright?"

"Yeah," Sideeq lied.

"OK, because if there is something bothering you, I'm happy to talk. Or if you rather, there is always the college counsel—"

"Nah, I'm cool, sir." Sideeq cut Mr Ghodstinat off. He knew where his teacher was heading and wasn't interested. Sideeq had seen and spoken to plenty of counsellors over the years and had no desire opening up old wounds with a new one.

"To be honest, sir, I like it up here. It's quiet. Sometimes the common room gets a bit too crowded for me, especially when the weather's bad."

"Ohh, well that makes perfect sense," Mr Ghodstinat said, peering out to the overcast skies. He walked over to the window and gazed at the looming clouds. Their grey and white marbling mass formed like warring monsters in the sky. Floating with puffy mouths open, they hovered high above, ready to devour the spirits of those below.

Studying the nimbus-made titans, Mr Ghodstinat spoke in a tender voice. "You know, Sideeq, in my country we have a saying for days like this. It comes in two parts, but the first goes like this: rich is the man who finds the sun on a cloudy day, for he knows his crops will still grow. Poor is his neighbour who spends his time mourning it. It's a beautiful saying, yes?" Mr Ghodstinat smiled, and for a brief second the two remained silent until Sideeq asked,

"How's the second part go?"

Mr Ghodstinat turned to face Sideeq. Smiling, he removed his spectacles and wiped the lens with his shirt. He sighed. "Well the second part says: when the rich man's harvest comes he will smile in abundance, while his neighbour will wonder why he has been forsaken. And that, too, is a beautiful saying, but it sounds sooo much bettah in Persian."

Mr Ghodstinat put his glasses back on and patted Sideeq on the shoulder. "You must always find the sun, Sideeq. For people like you and me it's imperative."

Walking to his desk, Mr Ghodstinat reached into his satchel and retrieved a pack of cigarettes and lighter. "And now I leave, the room is in your jurisdiction, but only until I return." Perhaps sensing he had done enough to plant a seed, Mr Ghodstinat smiled warmly at Sideeq one last time before leaving.

Looking at the dragons in the sky, Sideeq sat in deep contemplation waiting for the sun. Peeking in from the corridor, Nerissa quietly crept in. Slowly she pulled out the beagle-shaped statute and tip-toed up until she was right behind him.

"Awww, what's wrong lil Sid?" she said in a whiny baby voice. "What's that? You're sad. Well, tell me why you're sad? No, I won't tell. It can be a secret just between me and you. Yes, we'll call it classified."

A huge grin span across Sideeq's face and he turned to face Nerissa.

"What makes you think I'm sad?"

"Pardon?" she smiled, taking a seat on the central table. She leaned back with her legs slightly apart and propped up her weight with her arms so her chest poked out. Kicking her legs back and forth, she looked at him, waiting for a reply. Sideeq looked her over, thinking she looked quite chic today. She wore a pair of black suede penny loafers and black jeans that showed off the shape of her thighs, matched with a black sweater and a white-collared blouse underneath. Around her neck she wore the purple paisley patterned scarf, which complimented her purple nail polish.

"I said, what makes you think I'm sad?"

"Err, what makes you think I was talking to you?" Nerissa pulled a sarcastic face, flirting. She began stroking the statue's head. "I wasn't talking to you. I was talking to Little Sid. Ain't that right, Little Sid?" She lifted up the statue and held it to her ear. "Oh what's that, Little Sid? Ohhh, yes you may be right... Maybe we shouldn't talk to him... Yes, we don't want to get charged with conspiracy."

"Ha ha, very funny. You got jokes."

"Sometimes." Nerissa bit her lip. "Do you like his name?"

"It's alright. Not too original though."

"Whatever. You're just hating that Little Sid gets more girls then you."

"Hmm, that's good for him." Sideeq grunted. He swivelled back around in his seat and went back to his artwork, turning away from her. His action apparently surprised Nerissa and she misread his awkwardness on the subject of girls. Putting Little Sid down, she hoped off the table.

"What you doing?" she asked, peering over Sideeq's shoulder.

"Nothing," Sideeq chuckled. "Just looking for a muse. D'you know any?"

Nerissa hit him on the shoulder. "I hate you. I really hate you."

"What? I was just asking. If you know anybody that wants to be one, let me know."

Laughing, the two stared at one another's grins. It was only for a split second, but Sideeq found it strange that they both felt comfortable looking directly at each other. Then he saw Nerissa's eyes shift to his study his scar. Self-conscious, Sideeq swivelled enough to break her gaze.

"So how's the monologue ting going?"

Nerissa seemed to realise what she'd done. "Yeah, yeah, it's fine." She looked towards the open door. "Would you like hear it?"

Sideeq took a moment to think. "Yeah, why not?" He

shrugged.

"Oh wow, thanks that's very inspiring." Nerissa shook her head. "You don't have to if you don't want to."

"Nah, nah, sorry, I mean yes." Sideeq rephrased his words. "Yes please, I'd like to hear your monologue."

"Well actually, it's a theatrical apostrophe, but I'll let you off, because I like you." She waited for Sideeq to fire back, but he played it cool, watching her with a smile on his face.

"Come, let's go," she said, picking up Little Sid.

Sideeq frowned. "Go where?"

His question stopped Nerissa dead in her tracks, and she looked at him curiously. "To the drama room."

"Why?" Sideeq frowned harder.

Nerissa glanced at the open door. "Well I weren't going to say anything, but since you asked, I'll be honest. I didn't really appreciate how your friend tried to run me out the last time I was here. So I'd rather be in the drama room where no one can't accuse me of fastening up where I weren't suppose' to be. If I be totally honest?"

"Hmm," Sideeq mulled. She made a good point. Following her to the drama class would probably make it easier for them. Sideeq really wasn't interested in hearing any noise in his head today, but wasn't exceedingly keen on leaving the art room, either. He was comfortable here. It was a zone that he could control.

"Is that it?" he said in an empty tone.

Coiling back, Nerissa scowled at him.

"No, that's not it. Do you think I don't know what people say about me? Because I do. I use to go to an all girls' school, so trust me when I say I know when people are trying to chat me. I'm not dumb. I know too well."

Nerissa's words were sharp. They were filled with a cold anguish, but never once did she raise her voice. "Do you think I'm not used to people staring? Whispering and pointing their fingers at me? Or better yet, hearing them make up some stupid conversation mid flow to pretend they weren't talking about me when I enter a room? Do know what that's like?"

The irony was with his hearing aid and scar Sideeq did, but he chose not to interrupt her.

"Do you think it's fair that people like your friend can walk up in my face and tell me who I can and can't talk to because of something they think they know? Cause let's tell the truth, that's what it is. Your friend doesn't like me not because I've done anything to him, but because of what Gobbler's done."

Sideeq twisted his mouth at the mention of Gobbler's name.

"Yeah, look, it's written all over your face. Go on, say something?"

Raising an eyebrow, Sideeq coolly fixed his face. "What do you want me to say? It ain't none of my business."

"Yeah and it's none of my business, either. I never told Gobbler to beat up Olly or whatever his name is. I don't even know him, but I'm the one everyone's talking about. How's that fair?"

Sideeq smirked, thinking about his mum's saying.

"You think it's funny?"

"I'm not laughing."

"Good," Nerissa snapped. "Because I hate it. I hate not being allowed to talk to people, or how everyone avoids me because of him. I mean literally it's like I've got the friggin' plague. No one wants to come near me. Do you know what that feels like? Having to spend every lunchtime with Gobbler and his stupid friends, listening to them chat shit about robbing this guy or looking to stab that guy. And then at the end of the day having to hear it all over again, because Gobbler says I'm not allowed to go home alone. Why? Because he don't trust some boy won't try talk to me. I'm like, how the flipping hell they gonna do that? They're all bloody scared! In fact…" Nerissa broke the rhythm of her rant, "You're actually the first boy outside of my class that's spoken to me. The first."

Poker faced, Siddeq sat listening. He watched Nerissa, wondering whether to ask why she still stayed with Gobbler, but decided not to. He found it strange that although she complained, she had yet to say she didn't want to be with him. However it was clear that she did want something.

Hugging Little Sid to her bosom, Nerissa bit her lip and turned away to compose herself. "It would be nice to be friends with someone who… I don't know, saw me for who I am, not who everyone *thinks* I am."

She looked at Sideeq. He kept the expression on his face empty and unmoved.

"OK, so lemme clarify your answer," Sideeq said bluntly. "The main reason you want to go the drama room is for privacy. So my friend can't come and interrupt us?"

"Well yeah, more or less, if that the only thing you took from what I just said?" Nerissa shook her head, frustrated.

Sideeq stood up, nodding his head with a slight grimace. Walking over to the supply cupboard, he grabbed some Sellotape and a large black sheet of paper. Closing the classroom door, he covered the circular window with the paper and taped it fast. Turning the latch, he locked the door.

"No, don't lock the door," Nerissa said with a slight panic.

"You sure?" Sideeq asked, picking up on the alarm in her voice. "It's only so no one can burst in." From her reaction he gathered she had a thing about being locked in, especially with a boy she barely knew.

"No, covering the window should be enough." Nerissa smiled a little.

"Cool," Sideeq said, taking his seat. "No one ain't coming in here now. And if they do, you're my guest. So you don't have to explain yourself."

Nerissa bit her lip again, then twisted her mouth, looking around the classroom.

"What's wrong now?" Sideeq asked. He couldn't tell that his understated manner was giving Nerissa the flutters.

"The lighting." Nerissa said

Putting Little Sid down on the table, she skipped over to the door. She peered around again, then turned off the lights. Instantly, the room became smaller and more intimate. The natural light from outside evoked a sensual mood for theatrics. It was heightened by the glow from an uncovered lightbox in the corner, which cast shadows on the hanging art. Nerissa flicked the switches again, finding the right light at the back of the room and creating a new warmth inside the class. Suddenly the room appeared more like a set from a play.

Sideeq shook his head, chuckling at her extroversion, but he found it entertaining to indulge her. Happy with the ambience, Nerissa stepped away from the door, but not before she turned the latch once again. Now that the door was locked on her terms, she took the stage, ready to perform for her audience of one.

"OK, don't like laugh—my piece is called *Memoirs Of a Muse*."

As Nerissa began, she removed the purple scarf from around her neck and placed over it Little Sid. In her excitement, she seemed to have totally forgotten about the bruising on her neck. Sideeq's eyes fell on the discolouring around her throat, and took note of what looked like strangle marks.

CHAPTER 3.3

There were four things that Danny loved: dogs, money, music and weed—and he weren't too partial as to what order they came in. Which was why Thursday was Danny's favourite day of the week. Where some Weekend Warriors might look forward to Friday marking the end of a long week, or Saturday bringing the excitement of match day and party night, Danny took pleasure in the small delights of Thursday. Why? Because for dog walkers like Danny, Thursday actually brought about the beginning of his weekend, and was usually his busiest days of trade.

You see, most dog owners, like any modern parent, had two routines—their weekday routine and their weekend routine. The first generally consisted of: go work, come home, cook, and if you're not too tired, take the dog for a walk. However, their weekend usually involved the rigmarole of maintaining a social life—while trying to attend enough events to qualify as adequately sociable. In between this, their poor canine charge was usually left picking at the scraps and demands of their owner's weekend schedule. Instead of idyllic walks in the park playing catch, they could end up with two five-minute trips to the back yard to do their business.

And so the Thursday dog walk became vital, because Danny's regulars knew that no matter what they had planned, Thursday was usually their pampered pooch's last chance to hang out with their four-legged friends before the weekend. Added to the fact Danny's rates went up on the weekend. As a result, Danny's Thursdays usually consisted of at least sixteen dog walks from the local Ladbroke Grove and North Kensington area, and earned an easy minimum of three hundred and twenty pounds in a day. And although picking up dog's do wasn't appealing to the likes of Kyle, with no managers to answer to except himself, Danny happily professed, "Dog money is better than drug money, there's a lot less shit to deal with."

Rizla, on the other hand, was not so keen on Thursdays.

Waking at 6am, Danny washed and got dressed. He threw on a pair of black combat trousers and a black sweater that had Danny's Dogs stitched on it in white embroidery. Slurping down a bowl of cereal, he looked at Rizla who hadn't touched his bowl of kibble.

"Rizla," Danny called the dog. "Stop playing."

Lying on the floor, the ancient dog looked up with his one good eye. He acknowledged his master then closed his eye again, burying his head in his paws.

"Rizla, you're not funny. Come on, it's Thursday, we ain't got time for this. Eat your food."

Stretching, Rizla walked over to the bowl. Inspecting its contents, he sniffed the dry dog food and barked at Danny.

"No!" Danny jumped up from the table. He dropped his bowl in the sink. "I told you, it's Thursday, I haven't got time to cook sausages."

Ignoring Rizla, Danny checked his rucksack filled with balls and dog toys, making sure he had enough water in his bottle for the dogs to drink. Opening up a box of dog treats, he snatched three packs and shoved them in the side pockets of his combats. Picking up a set of six homemade dog leads, Danny threw them over his shoulder and fixed his rucksack. "Rizla, cmon!" he hurried the dog. Rizla trotted into the hallway, stopping by the kitchen. He barked at Danny again. "No Rizla, I'm warning you boy, you don't push your luck."

Rizla made a whining sound and looked back at the stove.

"Move." Danny shooed the dog out the way. He stomped into the kitchen. Ripping open the refrigerator door, he grabbed a packet of sliced ham and pulled out a slice. He tossed it at Rizla. "There. Now c'mon!"

Nonchalantly, Rizla looked at the slice of ham as it slapped onto the laminate floor, then back up at Danny, unimpressed. Fuming, Danny marched to the front door.

"Right, that's it, Riz, I'm serious. If you don't come now, I swear you not getting anything at lunch. I mean it. You can stay here all day. That means no saveloy."

Not budging, Rizla titled his head to the side and watched Danny, as if to say *your move*. Furious, he took off one of his homemade leads and grabbed Rizla by the collar. Putting the dog on the leash, he opened the door, letting in a gust of wind. As Danny dragged the old dog out into the cold, Rizla began whining again. Danny looked at the grey sky realising the inevitable. He knew Rizla hated to be on the lead, and gathered that if he had to drag the dog now, Rizla was only going to slow him down with another five dogs in tow.

"Bloody hell, Riz!" Danny said, conceding the battle. "I can't believe you. Get!" he said, unclipping Rizla's lead and sending him back inside. As Rizla scuttled indoors, he slapped the dog on the hind with the leash. "Oh no you don't! Don't you dare!" Danny bellowed as Rizla ran to the slice of that ham and wolfed it down.

"Right, that's it!" Danny warned. "Watch what happens at lunch time, you miserable so and so."

Slamming the door, he bopped down the stairs as Rizla appeared in the bay window of the Victorian terrace and started barking at him. "Whatever, Rizla!"

*

After walking his first five dogs, Danny was late. He didn't have time to drop off his gear, and went straight to college. When he arrived, Kyle and Sharkey were in deep discussion. Overhearing their conversation about someone getting stabbed in the back, he interrupted. "Stabbed who in the back?"

"No one," Sharkey replied giving Danny an unwelcoming look.

Still annoyed with Rizla, Danny had no interest in imposing himself on anyone today. "Cool, no worries, you ain't got tell me when I'm not wanted."

Taking off his rucksack and leads, he took a seat opposite Sharkey. Grabbing a pair of headphones, he logged on to his computer and began composing a beat he had been working on. Building a deep drum 'n' bass inspired track, he got lost in his tinkering.

At lunchtime Danny followed the others to the common room, staying long enough to strap a joint. After five minutes he left to go collect his next six dogs. Noticing Gobbler and his friend on the other side of the road, he held off from lightening his spliff and walked in the opposite direction. He thought it was dumb that someone who proclaimed to be such a gangster spent so much time outside the college waiting for their girlfriend.

Pondering how Gobbler made his money, Danny sparked his zoot. Filling his lungs with the lemon flavored kush, he began to work out the best route to pick for the six dogs on his list. Seeing as Rizla had misbehaved, Danny decided to leave the moody bull terrier inside, as dog walkers were only allowed to walk a maximum of six dogs on the leash at one time. Also it would teach the old dog a lesson. Blowing smoke in the air, he sniggered to himself. When he first started college, he had wondered how he was going to cope with the large number of bookings on Thursday. However, luckily for him he had been blessed with a double free period after lunch, giving him ample time. Making the most of it, he set off to complete his Notting Hill route.

When Danny finally picked up Rizla, he could tell the dog was in a foul mood. Ignoring the half eaten saveloy he presented as a peace offering, Rizla stretched his hind legs and shook the aches out of his joints. Walking to the door, he waited to have his leash put on. Collecting his last five dogs Danny head to the park off St Mark's Road. On days like these it was easy for Danny to see Rizla's eleven years catching up with him. A veteran amongst the dogs, he didn't even chase the colourful balls when Danny threw them out. Instead he wandered off, finding a small bundle of brown leaves underneath an oak tree and sitting peacefully until it was time to go.

Checking his watch, it was almost three o'clock when Danny dropped off his last two dogs. Last period would soon be over, and he decided to go back to drop Rizla off before he went back to catch up with his friends. As he made his way home, Danny was turning on to St Charles Square when he saw Gobbler and his goons posted up on the corner. Immediately he thought about crossing the road and taking the long way round, but it was too late. Gobbler turned and smiled at him.

"Yo, Justin Timberlake! Wha gwan? Come!" He beckoned Danny over.

For a moment Danny hesitated. He looked up the road beyond the gang of boys to the college gates. There was no one in sight, not even Pat the old security guard. He wondered whether he should run, but his instinct told him that wouldn't be a good idea, and to stay cool. He smiled.

"What's happening, Gobbler, what's happening, Hass?" He nodded his head like a bobble head toy.

"Yes, what you saying, dog boy? You cool?" Gobbler grinned, holding out his right fist as he crumpled some weed in his left. "You got a chip?"

"A chip?" Danny repeated the question. He was nervous, trying to calculate the best way of dealing with Gobbler.

"Yeah, that's what I said, blud. Are you deaf?"

"Nah, nah, of course not." Danny patted himself down. He knew exactly where his cigarettes were, but he was trying to work out how much money he had left in the box. Since his Gobbler robbed Olly, Danny had taken the precaution of carrying no more than forty pounds around college. Anything bigger than that he tucked in his boxers shorts.

"Ah, here they are," Danny said, pulling out the box. He took out two cigarettes and handed them to Gobbler.

"Bless," Gobbler thanked Danny. Slipping one cigarette behind his ear, he broke a chip of the other. He grinned slyly at Hassan. He admired the way Danny had managed to guard the box by surrendering two cigarettes, but they both knew it weren't gonna be enough.

"So where you coming from, blud? You look like you jump fresh outta Call Of Duty in all that gear and ting."

"For real." Squingey, one of Gobbler's cronies, laughed. He was a dark skinned boy with low cropped hair and a thin pyramid moustache, who got his name from the way he flared his nostrils. "All my man needs is an AR15 and he could be Black Ops."

"Yeah, man does look a bit Rambo'd off innit?" Danny joked nervously. He was waiting for the right time to exit the conversation.

"Oi, akh." Hassan stepped towards him. "What's all them rope tings?"

As Hassan reached for one of the leads, Rizla started barking, making the gang step back. Showing what was left of his teeth, he stood in between Danny and them, growling.

"Oi, akh, control you effin' dog, before I boot it in the face!"

Hassan snapped.

"It's true, man!" Gobbler stood to side, laughing as he built his spliff. "I thought I warned you about that oversize rat. Put it on a leash, you're scaring Hass."

"Sorry," Danny apologised. Taking a lead off, he put Rizla on the leash and stroked his chest to calm him down.

"Don't watch that." Gobbler smiled. "He's juss protecting his owner innit." Gobbler licked and fastened the corner of his joint. Taking out a lighter, he sparked the zoot and took a long pull on it. Blowing the smoke out, he offered it to Danny.

"You bun?"

Without thinking Danny said, "No."

"What you lying for, ahk?" Hassan pulled him up quick. "I seen you bunnin' bare times."

"Huh, me?" Danny stuttered. "Nah not me? More time I smoke roll ups."

"Oi, ahk do I look dumb?" Hassan spat on the floor. "D'you think I don't know the difference between a zoot and a roll up? Don't make me slap you. Your eyes are all red now!"

"Nah, I'm not calling you dumb," Danny said nervously. He looked to the gates and wondered whether now was the time to run.

"OK, so do you bun or not?" Gobbler asked.

"Yeah, sometimes, but not around here, not anytime I think Hass would have seen."

"What?!" Hassan laughed in disbelief. "Fam, what the hell is this guy talking about? Ahk, do you bun or not bun?"

Frightened, Danny looked at Gobbler taking another pull on

the spliff. Through the smoke the glowing orange ember stood out in contrast to the black glove on his hand. Danny's mind went blank as he looked between the three boys waiting, and he answered, "Yeah."

Shaking his head, Gobbler exhaled. He passed his zoot to Squingey, who sucked on it like a vacuum.

"So why did you lie?" he asked in a non-threatening voice. "After I try be nice to you?"

"Mmm, that's deep," Squingey said, passing the spliff to Hassan.

"He violated you, ahk." Hassan dried the end of the joint with the lighter.

Danny began stuttering. "I, I, I…"

"Hold on, wait," Gobbler stopped him. "Think before you answer."

"I don't know," Danny shrugged hopelessly. "I, I, I…"

Sighing, Gobbler held up his gloved hand, stopping Danny from continuing. Shaking his head he reached over and took Rizla's lead out of Danny's hand. He passed it to Squnigey and signalled for his friend to move back.

"Blud, you shouldn't lie, y'know. Didn't your mum ever tell you not to lie? Now it's gotta get all peak for you."

Stepping forward, Gobbler put his hand on Danny's chest. Exercising his strength, he slammed Danny against the wall then lined him up with a backhand. The slap reverberated in air and both Hassan and Squingey let out a chorus of "Ooooo" in awe of its power. Immediately, Rizla started barking. He tried to run to Danny's aid, but Squingey keep a firm grip on his lead.

"Oh my days!" Hassan cackled. "That was a violation reversal. Nah, ahk, nah. Stop."

"Stop what?" Gobbler laughed. He told Danny, "Turn out pockets!"

The sting of slap stunned Danny into a panic. "Sorry, Gobbler, sorry," he apologised profusely. "I'm sorry, I didn't mean to lie." Danny reached into his pocket and handed over his cigarettes. "There's thirty pound in there. That's all I got."

"What!" Gobbler snatched the cigarettes out Danny's hand and inspected the box. "What, is this it?" he said, pocketing the money. "Where's the rest? I know you got more."

"I swear to you, Gobbler, that's all I got." Danny held his hands up, pleading.

"Oi put your hands down," Hassan ordered. Danny did as was told and Hassan, who was still smoking, kicked him up his bum. "Stand up straight, man."

Trying to anticipate the next blow, Danny squirmed in front of Gobbler.

"Ah please, you man, allow it, please."

One half of Danny's face was covered with a huge red handprint as Gobbler toyed with him. "What, blud, you still don't turn out your pockets yet?"

"But I ain't got—" Danny started to reply. Before he could finish, Gobbler buried an uppercut in his stomach. The blow would have floored him, but Gobbler followed through with two quick left-and-right liver shots to his torso. Winded, Danny dropped to one knee. Ready to retch, he dug into pocket and pulled out his phone. Still struggling to breath, he hand it to

Gobbler, who then reached down and grabbed a hand full of hair. He yanked Danny to his feet. Shoving his forearm under Danny's chin, Gobbler pinned the boy against the wall and used his weight to crush Danny's throat.

"Oi fam, do you think I'm playing with you? I know you got more P's on you."

"I ain't," Danny tried protesting, but Gobbler started rifling through his pockets. He pulled out all the loose change Danny had on him and dashed it on the floor. Then he pulled out Danny's keys, along with a weed grinder and some rolling papers.

"And this guy said he don't smoke. Bieber, you're tekkin man for some ediot."

Gobbler gave Danny another slap then ordered him to take off his rucksack, socks and shoes. Hassan yanked the rucksack off Danny's back and started emptying it. He went through every compartment, pelting tennis balls and rubber dog bones at Danny.

"Nothing in there."

"Check it again," Gobbler demanded

Unsatisfied Danny wasn't hiding any more money or weed, Gobbler threw Danny's trainers over the wall. By now Rizla was barking in a frenzy, and the commotion started to draw attention at the top of the road. Gobbler noticed a couple of girls by the gates looking on with concern as Danny stood cowering, barefoot. He ordered Squingey, "Blud, shut that friggin' dog up!"

Squingey started kicking Rizla in the side. At first the old dog tried to fight back with a lunging bite, but when Hassan came in with a huge boot to the eye, Rizla yelped out in pain. It spurred

Danny into action.

"No don't, please don't hurt him!" Danny tried to run to Rizla's defence, but Gobbler grabbed him.

"Oi, where going, blud? I ain't finished with you."

"What!" Danny barked back. "What do you want? You already took my money and my phone. I ain't got nothing else."

"Blud, who you talking to?" Gobbler gripped Danny by the throat. "I'll tek your stinkin' dog and drown him in the river if you carry on."

That was a threat too far. Instinctively, Danny whacked Gobbler's arm, breaking his grip and pushing Gobbler back. He yelled, "GET OFF ME!" so loud that it could be heard at the top of the road. Outraged, Gobbler gripped Danny again but this time he didn't toy with him. He lashed out with his full force and plummeted his fist into Danny's face. Blood exploded from Danny's nose as his head smashed against the wall. As he fell, he felt a flurry of blows, but they were insignificant to the pain that erupted over his face. Blinded with pain, he heard Pat, the old security guard, yell in the distance, "OI! WHAT'S GOING ON?"

Whoever was kicking him stopped, and Danny heard Hassan say, "Oi, Gobbz come, come, come, I can't be seen here."

Blood poured from Danny's nose as he saw the three boys running off. Panting, he tried to call out for them to stop, but couldn't breathe. Grasping he was powerless, he saw Squingey turn the corner still dragging Rizla on the lead.

It would be the last time Danny ever saw his dog alive, and in that precise moment he knew it.

As Pat radioed for help, he sat. Eyes filled with tears, he dropped his head and began weeping. Soon a crowd started to gather, and Danny looked up as Kyle and Sharkey pushed their way through.

"Dan, what happened? What happened?"

Danny reached into his boxer shorts he pulled out a small wad of notes.

"Here, here," he bawled. "Tell 'em to come back. They can have the money."

CHAPTER 3.4

In the aftermath of Rizla's death, there were rumours that Gobbler and his friends had posted a video online of them smoking weed and tormenting the dog. One story surmised that Gobbler had sold Rizla to a local traveller who pitted the pet against others in an illegal dogfight. Yet more tales told that the gang had tied Rizla to the back of a stolen moped and dragged the bull terrier till he couldn't run any more. The demise of *'Danny's Dog Rizla'* became an urban myth and gossip-monger's delight. Each story had its own variant, but most ended with Rizla's body being dumped at the back of Wormwood Scrubs.

When the police finally did find Rizla's corpse, they informed Danny that there were clear signs his dog had been through a substantial amount of trauma before passing. Along with his mum, they urged Danny to let them know if he had any information on who would want to do this to Rizla, or whether he knew the boys that robbed him outside college. Not wanting to be labelled a snitch, Danny lied. The last thing he wanted was to give Gobbler another reason to come after him. Keeping quiet, he stuck to his story and told the police,

"I don't remember. It all happened too fast."

"Danny, a witness says you were seen speaking to the assailants?"

"Yeah I did. They asked me for a cigarette."

"Well do you think you would recognise them if you saw them again?"

"I don't know. I don't think so. It all happened too fast."

"Can you describe them, Danny? What they looked like, what they were wearing?"

"No."

"Do you know whether they're local boys, or perhaps one of them goes to your college?"

"No. None of them go to my college. I've never seen them before."

It was telling that last lie that hurt Danny the most. It reeked of betrayal and haunted him as much as seeing Squingey lead Rizla around the corner. Sitting in the common room watching Kyle and Sharkey play cards, he remembered the expression on the officer's face when he replied. She had a kind face, with ice green eyes and freckles. She was in her early twenties with a short dark brown pixie haircut that gave her an elfish look in her uniform. Under any other circumstance, Danny would've called her a *sort,* but instead he studied her face. He figured Rizla would have liked her. As she closed her black notebook, her gaze was filled with disappointment and pity. "OK, Danny," she said in a Belfast accent. "If you do remember anything else, please let us know."

Danny remembered. He couldn't forget. Grief had muted his soul. At night, he lay in bed replaying the events and asking God for one last chance to save his friend. When the morning came he would sit at the table with a cup of coffee, looking at Rizla's bowl. He contemplated again and again whether if he had just cooked those damn sausages, the day may have turned out differently. Would the five minutes it took to cook a string of sausages saved Rizla's life?

"Dan, are you listening?" The tone of Sharkey's voice broke Danny's train of thought. Snapping out of his trance, he looked around at the others, who were apparently awaiting his reply. He looked at them, lost. He was surprised to see Swank and Sideeq at the table, realising he hadn't noticed when they arrived.

"Huh? Sorry, I didn't hear you."

"I know." Sharkey smiled warmly. "I said I'm playing at *2AM's* house party next weekend, do you wanna roll?"

Danny shrugged hopelessly. "Nah not really, I'm not really in the mood."

"Nah c'mon Dan, bruv, come," Kyle urged. "We're all goin'. It's gonna be live."

"For real," Swank agreed. "I was speaking to one ting from William Morris, she said there's bare girls from her college gonna be going. Look." Swank pulled out her phone and they all swarmed around it. She flicked through a short array of photos of girls on a night out, posing for some group selfies.

"Woooo, see it dere," Kyle squealed. "That's what I'm talking about!" He high-fived Swank. "That one! That one!" He pointed to a cute little blonde in a gold dress.

"I know THAT'S you Danny!" He zoomed into the picture so they could all get better look.

"Ooh, that's Paige!" Swank slapped Danny on the back. "Yo, fam, I heard she's a freak. You can draw that, no long ting."

"Jeez!" Kyle chirped, as a cheeky grin eventually cracked on Danny's face.

"Wait let me hav' a look," he said, taking the phone. They all went silent as he studied the picture, and his grin split into a full on smile. It was the first since Rizla had been murdered. "Yeah, she's alright I suppose. What's that big bum ting saying?"

Danny pointed to a chocolate brown skinned girl in a peach maxi dress and braids.

"Ohhh, that's Tash."

"Yeah, she's a bit of alright, too."

"Nah, bruv, tek time." Kyle snatched the phone. "What makes you think you can handle dem tings dere? That dere is *me*," Kyle said, adding some bass to his voice.

"Lemme hav' a look." Sharkey peered over Kyle. "Oh, Tash," he said, raising an eyebrow. "Yeah, I know Tash, she's calm. One of you man should move to it, still."

He stepped back with a sly expression on his face. He looked at Swank and asked "Is that your people yeah?"

"Yeah." Swank returned the grin.

"OK, say no more."

The two started laughing. It was obvious they had a mutual understanding and the less said the better.

"Nah, whats' the joke?" Kyle demanded to know. He turned to Sharkey. "Did you hit?"

"Mm mm." Sharkey frowned and shook his head.

"Nah, bruv, don't lie," Kyle protested. "Coz when we go ta

the shoobs, I'm on this chick."

"That's good for you." Sharkey laughed. "Do your ting."

Not willing to reveal any trade secrets, Sharkey switched the subject. "What about you, Sid? You rollin?"

"Hmmm, for real big man." Swank beamed. "What you saying? We must can find you a little lightie to wind pon."

"I'm cool." Sideeq smiled bashfully. "I'm not really into the whole party thing."

"What you talking about?" Kyle interjected. "Don't listen to him, Swank. If Danny's rolling, you're rollin'. We're all rolling. No ifs, no buts, no maybes, I'm putting it in the air. Wallahi, it's written."

"Yes, it is." Sharkey patted Kyle on his shoulder, calming him down. "So let Sid decide for himself. Either way, just let me know."

"Nah man, he's coming," Kyle insisted.

"We'll see." Sideeq ended the conversation as a text alert sounded on his phone. Smiling, he read the message and ignored Kyle's griping as he text back.

"Right, I'm off," Sharkey said putting on his backpack. "I gotta check one breh in Bush about that 1 series Beemer I see the other day. All goes well, man could be whipping to this ting next week."

"Oi, hold up, fam." Swank jumped up. "Which way you going? I need ta rap to you about something real quick."

"Whichever way you want." Sharkey grinned. "I got time to talk."

The two walked off jovially, conspiring in cahoots. They

disappeared beyond the doors and Kyle turned to Sideeq, who still had his head buried in his phone.

"Who you texting?" he asked.

"No one," Sideeq said, putting his phone away. "It's just my mum."

"Your mum?"

"Yeah that's what I said," Sideeq replied.

Looking up, his eyes instinctively darted around the room. Kyle frowned, suspicious. He picked up on Sideeq's line of vision and saw Nerissa sitting at a table not too far from the snack bar. Sipping on a hot chocolate, she giggled and smiled at something on her phone. Stewing, Kyle said, "Tell your mum I said 'hi'."

Ignoring Kyle, Sideeq reached into his blue back pack and pulled out his folder.

"Yo, Dan," he said, taking out some sketches. "I don't know if these will help, but I done this for you. Just to let you know Rizla was in our hearts, too." He passed the pictures to Danny, who again had to break out of his trance. His hands began to tremble as he looked over the ink drawings of the gang and Rizla. His face filled with sorrow and joy.

"You drew these all from scratch?"

"Yeah, man." Sideeq smiled.

"Effin' hell, man." Danny passed them one by one to Kyle. "Look, he even got the scar on Riz's nose and the tear on his ear."

"Yeah, bruv these are hard," Kyle agreed.

He reached out his fist to touch Sideeq's. It took a special type of artist to bring joy to a grieving man. They both watched Danny as his eyes lit up, and for a moment sat nodding at the detail and accuracy of Sideeq's illustrations. Getting emotional, Danny took a big breath. Overwhelmed, he wiped away a tear in his eye.

"Let it out." Kyle rubbed Danny's back. "It's OK if you wanna cry."

"No, is not that." Danny smiled. "It's the picture. I mean, it's him, innit. Look at it. It proper looks like him."

"Yeah." Kyle looked at Sideeq, not knowing how else to answer. Then Danny started laughing to himself, and Kyle wondered whether he was on the verge of a break down.

"I mean, you can say whatever you want about Riz. I know he weren't the best looking pup in the park, but I swear to ya, there's no forgetting that face there."

He let out another laugh. "Flipping ugly dog." He got up and thanked Sideeq with a quick hug. "Thank you, man. I'm gonna take this home and frame it. Nah, better yet, I'm gonna put it on a T-shirt."

"You see what I keep telling you about your art, bro?" Kyle raved. "This shit is powerful. I promise you, bruv. Once we do this Art-Meets-Culture ting and both of our names is out there? Yume. We need to thinking about get some T-shirts done for this clothing ting."

"What clothing thing?" Danny asked.

Kyle looked at Sideeq, guarded now. It was the first time they had spoken about their entrepreneurial dreams in front anyone else. Kyle pulled a face. Holding back, he waited until Sideeq gave him a reassuring nod. They both knew Danny could be trusted.

"Alright, hear what I'm saying. I'll tell you, but you can't say jack to no one. Agreed?"

"Yeah course." Danny sat up, all ears.

"Well, me and Sid's got this idea. We're looking to set up our own record label and clothing line."

A master salesman, Kyle began to outline their vision step-by-step for Danny. He began by explain the concepts of having a yume and where this vision would lead them. As he spoke, he elaborated using case studies and business models from other urban entrepreneurs. Borrowing from Jay-Z and Rocafella to London's very own Trapstar, he conjured images that made it seem feasible to envision the possibilities. Most importantly, he explained the ethos of their labels and how they created a niche in the market. Danny was spellbound. Like a magician, Kyle's vision had dazzled him and left him enchanted with the prospects. There was only one problem.

"Sid's got load of designs here and there, we just need to raise enough capital to get started?"

"How much is that?" Danny asked excitedly.

"It depends." Kyle watched Danny suspiciously. "Maybe about six or seven hundred, why?"

"Well, it's up to you lot, obviously. I'm not tryna step on no one toes or nothing. But if you want, I'd be interested in investing some dough in that."

"How you mean?"

"I mean, putting something in to get started."

"You serious?"

"Yeah."

"Oi, Danny, don't play." Kyle tried to dismiss his excitement.

"I'm not. Obviously you man would have to sort me out a little something on percentage. But friggit, why not? It already sounds like you man know what you wanna do, so I'll be up for it, if you are."

"We are." Sideeq spoke for the both of them. "How much was you thinking?"

"Well I've still got that money from when Gobbler and dem tried to rob me the other day. That's almost three hundred pounds. You can have that, and I reckon if I go back to doing some more dog walking I can raise some more—"

"Nah, that will be enough for now," Kyle cut him off.

"You sure?"

"Yeah, yeah, yeah," Kyle said confidently. His mind had clearly shifted straight into business mode. "We can get some samples done first, so we can work out our production cost. Then after that's when we can all put our dough into a pot and work out the percentages then. But for now, all we need is those samples."

"So we're in business?" Danny asked hesitantly.

"Yeah," Kyle replied shaking Danny's hand. "Yeah."

He fell silent, looking at Sideeq, amazed. They both smiled at each other in delight. This dream that had started from a song lyric was slowly become tangible.

"So what about a logo?" Sideeq asked.

"Bruv, that's your department. The quicker you draw one up, the quicker we can get these samples printed."

"But we ain't even decided on a name?"

"Don't worry about it, you'll find one." Kyle grinned.

"What about Yume?" Danny said. "I like that. It kinda

sounds like you and me and could be like us sharing our vision, like you was talking about earlier."

"Hmmm." Kyle thought about it. "Yeah, that could work. Yume Clothing. Yeah, maybe? What you thinking, Sid?" Kyle asked. He hadn't failed to notice Sideeq was back on his phone, texting.

"Maybe for the records," he said, looking up. He saw Nerissa get up and head for the door. As she left she smiled, giving Sideeq a minute wave. Sideeq raised his hand pretending to rub his eyebrow rather than waving back.

"I think I got another idea," he said, turning his attention back to the conversation. He hadn't realised Kyle, who had positioned himself in his blind spot, and had just clocked his whole interaction with Nerissa. Annoyed, Kyle said nothing as Sideeq took out a piece of paper. Taking one of the smaller sketches of Rizla, he traced the dog's outline then doodled a shield around the silhouette. Finally, he spilt the shield in half, darkened one side, and scribbled three letters to create a badge.

"U.D.C? What's that?" Kyle frowned.

"Ugly Dog Clothing." Sideeq smiled. He looked at Danny, whose eyes lit up.

"Oi, that's it. It's got to be that!" Danny tugged on Kyle's arm. He didn't look too convinced. "Think about," Sideeq said, packing up his stuff. "We'll talk about it later."

As Sideeq rushed out of the common room, the last thing Kyle was thinking about was the label's name. He got up and walked to the large window. Watching Sideeq leave, he didn't like what he had just seen between his friend and Nerissa.

He knew it wasn't enough to say anything yet, but felt something dangerous was brewing.

Chapter 3.5

Sideeq wasn't really one to play truant, but mischief and adventure tickled his ear. Excited by their whispers, the jubilation of going in to business with Kyle and Danny had him buzzing. For the first time in ages he was brimming with confidence. It was a confidence he was yearning to explore. Fleeing the common room and Kyle's watchful eye, he snuck out the college gates and made his way to the tube station. Seeing as Swank had already absconded with Sharkey, Sideeq had been inspired to follow suit. He knew Mr Ghodstinat would ask him for Swank's whereabouts and if he was totally honest, he'd rather not lie to his teacher. Plus, the euphoria of the day had him ecstatic and he was anxious to share. Smiling as he hit the main road, Sideeq took out his phone and scrolled through his messages as he made his way to Ladbroke Grove train station.

Hmm u & ur Frndz seem very
hype in that crnr...

Wat U lookin at?

Dat's classified! On a need to
know basis lol

So it's GIRLS!!!

It's classified!!! I can neither
deny nor confirm.

Why don't you just admit it?

Ok fine I admit it's classified!
Lmaooooo.

USD!!!

Huh? What's that mean... US
Dollars?

NO!!!!! Ur So Dumb!!!! PSML!!!

I was playing! I know what it
means I just wanted to see
you smile.

Awww OMG that's so sweet...
But no you didn't lol

Whatever!!!! I'll just ignore you
then.

U wouldn't dare.

Oi don't try not look at ur
phone!!!

Oi! I'm not playin wid U... I'll
come over there!!!

Ok ha ha ha very funny... So I
won't come over, but answer
now plz.

SIDEEQ!!! I'm not playin' wid U
answer now.

ARGHHHH!!! Why R U so
annoying?!!!

Can U stop playin' I've really
got something I want 2 ask U

I swear Sideeq if U don't
answer me I'm gonna walk
out.

Ok FINE! Don't EVER talk to me
AGAIN!!!

Wow!!! Why so serious (Heath
ledger Joker voice)... Lol

I don't like ppl ignoring me.

I see lol.... What's Ur question?

It doesn't matter now! I'm
mad at U!!!

Oh dear ☹ 'NerdRissa is mad
at me... Help! Help! The end of
the world is upon us.

I H8 U!!! LMAO why R U like
this 2me???

Bcz Ur a pagan! Wats ur
question?

Me & Lil Sid wanna kno wat u
doing last period?

Lil Sid wants to kno dat?
Really?

YES!!! He misses you. Now
answer the question.

> Tell Lil Sid I've got art last
> period. He can come and
> check me if he wants.

He told me to ask U if U want
2 skip last period and follow
me Westfield?

There's a special screening
at the cinema. He thght u
might wanna come.

> Hmmm Lil Sid said to ask all
> that?

YES!!

> Hmmm

Hmmm, hmm, hmm!!!!

He also said don't OVERTHINK
IT!!! It's only bcz dogs aren't
allowed.

Lol

Ok seeing as Lil Sid can't go,
cool

But don't U have to meet ur
other fri3nd after college?

Wat other frnd?

The one that likes to wait for
U every day?

He's not my friend! We're
dun!!! I told him to stay away
from me.

Hmmm interesting   ☺

Hmmm, hmm, hmm!!! Actually
it's NOT!!!

Woooooooo touchy touchy
lol

OMG U are so annoying. Lol I
h8 U

R U coming or not? If we go
now we won't run into him.

                              Yeah go on then if it makes
                                                you smile

☺☺☺☺ it does!!! Do I make U
smile?

                              KMT!!! No Ur too corny 4 dat.

FINE!!! Be miserable. Meet at
Grove station in 15mins

                              Bye Nerissa (Ice cube Friday
                                                voice)

I bet I make U smile before I
leave this common room

                                    Bye Nerissa!!!

Was that a smile I saw? I
think it was LMAO!!!!

1 - 0 to the Muse!!!

No I had something stuck in
my teeth lol

LOOOOOOL... USD!!!

$☺$☺$☺$☺$ LOL

Smitten, Sideeq was still beaming at the text conversation when he heard the heavy sound of the train crossing the bridge above his head. Shoving his phone in his pocket, he sprinted into the station. Touching his Oyster card against the yellow reader, he rushed through the ticket barriers. Leaping up the steps, he could hear the train doors beeping, marking the train's imminent departure. He dashed onto the platform in time to see Nerissa take a seat inside the carriage. Diving, he squeezed through the train's double doors just as they shut. He dropped in the seat next to Nerissa, panting, and looked at her.

"Yes, for your information I ran. It was only up the stairs, but I ran. If you say anything, one word, I'm getting off at the next stop."

As always, Nerissa bit her lip and smiled, and the two sat silently grinning as the train pulled off

CHAPTER 3.6

When the movie was done, Nerissa wasn't in a rush to go home. Although they had spent most of their time in the dark, she was enjoying Sideeq's company. She found herself slowly becoming besotted by his charm. Despite the fact they weren't actually on an official date, to her the evening bared all the hallmarks of a real one. Like a gentleman, Sideeq had refused to let Nerissa pay for the tickets, and when she insisted on buying the popcorn and something to drink he just smiled and said he was alright. He wasn't fussed where he sat, and for once Nerissa was allowed to sit anywhere she wanted, rather than the back row. When they found their tier, Sideeq thoughtfully brushed off her seat before letting her sit down, and she wondered how many girls he had done that for. As they waited for the adverts and trailers to play, they had a short discussion about world film and cinema. Nerissa confessed it was her lifelong dream to act for both screen and stage. Sideeq asked what the major difference was between performing for each. As always he listened to her with a minute grin on his face. Nerissa began to realise it was his signature smile.

When the lights dimmed, she leaned closer to smell the remnants of his musk-infused deodorant, and she swore he moved closer to smell her, too. Throughout the film she felt herself drawn to looking at him. The skin on his scar seemed to shimmer in the light, making it almost twinkle around his eye, and from time to time he would catch her looking at him between scenes.

"What?" he would whisper.

"Nothing. I'm just making sure you're watching the film properly. Shh, be quiet."

There was magic in the dark. Secretly she had hoped he would try to put his arm around her but he never did, which made the few times their hands touched even more exciting. So she insisted on passing him popcorn. It was a welcomed change from being constantly groped by Gobbler. In one moment she even forgot herself, stroking the back of Sideeq's hand and the creases between his fingers with her little finger. He looked at her and she caught herself. Blushing, she apologised and he said nothing, turning back to the screen.

When the movie was done, all she could think about were ways to stay in his company. She suggested they go window shopping. Sideeq seemed reluctant, but when Nerissa begged him, he went along with the flow. However, after half an hour it was clear that he surely was uncomfortable. She noticed his mood change and he became somewhat subdued. Disappointed, Nerissa felt slightly rejected. She asked Sideeq whether he was worried about being seen out with her. "I understand. You don't have to stay if you don't want to."

"It's not you," Sideeq explained. "I don't really like crowded places." He paused for a moment, dropping his gaze and fidgeting like a little child. "Because of my disabilities, I don't really like places where there's too much noise or people moving around." Looking up, he sighed as he struggled to elaborate. "It makes me anxious, coz I can't hear everything properly and I don't like people approaching on my blind side." Sideeq's face tightened as he slurred the last word, and he cursed himself under his breath.

"Awww, Sid, I'm sorry," Nerissa said, feeling awful. She was so wrapped up with her own insecurity that she couldn't fathom his change of disposition had nothing to do with her. "I didn't realise."

"It's cool."

"No, it's not. Come, let's get out of here."

Nerissa linked arms with Sideeq, and the two walked out into the cool air. Night had fallen, and the promenade was lit with a huge drape of fairy lights. Nerissa looked up, taking it all in. Happy again, she snuggled closer to Sideeq, feeling his huge bicep. He literally amazed her. At times she found him hard to read, sensing he could be very guarded. While other times he exuded a blunt confidence that aroused her. The blank expressions he wore on his face were a constant oxymoron. On the surface, they told nothing about him, but they somehow also conveyed that he was full of character and depth. Watching him again, she asked, "What you thinking?"

As they turned on to Shepherd's Bush Green, Sideeq replied, "You know this isn't the way to neither of our houses, innit?"

"So?" Nerissa pushed him. "Are you in a rush to go home?"

"No, but I'm just saying, innit. My house is the other side of Westfield and yours is that way." He pointed to the 94 bus stop on the other side of the green.

"Maybe I wanna take the long way home," Nerissa flirted. "Do you have a problem with that?"

"Nope." Sideeq smirked. "Do whatever makes you happy." He chuckled to himself and Nerissa saw a private joke playing in his mind.

"Now what you laughing at?"

"Nothing."

"Oh tell me, please. Please."

"Honestly, it's nothing."

"Don't be like that, Sid. Tell me. Otherwise I'll think you're laughing at me."

Sideeq shook his head. The more time they spent together, the wider his smile grew.

"I was thinking about today," he said in a soft voice. He peered up at the light of the red man on the pedestrian crossing and waited for it to change colour. As the traffic came to a halt, he led Nerissa on to the green.

"I was thinking it's been a good day. Then I thought about something my teacher said." That's all Sideeq came out with before falling back into his own thoughts. Eager to know more, Nerissa tugged on his arm.

"What did he say?"

"Oh." Sideeq came back to the conversation. "He told me this Persian saying: rich is the man who finds the sun on a cloudy day, for he knows his crops will still grow. Poor is the man who spends his time mourning it."

"Wow, that's deep."

"Yeah." Sideeq frowned. "But there's a second part. I can't remember it properly. It's about the rich man's harvest, and his neighbour thinking how come he's been blessed and the neighbour forgotten."

"Hmm, oh ok." Nerissa was puzzled. "What's that got to do with today?"

"Nothing exactly. Just, my teacher said that some people need to find their sun."

"Ohh." Nerissa made the connection. "Like a metaphor for what makes them happy?"

"Yeah."

"Wow, that's really beautiful."

"I know." Sideeq laughed. "But apparently it sounds much better in Persian."

"Oh my gosh, you are so dumb." Nerissa rolled her eyes.

Reaching the bus stop, she looked up at the LED display. She had three minutes to make her move before the next 94 bus came.

"So what makes you happy?"

Raising an eyebrow, Sideeq took a seat and looked at her with his signature smirk. "Why you always ask so many questions?"

"What! What's wrong with asking questions?"

"Nothing, but I noticed you do a lot of asking and not so much answering."

"That's because you never ask anything, do you Mr Know-It-All? Do you?"

Nerissa stepped between Sideeq legs, pointing her finger in his face.

"Move." Sideeq lowered her hands and tried to push her back.

Looking at the display, Nerissa started poking him in his chest. "Go on, ask me something. Ask me something. Anything."

"OK, OK." Sideeq restrained her at arms-length. He laughed as she tried to use her legs to push against his hold, to no avail. "Alright, cool—tell me one thing you've always wanted to do, but never had the chance?"

Trying not to bite her lip, Nerissa looked at him with a goofy grin. She thought about saying *kissing you*, but she wasn't ready to take that gamble. Instead she took a seat beside him and wrapped his arm around her shoulder.

"OK, but don't laugh. I've always wanted to go to the theatre to see a play."

Rearing back, Sideeq frowned at her.

"What?" Nerissa said, feeling embarrassed. "Why you looking at me like that?"

"You've never been to the theatre?"

"No!" Nerissa laughed at his expression. "Not a proper one. I went to see a panto of Jack and the Beanstalk in primary school, but I've not been to a proper play."

Flabbergasted, Sideeq continued to stare at her in disbelief. "Stop lying."

"I'm not." Nerissa said, pushing his face in the other direction.

"But Bush Theatre is just over there."

"OK."

"And the Lyric is down the road."

"OK, what's your point?"

172

"You're a drama student that's never been to the theatre." Sideeq stood up for emphasis. "That doesn't make no sense."

"No, it doesn't." Nerissa stood up as well. Taking Sideeq's arms, she guided him back down to his seat. "But you told me to tell you something that I've always wanted to do, but never got the chance."

Looking towards the oncoming traffic, she saw a red double decker bus in the distance. As it approached, she knew her time was up.

"Maybe someone will take me some day," she said, taking his arm and putting it around her again.

"Maybe," Sideeq replied. Apparently wondering what to do next, he stood up, looking at the large yellow numbering on the 94 bus. As it approached, Nerissa got up and held his hand. She wished he would kiss her, and stroked his little finger. It was almost the same size as her index finger, and she pictured him caressing her. When the bus pulled up, Nerissa knew her perfect night was over. For whatever reason she could tell Sideeq didn't like being too forward and he would probably take his time pursuing her. That was if he *wanted* to pursue her. The lack of an answer frustrated her, and Nerissa knew if she didn't do something the question would be in her head all night. Impulsively, she asked, "Sid do you want me to come to your house?"

Speechless, Sideeq stood there, staring at Nerissa. He looked as though he didn't know how to answer.

*

But as the two stared at each other, they were unaware they were being watched. Tucking into a box of chicken and chips smothered in burger sauce, Hassan sat at the back of a single decker bus licking his fingers. As the bus passed the W12 Shopping centre in traffic, he looked back to check his mind wasn't playing tricks on him.

He saw Nerissa standing at the bus stop, holding hands with Cyclops.

CHAPTER 3.7

On the way home, Sideeq listened to Nerissa chatting away and responded when necessary. She seemed to be enjoying herself. Gripping his arm, she continually snuggled against him and giggled at his blunt jibes and banter. He gathered that she was still oblivious to the idea that this whole adventure was uncharted territory for him. However, the real test was yet to come.

Sliding his key in the front door, Sideeq told Nerissa to be quiet as he listened to hear whether his mum was indoors. Being the first time he'd brought a girl home, he had no idea how his mum would react. He was nervous, and didn't welcome the awkwardness of having to introduce Nerissa to his mum. Luckily, to his relief, the house was in darkness. Wiping his feet, he switched on the passage light and found a note on the side table: *Food in the microwave, I've gone bingo with Aunt Janet, Love mum xxx.*

He smiled. The gods were making it easy for him. He whisked Nerissa upstairs to the sanctuary of his room. Like the very few that had the privilege of entering the room, Nerissa stood in awe at all the artwork on display. "Oh my God, Sid, did you do all these?"

Sideeq didn't answer. Instead, he raised an eyebrow with a sarcastic look. Nerissa cut her eye back at him.

"You do know how much I hate you, right?"

"So you keep saying." Sideeq smirked and turned on the TV. Brushing past her, he gave Nerissa a light shoulder-barge, then dodged her retaliating slap.

"You wanna drink?" he said tossing her the remote.

"Yes please."

"Juice or fizzy?"

"Fizzy."

"Hmm," Sideeq pulled a face, looking at her. "Makes sense."

Nerissa frowned "What does?"

"You like bare gas," Sideeq joked.

"Oh, really?" Nerissa retorted. "Is that why I like you?"

Her comment caught Sideeq off guard and he started to blush, saying "Whatever" as he slipped out the door. Making two drinks, he dropped two ice cubes in each glass and headed back upstairs. When he returned, he found Nerissa singing along to Destiny's Child 'Cater 2 U' with her eyes closed. To his surprise, she was pretty good, and he stood admiring her. She followed the riffs of Beyoncé's voice, holding the remote like a microphone. Twirling around, she threw her head back and reached out her free hand as she went for a high note. Hitting it, she opened her eyes and was startled to find him watching.

"Oh my God," she gasped, holding her chest. "What you doing? You frightened me."

"I didn't know you could sing."

"There's a lot of things you don't know about me." Nerissa

smiled, taking her drink. She took a sip then looked around for somewhere to rest her cup. Sideeq pointed to a spot near the bedside cabinet, and laid the tray down.

"Where did you learn to sing like that?"

"That's classified." Nerissa laughed.

"Really?" Sideeq scowled at her playfully.

"No. Not everyone's like you. Not everything's classified."

Nerissa kicked off her trainers and sat on the bed. "I've always sung. When I was little I used to drive my mum crazy sometimes. I was convinced I was going to be the next Beyoncé. So my mum sent me and my sister to this little gospel church in Fulham. She said that all the best singers—Aretha franklin, Dionne Warwick, Whitney Houston, Tina Turner—they all started off as choir singers. So that's why she sent us. I use to love it."

There was a glimmer in Nerissa's eye as she spoke. Listening, Sideeq enjoyed seeing her smile.

"It was nice. They'd do all these gospel songs, and show us stuff like pitch and control. It was really good."

"Did you get to wear those funny robes?"

"No, but I used to pretend I was one of the kids in Sister Act II..."

"...Because they never had robes in the end," Nerissa and Sideeq both said at the same time, laughing.

"Yeah!" Nerissa sighed. "It's a shame, I really liked that church."

"Why, what happened?" Sideeq queried.

"Oh, it's a long story." Nerissa took another sip of drink. "I'll tell you another time."

"Cool." Sideeq nodded. He decided not to probe, but Nerissa seemed to have an urge to tell him.

"Actually, wait," she said, covering her mouth and trying to crunch on an ice cube. "I'll tell you now. I haven't got nothing to hide."

"Basically, there was this girl there who was one of the deacon's daughters. I think her name was Tanya or Tarnya I can't remember—but she started spreading some rumours about me, so my sister beat her up and then attacked her dad. It's really kinda dumb. Trust me, but that's how things sort of go in my family."

"How'd you mean?"

"I don't know." Nerissa shrugged. She repositioned herself so she was right beside Sideeq with their backs against the wall. As was becoming her habit, she took his arm and put it around her.

"Things always seem to happen in my family. Mad things," she said in a sombre voice. "My nan used to say the women in our family are cursed. She said we can only attract bad men and bad things. That's probably how I ended up with Gobbler."

"Hmmm," Sideeq murmured at the sound of Gobbler's name. Unfortunately, Nerissa didn't pick up on his unease.

"I hate him, you know. He's such a bully. I heard what he did to your friend. Why didn't he go the police?"

"You know how it goes." Sideeq shrugged. He removed his arm from around Nerissa. He shuffled off the bed and got up to pull the curtains. "He didn't want everyone calling him a snitch."

"So? He should've still said something."

"C'mon," Sideeq scoffed. He took a seat by his desk. "You

know it's not that simple."

"I know, but it makes me mad." Nerissa looked annoyed. "I hate the way he thinks he can walk around with that stupid glove on and hurt people. Then just get off scott free. He thinks he's some badman. He hasn't even got a gun. "

"What?" Sideeq looked at her, surprised.

"He hasn't got a gun."

"But I thought that's why he wears the—"

"No," Nerissa cut Sideeq off. She jumped off the bed, ready to vent.

"He wears that sweaty thing because he's got a scar on his hand. He got burnt by a boiling kettle or something when he was little and the scar deformed his hand. His last two fingers are crippled because he was supposed to have surgery and never went. By the time he did, it was too late. They were going to cut his fingers off."

"What?" Sideeq sat perplexed. "Are you sure?"

"Of course." Nerissa walked over to Sideeq. Taking his hands, she stepped between his legs and sat on his lap. Leaning back she played with his fingers, lacing them between her own and resting her head on his chest.

"You don't know what it was like being with him," she said in a sad voice. Pivoting her feet, Nerissa encouraged Sideeq to slowly swivel the chair from side to side in a rocking motion. "He used to scare me so much. One day he would be so nice and the next he would just switch."

"Hmm." Sideeq placed his free hand underneath Nerissa arm so he was cradling her, and the two began to rock as one.

Stroking her hair back, he asked, "Why was you with him in the first place?"

"I don't know." Nerissa lifted her legs, moving them to rest them over his. "I didn't even like him at first. But he kept coming down to my school to ask me out. I thought he was being sweet. I thought wow, he must really like me. And all my friends were saying to go out with him. But really he's just one of those guys that don't take no for answer. He's not interested in me. He only wants to be with me coz people say I'm pretty and it makes him look good. Gobbler would never treat me like you've treated me today."

"If you say so." Sideeq blushed.

"He wouldn't, Sideeq." Nerissa remained adamant. "You're different. You're not like all the other boys I've met. You're kind, thoughtful, caring. You're practically perfect. I've never met anyone like you."

"Perfect, with one eye and one ear."

"Oh don't, be like that, Sid." Nerissa sat up. "Don't put yourself down like that." She started stroking his face. "I think you're wonderful. You're the only person in my life right now that sees me. The *real* me, not some peng ting or Gobbler's girl. Just me."

Blushing more, Sideeq dropped his gaze. Nerissa turned around to straddle him. Placing her forehead against his, she ran her finger gently long the length of Sideeq's scar, stroking it. Cupping his face she whispered, "It's OK, Sid, I see the real you too."

Twisting her head, she leaned forward and pressed her lips against his. He pressed back, then suddenly pulled away. He still

"You don't need to do this because you feel sorry for me."

Still holding his face, Nerissa smiled. "Why would I feel sorry for you?" Giggling she hugged him, then kissed him on the forehead. Standing up, she took his hand and pulled him up, too. "Dance with me."

Feeling shy and awkward, Sideeq had his first dance to the sound of Destiny's Child. Nerissa told him that the song had been especially for him, and she whispered, "I think this is gonna be our song."

Holding Nerissa tight, Sideeq counted to five and leaned in for his first kiss.

181

CHAPTER 3.8

The power of a secret can affect a person's psyche in a multitude of ways, for each secret holds its own intricate weight. There are those that are so dark and obscure that they manifest themselves like a burden of stress, heaping deep-rooted fears upon their owner. Their conscience shackles our souls with the trauma of the weight and paves the paths to self-loathing and depression. These are the secrets that most people like to bury deep into the abyss, never to be discovered or visited again. They come with warnings. More fool is he who goes in search of toil, and pay heed to those who willingly lighten their loads on your shoulders. For these people can be as dangerous as their secrets, and in life the two remain entwined.

However, on the other side of the spectrum there are those secrets that bring about a reverent light. That dance a ballet on the tips of our tongue and pirouette with delight. These secrets are infectious, creating energies teeming to explode. Their mere existence seduces, consumes and dilates. Burning hot, they inspire the enthusiasm to share and tempt our powers of discretion. These types of secrets come gift-wrapped in excitement, tinged in euphoria. They leave us with a fleeting madness, an ecstasy of recklessness to blurt them out or release them upon trusted ears. They are a force to be reckoned with, for what happens in the dark must come to light. In their eagerness to escape, they embody our whole being and make themselves visible in the smallest way. And sometimes in their subtle detection lies the capacity for our mistakes. Because all secrets hide in plain sight and are waiting to be unravelled.

The day after the cinema, Sideeq sat in art class with an ever-lasting smile on his face. Unlike his signature grin, it beamed with curiosity and captivated those who came into his presence. Swank looked him over as he prepared his portfolio for assessment. Humming away, Sideeq checked off his artwork against the unit criteria and reflective essay requirements.

"Rah, wha gwan fam? Why you look so happy today?"

"I don't know." Sideeq shrugged. "How do I usually look?"

"Like this." Swank straightened her face until her eyes were blank and expressionless. She deepened her voice with an Arnold Schwarzenegger impression and mimicked Sideeq's mannerisms. "'Wha gwan people, my name is Sideeq. I'm a cybernetic unit from the future, sent back in time to destroy Sarah Connor, but first I must paint.'"

"Whatever, you waste girl." Sideeq smiled as the text alert sounded on his phone.

"Ohhh, now I see." Swank tried peeping at his screen. "Who's *The Muse?*"

"Don't watch that." Sideeq hid his phone under the table, grinning. "That's my business, innit."

"Ohh, it's like that, fam." Swank reeled back playfully. "OK, say no more cuzzy."

Swivelling his chair away from Swank's prying eye, Sideeq replied to Nerissa's text then put his phone on silent. He knew if he didn't, he would probably spend the rest of the day texting her. There was something insatiable about her that excited him. She had a feverish quality that demanded his attention, and peculiar to his manner he felt good feeding it. Thinking about the relationship between famous artists and their muses, Sideeq began to recall the events of last night.

After their first kiss and a lot of canoodling, Nerissa had begged him to allow her to sit for him. Yet, like an infant, her natural energy wouldn't allow her to sit still for longer than ten minutes. In the end, Sideeq had her pose while he took her photo on his mobile. Taking out his phone again, he flicked through the images. Like a besotted artist, he studied every detail on his muse's face as though it were both the first time and last time he would see it. He recorded every facet from the shape of her lips to the slight chicken pox scar on her cheek, trying to understand how a person could transfer such energy and influence into another's soul. Zooming in, he looked at the bruising on her neck. It had faded since he had first seen them and were beginning to return to her normal colour. He smiled, thinking that when she came to his house again, he would replace them with his own type of mark. Nerissa had tried her best to give him a love bite but he kept wriggling away before she could blemish his skin.

Digging into his backpack, he pulled out his pad and looked at the sketches he had stayed up to early hours fever-ishly completing. Checking his composition and scaling, he cross-examined his version against the photos to judge the likeness of his drawings. He couldn't wait to give them to Nerissa. Revelling in his work, he was wondering whether he should wait and try and buy a frame when Swank asked,

"Is that Nerissa?"

Sideeq jumped. Immediately he closed his pad and tried to put his phone away. He looked around to see if anyone had heard Swank question when she asked another. "Why you got pictures of Nerissa, fam?"

"Lower your voice," Sideeq growled. His change in demeanour surprised Swank, but clearly not as much as the sketches and photos.

"Fam, what are you doing with pictures of that girl? Y'know is she a no-go, bro."

Sideeq didn't reply. Ignoring Swank, he put his pad back in his backpack and turned to his other work. However, Swank hadn't finished.

"Is that who was texting you before, *the Muse*?"

Sideeq continued to ignore her.

"Yo, fam, are you listening to me? Coz if that was Nerissa… Bro, you need take a step back and think about what you're doing."

"And what am I doing?" Sideeq finally answered. He waited for Swank to reply.

"I don't know, but whatever it is, it's not a smart move."

Sighing, Sideeq rolled his eyes and tried to continue with his work. "OK, noted. Can we move on?"

Swank frowned and decided to work another angle. "Yeah

cool, we can move on when you tell me what you gonna do when Gobbler finds out you're drawing pictures of his girl? Because he will find out."

"I'm not gonna do nothing." Sideeq sat up, agitated. "Because it's none of his business, same way it's none of yours. Besides they're not even together."

"That's for now," Swank scoffed. "Fam, listen to what I'm telling you. Truss me when I say you don't wanna get in the middle of them. You'll get yourself hurt."

"Do you think I'm sacred of Gobbler?" Sideeq snarled.

"I didn't say that."

"Good. Because I'm not."

"Fine, you ain't gotta prove nothing to me, my G, but deep this. You don't know Nerissa like I do, and I'm telling you. Whatever's going on between you and her, at some point Gobbler is going to get involved. He's going to see those pictures and he's gonna wanna know who drew them. You feel what I'm sayin?"

Annoyed, Sideeq didn't want to hear what Swank had to say. She was getting vex, but he wasn't foolish enough to completely dismiss her.

"Fam, lemme ask you this. When the time comes, hand on your heart can you guarantee my girl not to tell him your name?"

Sideeq turned to Swank and cut his eye at her. "I don't need to guarantee shit," he said coldly. "You need to stay out my business." He stood and backed away from the table. "Trust me, if you value our friendship, you'll let this go. I don't want no one talking my business, especially to Kyle."

*

Sideeq left Swank with a huge dilemma.

Beating her brow, she sat down wondering to what to do next. She contemplated her options, realising the affliction of holding certain secrets led to the birth of new lies. For when high tide comes, friendship and honesty find little reward in wading in a mangrove of secrets. Both run the risk of being washed away.

Chapter 3.9

For the rest of the day there was a frosty atmosphere between Swank and Sideeq. At lunchtime they met up with the others. Walking to George's, the two friends naturally gravitated away from each other, finding solace amongst the group. However, when Kyle—who was forever the glue between the five—directly addressed or drifted behind to speak to Swank, she could feel Sideeq keeping a watchful eye. It annoyed her to see his blatant mistrust, but she managed to ignore it in front of the others.

In class, however, she sat at her desk fuming. Even the jesting jibe Mr Ghodstinat threw at her did little to pull her out of her funk. To Swank there were three types of mistakes. There were good mistakes, bad mistakes, and some that don't need to be made at all. For some time she believed the first two may be inevitable—sometimes a case of simple dumb luck—whereas the last kind were usually the result of a conscious decision, and invariably a poor one at that. Whatever the outcome, Swank concluded these mistakes left us with the experiences that govern our lives. Either you were given the chance and ability to learn from them, making wiser decisions the second time around, or you continually make the same mistakes, proclaiming the circumstances around them were completely different from the first.

Irrespective of quantity, Swank figured these mistakes and experiences influenced our choices, and gave us the insight to warn others. The problem she was struggling with was what to do when your friend refuse to *heed* that advice. In Swank's experience, there was a time for discretion and a time to intervene. The pragmatist in her told her that Sideeq was absolutely right to tell her to back off. He had a complete right to privacy. Whatever was going on between him and Nerissa was his business. Who was she to start meddling in his affairs? In fact, why did she feel the need to interfere at all?

At first, her answer was due to their friendship. Being a concerned friend should have been good enough reason, but her pride started to get the better of her. Watching Sideeq at the table next her, Swank thought more fool him if he didn't want to listen. *'Coz who cyan't hear must feel.'* However, as he smiled away at the stream of text messages on his phone, her frustration started to build. It was a simmering anger like a stove kettle on a slow boil. There was something about the whole situation that didn't sit right with her. Swank could feel it niggling away at her to the point of irritation, but she refused to scratch the itch. As she packed up her stuff to finish the day, she began to realise what it was that irked her. She *liked* Sideeq. She liked him and thought he was too good for Nerissa. She didn't want to see him make the same mistakes that she had.

Leaving the room, Swank tried to make peace with Sideeq by biding him a friendly goodbye. He replied with an awkward, "Yeah cool I'll catch you tomorrow." She hoped that was enough for them to reach an understanding, but was unsure.

Disappointment filled her heart as she headed downstairs. She checked the time. She still had over an hour before her women's football training started at the Westway. Rather than going to the common room to chill, Swank decided to get there early. She knew her coach would probably be happy with that, and after a long day wrestling with what to do about Sideeq and Nerissa she welcomed a stress free kick about.

Spotting Gobbler and his cronies at the bottom of the road, Swank waited for a herd of students to exit and used the cover to dip down a side road in order to avoid them. Rummaging through her sports holdall, she pulled out her wireless headphones and was about to play some music when someone grabbed her from behind.

"Yo, wha gwan!"

Instinctively, Swank bent down and weaved out of the hold, pushing the person off her. She was about to start swinging when Kyle said, "Whoa, whoa, whoa, easy Nicola Adams, easy!"

"Move, man." Swank pushed him again. Her heart was still racing. She actually thought it might have been Gobbler or one of his friends that grabbed her. The notion, more than Kyle's actions, infuriated her and she lashed out at him again. "What's wrong with you? That shit's not funny. You don't grab a woman from behind like that!"

"Sorry." Kyle held up his hands. "I wasn't thinking."

"That's you manz problem, you never think," Swank snapped. "You just think its funny to run up on people. What if I had a shank? You wouldn't have found it funny then, would you?"

"*Do* you have a shank?" Kyle asked.

"No, but that's not the point."

"So what's the point?"

"Ahh, don't worry about the point. What you doing following me anyway?"

"How d'you mean?" Kyle smiled at her with a puzzled look. "You said you was gonna show me where that recording studios was that Sharkey was talking about. The cheap one."

"Oh. Oh yeah," Swank said, remembering she had promised him at lunch. "Come we go."

The two cut down the Chesterton Road and took the back streets towards Latimer Road. As always, Kyle was his energetic self and he couldn't stop talking about the new logo design Sideeq had done.

"Oi, I'm telling you, Swank, when you see the design… It's 'ard, 'ard 'ard. Even the name, Ugly Dog Clothing, it's got that proper ring to it. I'm telling you, as soon as we get our samples, this thing is gonna be on. I swear. I'm surprised Sid ain't shown it to you yet?"

"I'm not," Swank said as they cut under the concrete shadows of the Westway flyover. "I'm beginning to learn my man's like that, fam. He likes his little *hush-hush* moves, still. He probably wants it to be just you man."

"What you talking about?" Kyle said, already dismissing Swank's negativity. "You know what Siddy's like, he ain't no big talker. Don't watch no face, when we finish building this ting, this label is gonna be for all of us. I want you to bus one, two designs as well."

"Nah, I'm cool," Swank declined. "I can find my own ting. I'm not inner pushing myself up into other people's business."

"Fair enough." Kyle decided to leave the subject. "Yo, have you spoke to that Tasha chick again?"

"Last night, why?"

"You know why. I'm on that. I thought you was gonna put in a good word for me."

"I did, but she said you're not her type."

"What d'ya mean?" Kyle whined. "How can I not be her type, what's her type? Tell me?"

"What for? She said you're not her type."

"So I don't care, I'll make her change her type."

"You do that then," Swank replied bluntly.

As they walked past the vibrant shapes and colours on the mural of the Maxilla Social Club, Kyle said, "Yo, hold up hold up." He came to a halt. "What's going with you today?"

"Nothing."

"So why you acting all off key then?"

"How am I acting offkey? Coz I'm not jumping around all hype enough for you today? Does that make me offkey?"

"No, of course not."

"OK then, fam, you tell me what makes me offkey? Tell me," Swank demanded. "You don't know about my life but you wanna call me offkey."

Swank was a ball of pent up energy, and Kyle tried to diffuse the situation. "Alright, alright before you get upset, calm down innit. Are you on your period or something?" Screwing up her face, Swank cut her eye at him. She wasn't in the mood to entertain his foolishness. Kyle laughed. "OK, my bad. Offkey, that's a poor choice of words, my bad. I apologise. I shouldn't have said that. But hear what, it's obvious that something's got you rattled today, so why don't you just talk to me?"

"It's nothing," Swank said between gritted teeth. There was water in her eyes and she was trying her best not to cry. "Truss me, my G, it's nothing. I just don't have to be out here every day looking like everyman's fool. Coz truss me, fam, I ain't no one's fool. I'm not! You don't know about me!"

"OK, I hear that, I hear you. Hand on my heart, I would never try and take you for no fool."

"I dint say you. Did you hear me say you?"

"OK then, who? Tell me," Kyle pleaded "What's going on, man?"

"Fam, I said nothing." Swank wiped the tears from her face. "Can't you just leave it at that?"

"No!" Kyle shouted. "Why should I? You're my bredrin. If someone has hurt you or upset you, I wanna know. Tell me."

"I can't." Swank shook her head. Taking a deep breath, she put her hands over her face and tried to compose herself. Wiping her face, she looked at Kyle, then gazed up to the sky, filled with a cocktail of hurt. "I can't."

Kyle stepped forward. Embracing her, he tried to comfort her with a hug.

"No, don't touch me." Swank pulled away. "Don't touch me, I'm fine."

However, it would have been obvious to anybody walking by she wasn't. To those who were driving past it may have even looked like two young men having an intimate moment as Kyle tried to hold and wipe her face.

It took him another five minutes to calm Swank down. Running to the shop he brought a bottle of water and pack of pocket tissues, and the two sat on a wall underneath the Westway. As all heart-to-hearts go between friends, Swank opened up with the obligatory disclaimer.

"Fam, if I tell you, swear down, anything I say stays between me and you."

"A hunna percent. I swear on my life, it's strictly between us."

Satisfied that Kyle was now bound to silence, Swank began to divulge what she knew about Sideeq and Nerissa, which on the surface wasn't much, but enough for Kyle to be furious.

"Is this breh dumb? Is he dumb? I knew he was up to something with that chick. I knew it. Flipping idiot. I saw him texting her in the common room. *Idiot.*"

"Don't blame him, Kyle. It's her."

"Nah man. After what happened to Olly, he should know better than to go round that girl. I told him to stay away from her. I said she's trouble"

"Yeah I know, but she has her way."

"Nah man, that's not good enough."

"Kyle, listen to me. It's her." Swank waited for him to stop pacing. "Don't get angry with Sid. You have to understand how people like Nerissa work. She's smart you know, very, very smart, and sneaky. She's one of those people who have a way of getting inside your head."

"How'd you mean? Like a whatcha-me-call-it, a narcissist or

something?"

"Not like exactly that. Fam. I swear to you, no lie, some of the girls at our school used to call her Narcissistic Nerissa, coz she's one of them chicks that craves bare attention. And she doesn't care who she gets it from. Truss me, I know. If she don't get it from one person, she'll run to the next and she say whatever she needs to say to get it."

"Like what?"

"All sorts, fam, just allsorts."

Swank could tell from the look on Kyle's face he wasn't going to settle with that answer. "Nah, c'mon, Swank, don't hold back. Elaborate."

Swank sighed. "She'll tell you all this stuff about how much you mean to her, and how you make her happy, how she thinks she's falling in love with you and that you're special, and no one has ever treated her like you. You get what I'm saying, fam?"

"Yeah," Kyle nodded his head listening. He was slowly starting to understand.

"Then she starts telling you all this mad stuff about when she was young and some deep things that happened in her family. I mean deep stuff, fam. You know the typa tings you don't repeat to other people. And you know what that's like. It's like when people entrust you with dem tings, you kinda feel you're connected."

"Yeah, I get it, I get it." Kyle sat back on the wall next to Swank. "Especially if you add it to all the other stuff."

"Exactly, that's how she lures you in, fam. It's mad. You can't blame Sideeq for getting caught up. She's dangerous. She knows how to play people, and she don't care who it is or who gets hurt. It's all about her. So long as someone's paying her attention. That's what she does."

"Is that was she did to you?"

Swank paused, looking at Kyle. She thought about lying, but realised it was time to tell her truth. She couldn't hide it any more. Sitting on the wall, she took a deep breath, letting out another long sigh. "Yeah," she said in sullen voice. Her hands were shaking and she nodded her head repeatedly. "That's how she played me." Swank studied the graffiti tags on the Maxilla wall, waiting for Kyle's next question.

"What happened?"

She could tell from his tone he was trying not to be intrusive, more fulfilling a formality. How could he not ask? Swank knew she could decline to speak, but she had got this far and there was no turning back now.

"We use to be cool. I never had no problem with her. When she first came to my school, certain girls dint like her, for what reason I don't know. I just thought they were being bitchy. You know how it is at an all-girls schools. The gyal dem are all cliqued up. It only take one not to like you and that's it, and you know me I'm not really inner that. I used to do my own thing, so we kinda just started moving together.

"Anyway you know how it goes—a few people used to say things about us being offkey and on a munching ting. That's where the name Swank from comes. When I cut my hair, they try say I was moving like Hilary Swank in that movie *Boys Don't Cry*."

"Yo, ain't that one about that chick that got murdered for pushing herself off as a boy?"

"Yeah Brandon Teena. One girl in my class, try call me Brandon, and I smacked her up after school. I told her straight, next time, she better go and watch Hilary Swank in *Million Dollar Baby* before she try call me anything again. After that the name Swank kinda just stuck, but I dint mind it. Nerissa loved it. She said it was like reclaiming the word 'nigger'. And she would do all these dumb things, like sitting on my lap or playing with my hair to provoke people to say something."

"So how'd you fall out?"

"When she started seeing Gobbler, things started to change. She told me he used to ask her whether we ever had something, or had done anything together. But we didn't, we was just tight. But true I knew Gobbler from back in the day, and I know how he stays. From the time I knew he never really checked for how close we was, I thought it best to kinda fall back for a bit. You get me, fam? But after a while Nerissa started turning up at my yard with bare bruises and ting. Telling me how Gobbler gripped her up or boxed her. So obviously, I just tried to do the good friend ting and tell her she needed to get herself out dat situation. But she kept going back. Then one day she was staying at my house. I used to let her stay every so often coz Gobbler would wait outside her house or turn up throwing stones at her window till she answered. Anyway, it was late and we were laying on my bed chilling and I was trying to comfort her and that coz she was upset. Then she started rubbing her leg on me and tryna stroke my crotch. At first I thought she was mucking around, so I told her to stop playing. But she tried to make me squeeze her breast and kiss me."

"What! Don't lie." Kyle's eye widened. "She proper moved to you!"

"Proper, fam. She was bang on it."

"So what did you do?"

"I told her to 'llow it. I told her I weren't on that flex."

Kyle looked at Swank baffled. "What? Whad'you mean? I thought you were."

"Not even." Swank shook her head.

Kyle frowned, obviously trying to compute the information. "Are you sure?"

Swank looked at him, lost. She rubbed the back of her neck, thinking. "Maybe a little, I don't know."

Again, Kyle frowned. He took another moment then asked, "But you like girls right? I mean you're not into boys, are you? Or do you like both?"

"Nah," Swank shrugged. "I'm not really into dudes. I mean, I don't mind jamming with them, but not like that."

"So, you like girls?"

"Yeah, I guess. I don't really know," Swank said, feeling embarrassed. "Fam, lemme just finish telling you the story."

"Oh, yeah, yeah go on." Kyle let Swank continue.

"So my girl started getting deep, saying things like please don't reject her, I'm the only one who cares for her, and saying she's always wanted to be with me but was scared what people would say. So I'm like cool, I hear that, but I'm not on that flex. Well, at least I weren't then, anyway. Then she just went mad on me, telling me I'm a bitch and saying why I been leading her on and I don't care about her and everything. And I tried to calm her down, but she sprang out the house like a mad woman."

"Oi, you're lying, stop lying," Kyle said, laughing with glee.

"Nah I'm being serious, fam! Don't laugh. I swear down. I think she's slightly gone in the head. Something's not right with her. Imagine a couple of days later, I was walking home and Gobbler came up to me and he was like *we need to talk*. And I was like 'cool', coz I didn't have no beef with him. Then he started asking me what happened with me Nerissa, and was like 'nothing'. Then he was like 'so you didn't try to move to her?' I musta laughed, and then he started getting vex and switched, so I tried bop, but he started gripping me up and dragged me round the corner. I ain't gonna lie. I weren't even tryna fight with him, coz I didn't think he was gonna really do anything, just try coarse me up. Then he started getting up in my face asking me if I like girls, and I keep saying nah I'm not on that." As Swank spoke, she started to get a little flustered again. "Then he pinned me up against the wall and put his hand down my trousers."

"He did what?"

"He put his hands down my trousers."

"Are you friggin' kidding me?"

"No. He started touching me up and asking me 'do you bang brehs. If you don't bang girls, you gotta bang brehs.' And I told him no I don't do none. Then he started laughing, saying 'so you're a virgin?' And I dint know what to say, so I just went quiet, and he just kept pulling and poking and groping at me, saying don't cry boys don't cry, and I knew exactly what he was talking about. I knew Nerissa had told him about that film. So I told him to 'llow me. I begged him. I said I'll do whatever he wanted. If he wanted me to stay away from Nerissa, I would. I'd never go near her again. But he kept laughing and feeling me up. Then he leaned in like this, crushing my neck with his arm—" Swank demonstrated for Kyle. "And he was like 'I'll let you go if you give me head.'"

"What?" Kyle said. He looked at Swank, waiting for her to finish.

"He said he'd let me go if I gave him head."

"So what did you do? Don't tell me you did it."

Swank could hear the disgust in Kyle's voice and felt ashamed to tell him what happened next. Her eyes started to well up again and she could feel herself shaking. "I did," she said, wiping her eyes. "I didn't know what else to do. I just wanted him to get off me so I did it."

In Swank's mind it was the only rational thing to do. She had to. She'd seen what Gobbler had done to Nerissa before, and he had her under duress. It was either do as she was told or get beat up, or perhaps worse. However it didn't help to hear Kyle say—

"Are you serious? Tell me you're not serious. Tell me you didn't do that."

"I did. I gave him head." Swank snapped. "So what! I don't care. Get over it." She felt shitty.

"Swank you're not serious right now. You didn't give it to him. He *forced* you. That's eff'd up."

"So what! I said I don't care. I'm dun with it." The more Swank said she didn't care, the more her own lie hurt her. "I don't want to talk about it. I only told you because my girl is trying moving to Sideeq."

"Yeah I hear that, but…"

"Nah, no buts, fam. I swear, if you tell anyone Kyle, I'll never speak to you again. Truss me, if you tell anyone, dats me and you dun."

"So I'm just suppose' to sit on it?" Kyle roared.

"Yes! You're the first and last person I'm telling."

"Why?" Kyle shot back at her. "You just said you don't care. So why shouldn't we do something?"

"Because I don't want my family finding out I'm gay."

It was the first time Swank had ever said it out loud. It was the first time she had allowed herself to accept it. After years of repression, confusion and taunting, she finally realised her own truth. *She was gay.* The words felt alien to her tongue, but she was willing to live with them. Looking at Kyle, she realised that this was her moment. This was the one she would describe again and again, and he would be the one she'd refer to as the first person she came out to. She wanted to explain more—that she came from a deeply religious family and was scared that she would be shunned, but then Kyle simply replied, "OK, fair enough. I hear that."

That was it. Any anger he had disappeared like vapours in the air. They faded into nothingness, and he stood looking at Swank with a peculiar look. She sensed he wanted to smile, and preferred he say what was ever on his mind.

"What? I am I joke to you, fam? I just told I'm gay and you're laughing at me."

"No way, it's not even that." Kyle smirked. "I was just thinking, are you sure your family don't know you're gay?"

"I don't know. I don't think so."

"Are you *sure*?" Kyle raised an eyebrow.

That afternoon Kyle shared a family secret about his Great Uncle Kenneth. He was a tall, slim, and soft-spoken man that everyone loved. Before he died in his seventies, he wrote a letter to his sister, Kyle's gran, saying he was sorry he was a disappointment to the family for never getting married or having any kids, but life never had that in store for him because he was not that way inclined. On his death bed, he asked his sister to forgive him. Kyle told Swank his grandmother said, "Kenneth was so foolish. I never had nothing to forgive him for."

Kyle even tried to put on his grandmother's West Indian accent. "The same way she knew her other brother Keithley was a teef from the age five was the same way she knew Kenneth was dandy. Her only disappointment was she never knew why Kenneth spent his whole life hiding it. There are certain things you can't hide; especially from family. She said that was truly Kenneth's biggest mistake."

As they finally made their way to the studio, Kyle told Swank that whatever she decided to do, he would be there for her and there was no need to stress. His gran had also taught him that God had a way of turning friends into family. If you lost one, He shall replace them with another one.

Swank smiled, overcome with a warm feeling of hope and a sense of belonging. The idea of mistakes dominated her mind no longer, and regardless of the outcome with her and Sideeq, she didn't regret speaking with Kyle. She was gay and he was the first to officially know. The only problem she had now was how to break it to Kyle that she was looking to move to Big Batty Tash…

CHAPTER 3.10

Whenever Sideeq had the chore of designing something, Kyle had the annoy habit of hovering over his shoulder. To make matters worse he would groan at every click of the mouse then ask, "Why you doing that?" to which Sideeq would always reply, "You'll see in a minute."

As Sideeq neared the end of each task, Kyle would inevitably signal his approval by coming closer and murmuring, "Hmmm, OK, OK. I see, I see."

Sideeq would almost always ignore him and continue with his next sequence of tasks. He didn't necessarily mind Kyle being a backseat designer; micro-managing was in his nature. However, the thing he found totally unacceptable was the way every so often Kyle would reach across to grab the mouse or tamper with the design if he left the room. On one occasion, when Sideeq had gone downstairs to get some beverages, Kyle naively tried to adjust an e-flyer they had been assigned for school work. When Sideeq returned, he found Kyle hunched over the laptop in a panic having lost half their design. A furious Sideeq banned him from ever touching the mouse again, and whenever they were designing anything together, he wasn't allowed to enter Sideeq's designated technical area.

So when Kyle came around to draft up the final designs for the UDC clothing samples, he sat eagerly perched on the edge of the bed, eyeing the computer screen and giving commentary from afar.

"Bruv, why don't you put the logo on the right side at the top? I think the right side would look better," he said, as Sideeq dragged and dropped the new shield-shaped logo on the left side of their T-shirt template.

"Coz there's no need. Logos go on the left side of the chest."

"No they don't." Sideeq ignored him. "Are you sure? I swear I got a few tops where the logo's on the right."

"A hundred per cent sure." Sideeq's eyes remained transfixed on the screen. "Go and look in my wardrobe if you don't believe me. I guarantee you won't find one logo on the right."

Kyle got up and started riffled through Sideeq tops. Checking the alignment of the logo on the design Sideeq smiled to himself.

"Brother, why you don't you ever like to listen?"

"I do," Kyle said, still searching for at least one top to prove his point. He flicked through the whole rack twice before he eventually conceded. Looking back, Sideeq smirked at him and said, "So you happy with left side, yeah?"

Kyle kissed his teeth. "Bruv you've changed you know. When I first met you, you was a calm yoot. I used to like you. But now you tryna deal with me like you're some boss."

"Now?" Sideeq laughed. "Fam, I been a boss from day. I just let you do a lot of talking."

"Whatever, you fool," Kyle replied, kicking the back of

Sideeq's chair. Dodging a retaliating blow from Sideeq, he moved further down the bed and rested his back against the wall.

"Bruv, I know we kinda named the label after Rizla, but why did you choose Ugly Dogs?" Kyle asked. "I don't know," Sideeq shrugged. He turned to face Kyle. "Its something I use to hear my Aunty Janet say whenever there was drama. She always be like *'Ugly dogs don't cry.'*"

"What's that meant to mean?"

"It means ugly dogs don't cry because they're ugly. They still have to learn to persevere or get on with things regardless. It's kinda like saying *no use crying over spilt milk*. Get on with it."

"Bruv, umm umm" Kyle shook his head. "You're aunty is from one dem small islands innit?"

"Shut up you fool," Sideeq laughed.

"Nah, bruv swear down, only small island people come with those mad sayings there. Where's she from Montserrat or something. Nah I bet she's from Carriacou. You know dem people there with dem mad accents."

After having his fun Kyle left Sideeq to get on with the last few amendments. He looked up at Sideeq's current artwork, studying it carefully. The panelled paintings of Shepherd's Bush Market had long gone, and he wondered what was now dominating Sid's mind. After what Swank had told him, he half expected to see a collection of sketches of Nerissa posing nude with a sheet half-draped across her, like one of those real-life models in an art house movie. He pictured Sideeq sitting opposite her sketching her curves, and the two smiling and flirting. He chuckled to himself, wondering how their relationship worked. Had it been any other girl, Kyle would have probably been happy for Sid, but there was something about Nerissa that irked him; something other than the Gobbler connection.

Mulling it over in his mind, he scanned the rest of the art, looking for any imprints and impressions of Nerissa. At first glance there didn't seem to be anything that stood out. It was more of Sideeq's usual stuff, with a strong focus on images of his family. Then Kyle was slowly drawn to two individual A4 pieces. His eyes darted from one image to the other. On the surface there was nothing that connected them. In fact they were on opposite sides of the wall in two different mediums, with zero relevance— but that was the point. Even if they had been side-by-side, most people would have probably still missed their significance, but not Kyle. He knew Sideeq too well. They had spent countless hours in that room, playing music, videos game, writing lyrics and talking about their dreams. They'd grown up unlocking each other's minds, and he knew Sideeq was all about details. Subtle details that even the devil would be proud of. Like many artists, he liked to hide things in plain sight, and so rather than the two pictures themselves speaking volumes to Kyle, it was the way they were hung.

The first was on the far left of the wall, amidst a collection of family pencil drawings. To the untrained eye, there was nothing unusual about it. It was a delicately drawn self-portrait of Sideeq, which had been masterfully shaded. The dark grey shades of the graphite had been smudged to create a natural skin tone on the portrait. With Sideeq's face at a slight angle, the drawing skilfully captured most of his features, but not all. The long winding scar that tore a divide in his face, and the cloudy pupil of his dead eye had been replaced. No longer did his face carry the leaden look of his scars. Here lay a version of Sideeq, the world had never seen. Not even Kyle. The drawing sat right under a picture of Sideeq's older brother holding his daughter, which became Kyle's first clue. Kyle remembered when Sideeq had first drawn it. Seeing as his brother had died before his niece was born, he had described it as his way of rewriting history, or spying on an alternate reality. At the time Kyle thought the concept was deep—the idea of time travelling and crossing realities through art. Sideeq, on the other hand, downplayed it as just a concept, no different than if Kyle wrote a rap about Malcolm X surviving his assassination attempt. That was Sideeq, always dismissive. However, here he was now rewriting history and spying on an alternate version of himself.

Kyle would have stared at the portrait for ages if he eyes hadn't been scanning for other clues when he found one. Like a hidden Easter egg, it sat on the far right of the wall. Again, the picture sat amongst a cluster of other work. This time it was an assortment of ink Transformer drawings. After discovering the original 80's animated *Transformers* movie and comic books, Sideeq had been inspired to master the technique of drawing the man-like robots. As always, he added his own twist to the style—one day he drew Optimus Prime in a black suit and tie. This later developed into an ongoing theme where he depicted Transformers in everyday clothes and scenarios. When Kyle asked Sideeq why, he simply said, "What if Transformers didn't need to hide? How do you think they'd cope without their disguise?"

It was something Kyle had never thought about. To him it was just a film. Only Sideeq would think about something like that. Then he'd asked, "K, if you had the choice, would you rather be a Transformer or a human?"

Kyle replied, "I'd probably be a Transformer, that way I could just change into a plane and fly to wherever whenever I want."

When Kyle returned the question, Sideeq had shrugged and said in a solemn voice, "I don't know. Some people spend their whole lives trying to transform, while others prefer to hide in plain sight. So I suppose there's not much difference being human or a robot, other than being able to fly off when they please."

It was one of their many strange conversations. Kyle had a profound love for the way Sideeq looked at things, which was why when he saw the second picture, he was worried. The ink drawing portrayed two robots, one male and one female, romantically embracing. They were entangled in a bed of wires, and the female robot seemed to be helping to free the male robot, whose missing eye and a deep gash along his metal face Kyle recognised.

Again he sat back, studying the two pictures. As his eyes roamed from one image to the other, and the space between, Kyle knew what he was looking at. They were polar ends of the same spectrum. Together the two pictures symbolised Sideeq's recent thought pattern. Kyle figured he was comparing the 'what if's' of his past with the 'what now's'—his ability to transform.

"Hello, Earth to Kyle? Are you listening?"

"Huh?" Kyle turned around to Sideeq, who stared at him waiting for a response.

"I said, I need the card number so we can process this order."

Kyle looked at the screen and Sideeq had already started the ordering process. "What, you finished all the designs already?" He fished out his bank card and handed it to Sideeq.

"Yeah." Sideeq started entering in the card details. "I ordered two mediums and one large tee in all three designs. Three black hoodies with the shield design on the front and back, and three black snapbacks with the embroidered logo. "

"OK." Kyle started rubbing his hands together excitedly. "How much was it?"

"All in it came up to £521."

"£521?" Kyle looked at the screen to see if Sideeq had made a mistake on the order. "You sure?"

"Yeah," Sideeq slid to the side so that Kyle could see the screen. "It's £120 for the hoodies and £225 for the tees, £36 for the snapbacks plus £140 set up fee and VAT."

"Rah, man, these samples are bloody expensive."

"I know, but that's the price for their quality stock. It's either that or we get the Fruit of the Loom stock."

"Nah, man, we ain't getting no boog Fruit of the Loom bits. These samples have to be proper, proper. When man's rocking dem, people have to be like 'rah, what's that you got on?'"

"I hear that," Sideeq said, passing Kyle the keyboard. "Put your address in."

Kyle typed in his address and confirmed the order. "Rah, bruv imagine this. In seven to ten working days, we're gonna have our own clothes label."

"I know! Nuts innit," Sideeq said as he took out his phone. He began to write a text. From the goofy grin on his face, Kyle guessed it was to Nerissa.

"Who you texting?" he asked.

"No one," Sideeq replied. When he finished texting, he put his phone down on the side and started closing some of the windows on his desktop. The two fell silent and Kyle watched Sideeq for a moment. He didn't like the idea of Sid keeping secrets from him, and he didn't like pretending that he didn't know. Taking another brief look at the picture on the wall, he decided to broach the subject with Sideeq.

"Oh bruv, I forgot to tell you, I booked a session in that studio under the arches for next week."

"OK." Sideeq turned around, lending Kyle his full attention. "What's it saying?"

"It's live, you know. Me and Swank went there yesterday."

"OK," Sideeq murmured. His face completely dropped at the mention of Swank's name. "How comes you went with her?"

"Sharkey weren't about." Kyle noted shift in mood. "So I got her to show me where it is. When we were bopping there, me and her got talking."

"Yeah I bet you did," Sideeq said, getting up. He walked over to his art supplies and started to pick out some marker pens.

"What's that meant to mean?"

"Nothing." Sideeq tried to down play his remark. "You know what Swank's like, she just yaps on a bit, that's all." He took out one of the custom trainers he was working on. He sat down and started doodling. "What d'you talk 'bout?"

"Nothing much, mostly music." Kyle decided to let the matter go. He could see Sideeq already had his back up, and he didn't want Swank taking the blame for any secrets Sideeq was hiding. "You know that beat Sharkey wants me to jump on? He's tryna get me to perform at the party, but I'm feeling like I should wait. What you reckon?"

Seeming relieved, Sideeq put his pen down and turned to face Kyle again. "Boy, that might be a good look, you know. That beat is a banger. If you murder it the party would go wild and you could stream it on your Insta."

"Oi, oi, that a heavy idea." Kyle sat up, excited. "That would look proper mad. The only thing is…" He hesitated, thinking.

"The only thing is what?"

Kyle frowned. "I ain't got no hook. I kinda wanted a chick on the chorus before I put it out there."

"Hmmm." Sideeq thought about it. After a second he had an idea. "I got it. Why don't you just perform the intro and the first verse, then when the chorus comes just say that was a little preview and ask the crowd if they want some more?"

"OK, I see where you're going." Kyle beamed. "Then drop the second verse."

"Yeah, and then later you can find someone to record the chorus."

"Yeah man, that one can work." Kyle held out his hand for Sideeq to slap. "You see why I always come to you. You're friggin' genius. Now all we got to do is find a chick to record it."

Smiling, Sideeq laced his fingers together and cracked them. "Don't worry about that," he said, putting his hands behind his head. "I think I know somebody who can help."

"Who?" Kyle frowned.

"Don't worry." Sideeq grinned and picked up his phone. "All you got to do is trust me. Send me the words and I'll find out if they're interested."

Kyle typed out the lyrics, but for the first time in their friendship, he had a grave wariness for Sideeq. Taking a seat at the edge of the bed, he looked up at Sideeq's wall. Hypnotised by the two pictures, he studied every detail with a great unease.

An hour later, Kyle said his goodbyes and headed home. On his way, he noticed a pair of old Air Force Ones dangling from a phone wire. As the two trainers swung in the night breeze, they batted against each other, barely making a sound.

In years to come, Kyle would remember that night. He would remember every line from those two pictures Sideeq had drawn vividly, and recall the impression they'd left on him. He would also remember the two beaten and battered trainers tied together and slung over that wire. He had admired how they weathered the storm and had contemplated what would happen if one shoe were to break and fall. The image of the trainers had made Kyle wonder how naïve his friend was. It had also made him question his right to query Sideeq.

That night, Kyle had envisioned alternative realities and came to the simple conclusion: no man can rewrite history, but they can always transform the future.

Part IV

Party & Bullshit

CHAPTER 4.1

If the first day of college gave students the chance to forge a new identity, then the first major party of the year provided the chance to solidify that persona. It was a time when those who had safely been strutting around the proverbial watering holes of college for weeks were now called to venture further into the teenage jungle. The moment when those who have been eyeing other's ascension eagerly waited to see what their rivals could do. Yes, that girl looks good in her everyday wear at college, but does she know how to step it up to the next level? What little number does she have in her wardrobe that could make her untouchable, or a new contender to the throne? Does she know that her status can drop ten points if she turns up wearing something from her weekday attire? Hmmm, and what about my guy over there? The one who's been flexing like an apex predator all this time. Can he walk with elephants, can he hunt with the pride, or is he just another big fish in a small pond? All these questions needed to be answered, and the 2AM Girls' birthday bash was going to be the place.

For the last two years, Ashani Benn and Mya Kerr's joint birthday bash had been labelled the autumn party to be at. What started as a modest drink-up in Ashani's parents' three-bedroom house in College Park had turned into one of the best teenage house parties West London had seen in a generation. With hordes of teenagers arriving unannounced, Sharkey was asked at the last moment to set up some decks. All it took was two phone calls, and 40 minutes later they had a full sound system and speakers. Then when the jerk man turned up outside and started selling jerk chicken from his oil drum, the party hit legendary status and became known as the famous '*Shoobs at Holberton Gardens.*' Those who were there partied to the early hours of the morning, revelling with delight—and those who weren't would have to hear about it year after year, wondering how they missed out.

And so when the girls asked to throw another party the following year, Ashani's father refused to accommodate their wishes, which caused the party to migrate to the local community hall. This migration created a knock-on effect. What should have been an invite quickly morphed into a flyer, a two-pound fee was added at the door, alcopops were sold at the bar, and without any explanation the jerk man turned up again. The second shindig was christened '*Da Big Shoobs Part II*', and inspired the girls to throw their first summer all-dayer, '*Shoobs in da Sun*' under their newly formed events company '*2AM Promotions.*' Renting a garden flat on Airbnb, the 2AM girls' fourth instalment saw them return to the house party set up with a secret location and a night to be called '*Da Secret Shoobs.*'

However, the events that were to play out on this night would not stay secret, and this was one party that was bound to make history.

218

At eight o'clock, the party's secret location went out to all those who were on the guest list or had bought tickets. By nine o'clock, the early birds started to arrive. By ten o'clock the party was streaming live on Snapchat and by twenty-fve past ten the first casualty was being carried outside, white girl wasted.

Kyle, Sideeq and Danny arrived just after ten thirty to a mass of people waiting outside, and a group of girls tending to their drunken friend. One of friends held her hair back as she threw up by the side of the road, while another rubbed her back saying, "Carly, are you alright?" A third stood by repeatedly saying, "She needs water, somebody get her some water..."

As the trio approached, Ashani's uncles stood on the door, cordoning off the front gate to control the flow of people. The two man-mountains, Big Reg and Benga, were ideal for security and guarded the door like a pair of grizzly bears. Diligently, they patted down and searched the boys for any weapons, then took their photos for extra precaution before letting them in. They were a few questions as to what was to be done with the pictures, but when Benga said, "Act up and you'll find out," no one bothered to inquire again. Mya's Aunt Carla checked the girls' bags, and Twitches, the oldest of Ashani's uncles, ordered the crowd to make two lines. Although he was small in stature, it was easy to see from the way he bellowed at the revellers that door work was nothing new to him.

"Ticket holders, stand to the left. Guestlist, come over here! If you're not one of the two, go home now! You're not getting in here tonight."

He looked directly at a group of boys who had gathered not

too far from the drunken girl. They'd been outside for a while and were still trying to work out how they were going to get inside. One dark skinned boy in a blue hooded top told his friend to call Mya and tell her to come to the door, while another in a dark grey tracksuit stepped forward, attempting to speak to Ashani's uncle.

"Oi bossman, talk to me. What you saying, if man slip you a little extra p…?"Big Reg looked at him with an unconcerned eye. "Who you wid?"

"It's just me." The boy quickly disowned his crew at the chance of getting in. Raising an eyebrow at Benga, who returned it with a dismissive grunt and a sneer of the top lip, Big Reg told the boy, "Stand over there, I'll talk to you in a minute." Excited, the boy stepped to the side while his friends grumbled, "Rah, is that how you moving, Kwamz? Nah you're a pagan of the highest."

Danny and Sideeq followed Kyle to the back of the guest list queue. Clutching his Armani man bag, Danny whispered, "Mate, you didn't say they were gonna be searching us."

"Bruv, minor formality. Don't watch no face. You ain't got nothing to hide, have you?"

Danny went quiet, scratching the back of his head. "I ain't sure about that."

Turning around, Kyle gave him the stink eye. He was about to ask Danny what he had when Ashani appeared at the door with a small entourage. The three girls who wore loose white sleeveless tops over dark denim miniskirts with gold stitching, looking like backup singers as Ashani out staged them in a stunning white dress with gold trim and a slit on the leg. It complimented her slim figure and dark skin. Her thick mane of lush black hair was plaited in a Dutch braid with delicate gold ribbons entwined in it that matched her eye shadow. Gold glitter enhanced her mix of Yoruba and Antiguan features, and she scanned the outside, apparently looking for Mya. Overwhelmed by calls from the waiting crowd, she was about to go back inside when she spotted Kyle.

"Rah, man like KJ Wheeler! Wheel up! Wheel up!" She roared Kyle's emcee name.

"Yo, wha gwan?" Kyle smiled. He tried to play it cool as people turned to see who he was. Ashani called to Twitches, "Uncle D, Uncle D! Let him and his friends in." She pointed to Kyle. Twitches waved them forward and sent them through with no search. Kyle looked at Danny, who gave him a cheeky wink, knowing he got a touch.

"Come, come," she said, giving Kyle a big hug and kiss on the cheek like they hadn't only just met earlier on that day when Kyle had helped Sharkey deliver the set. She greeted Danny and Sideeq, too. "Hi guys, what's your names?"

She clicked her fingers when they replied. Two of her entourage stepped forward, putting gold wristbands on their arms. Kyle noticed other people in the corridor had red wristbands and asked what the difference was.

"These are VIP," Ashani explained, ushering them inside. "Which means you can use the toilets upstairs and go to the back room. Sharkey's inside. He said you're gonna do you're new track?"

"Yeah, maybe, we'll see." Kyle grinned, trying to play it

humble. Secretly he knew any chance he got, he was going to pepper the mic with lyrics and murder the party.

"OK, well you guys go inside, find a girl and have fun. There's drinks at the bar."

Ashani gave Kyle another hug and disappeared with her entourage.

Inside, the party was heaving and the place was packed with sweaty bodies. Music blared from the speaker boxes and the bassline thumped away at the walls. The steamy windows rattled with the reverb, and the potent smell of skunk weed caught the boys' noses. There was a small queue by the kitchen, which had been turned into a makeshift bar, and outside there was a marquee for people to smoke. Venturing into the main room, the trio scanned the party. The ratio of guys to girls was healthy, and leaned in favour of the girls. That was always a good sign, as it gave less excuse for any trouble. Nevertheless, there were still prominent roadmen dotted around. In one corner, a crew of Grove and Latimer boys lead by Giant and Mint held their spot, while in another the Bush Squad did the same. You also had one or two representatives from White City and Zart as well, but with Sharkey's involvement, the 2AM promotions were one of the only dances that most of these fractions could go to without any drama. Everybody knew they were a strictly gang-free zone. However, if you went outside and shook a few bushes, you would probably find an arsenal of weapons in various spots.

The decks were set up at the far side of the room and Kyle made a beeline to where Sharkey stood chatting with one of the other DJs. As always, he was freshly dressed in a black Gucci polo top, black jeans, and fresh black Jordan 11s. He smiled, greeting them. "Yes, yes, family."

He made a point of hugging each of them, so those who were watching knew they were affiliated. Reaching for a small stack of red plastic cups and a bottle of Courvoisier, Sharkey handed them a cup each. He poured out generous portions of the brown liquor, then raised his cup.

"Salute, salute, my Gs, salute."

Taking a sip, Kyle tried to firm the burn in his chest, but almost choked when he spotted Swank up against the wall dancing with Tash. Meeting eyes, the two friends smiled at each other as Tash bent over and grinded her bottom on Swank's groin. Kyle pulled a face, exaggerating his surprise. Pushing up his lip and widening his eyes he nodded his approval and clapped his hands, finally understanding why Swank had said he wasn't Tash's type. Nodding back confidently, Swank gave him a wink. Then she put both her hands on Tash's shoulders, encouraging her to bend over more. Taking full advantage of Tash's dexterity, Swank gave the girl a serious wind that would have made any man stand to attention.

"Cor blimey, check the pounded yams on that," Danny said, pulling out a pack of balloons. Tearing into the packet, he quickly filled up a balloon from a canister of nitrous oxide, glaring as a group of girls started to cheer Swank and Tash on.

"Swank looks well in there, mate," he said, sucking up half the laughing gas in the balloon. "Oi, she ain't playing. I'm goin' over there before she takes all the gash."

He handed the balloon to Kyle and loaded up another one

before dipping into the crowd. "Easy, easy white boy coming thru."

In seconds he popped up on the other side. Using the balloon as his way in, he offered it to Swank, who hugged him. She inhaled the balloon twice then passed it to Tash, who devoured the gas while Swank introduced Danny to her friends. She waved Kyle and Sideeq over. Playing cool, Kyle put up a solitary finger, gesturing 'one minute', and turned to speak to Sharkey, who was already glued up to his game.

"Fam, I beg you don't play that too cool for school ting. There's too many man in here watching. Go chat to some gyal."

"Allow me, bruv." Kyle laughed, picking up the microphone and pretending to inspect it. "Man have tah try and make it look good, innit."

"There's plenty time for that later. The mic ain't going nowhere."

Sharkey topped up Kyle and Sideeq's cups and sent them over to Swank's corner. It was time to mingle.

*

As they settled in, it wasn't long before Sideeq started to feel out of his comfort zone. The dimly lit room with its red light and neon strips cast shadows across the mass of faces and bodies. Conscious he was surrounded by a gaggle of girls, Sideeq became aware of the different dudes scoping their corner. He could tell some were trying to figure out how to infiltrate the girls, while others were trying to figure out who he and his friends were. It put him on edge. Instinctively, he backed up against the wall and put his hood on, but he didn't remove his hearing aid. The music was too loud for that. It was so loud that every time someone said something to him he could barely hear what they were saying. He just nodded his head or smiled politely, hoping that was enough. Slowly, he sipped his Courvoisier, trying to relax. He needed to. This was his first real party and he had waited a long time to feel confident enough to come to one. He didn't want to spoil his experience by being on guard all night. Taking another sip, he tried to eavesdrop on Danny's conversation with Paige. From what he could make out, she was asking if he wanted to sell a balloon and Danny was saying she could have it in exchange for a dance. The banter seemed lively and reminded him of his own with Nerissa. He wondered whether she would turn up. Reaching into his pocket, he took out his phone to text her when he saw she had already sent him a message.

Woooo Mr popular yh???

Smiling, he texted back.

Wat U tlkn'bout?

I heard u got VIP??

Who told you that?

That's CLASSIFIED!!!

Ur so dumb!!! Nothing's classified 2 me I got full clearance!

Whatever Mr Goldwrist, just know my spies are watching you!!!

Is it?? I think U need some new spies.

They might be feedin u da wrong information LOL

Really? So U don't have a Gold wristband on no?

Nerissa texted a picture of Sideeq entering in the party. She circled the gold VIP band on his wrist.

LMAO!!!! That's my watch...

Watch yeah?!!!

Nerissa sent a video. This time it was recorded footage from her Snapchat. Her friend had posted a Snap showing one of Ashani's entourage putting the band on Kyle and Sideeq's wrist with caption, *'Wheel up!! Wheel up!! KJ Wheeler.. just land'*. Laughing,

Sideeq almost spat his drink out as Nerissa's next text came through.

Err hello 999... Yh I need the
fire brigade, my friends pants
are on fire!

PMSL !!!

That joke is so dead!

So is ur Spy career LMAO
☺☺☺

Whatever!!! Wat time U
landin?

I'm not...

Y? ☹

I heard Gobbler is going. Not
up for no drama

Hmmm...

So what u sayin... I can't get a
one dance?

Nope!

So its like dat?

Wateva.... Plenty girls at party
4U 2, dance with.

True! I shud go find a wifey.

Really!!! Lemme see U find a
wifey. Bare Sketz & Hoes in
there

Meoooooowwww! Put ur
claws away girl. U2 sensitive

LOL whateva... call me when
U get in U fool xxx

Cool... I'll have to duck the
new wifey 1st looool

KMT USD! Carry on... don't
4get my spies are watchin U

Bun ur spies!!!

Smiling, Sideeq slipped his phone back into his pocket. Sipping the rest of his drink, he leaned up against the wall taking in the vibe when Kyle shouted over the music,

"Oh, so you finally come off your phone, yeah? I thought you was gonna be on that all night."

"Not even." Sideeq grinned.

He could feel Kyle's eyes on him, but he just bopped his head to the beat. He could always tell when Kyle had something more to say, but he wasn't in the mood to be lectured tonight. He was feeling good and was ready to party. After a moment Kyle asked, "Yo you wanna roll to the bar?"

"Yeah," Sideeq said, knocking back the last of his drink. "Come we go."

CHAPTER 4.2

By midnight, Mya and Ashani's party was jam-packed to capacity with sweat dripping off the celling. As people wandered to the front door looking for fresh air, Twitches warned them, "If you want air, go to back garden. It's a one in, one out policy. If you go out this way there's no guarantee you're coming back in."

Those who took heed found their way back inside, and those who didn't found themselves at the back of the queue or on their way home.

Around quarter past, Sharkey took to the decks and called Kyle to the mic. Grabbing the microphone, Kyle seized his moment. Knowing whatever he spat was likely to go viral, he blessed the mic with a series of shout-outs, and an introduction to set the vibe.

"Yes, yes, yes, people, you dun know who it is, KJ Wheeler in the house, all day every day, yeh!!"

There was a chorus of 'brap-brap' and two finger gun salutes as Kyle introduced himself.

"Before we get this bumbaclart party started, I wanna big up my birthday queens Mya and Ashani, for throwing this bash. You dun know, you bring the fire each and every time! Secret Shoobs,

2AM girls, you're big, big, BIG! Make someone say something!"

As Kyle toasted the mic, there was a wild cheer for Mya and Ashani and Sharkey scratched the record back and forth, hyping the crowd.

"Yeah! I wanna give a big shout to my real Gs in the house, you dun know who you are I don't need to mention no names. Nuff Love to my Ugly Dog Crew, man like Deafeye1, Dutty Dan the Dog whisper and load up the bank, Swank, we dere, we dere. WE DERE!!! And lastly but not leas', I wanna big up my don, my partner in crime, da Prince of Reload, da original bad boy Sharkey G. Yo what you saying, fam?

"I'm here, family, I'm ready," Sharkey replied. "You ready?"

"Definitely, my G. RUN DA RIDDIMMMMMMMM!!!!"

He dropped the beat on the first track, and without warning Kyle unleashed a barrage of bars. It was like a blaze of lyrical fire, and the crowd erupted in a frenzy of excitement. Roaring into the mic Kyle chanted his catch phrase, "Who wants a wheel up!!" and the crowd howled back, "WHO!! WHO!!"

Going back to back, the duo tore up their set. Anybody listening would have thought they were playing on the main stage at Wireless or another festival. Throwing down a cocktail of beats and bars, Kyle and Sharkey created the same intensity as their radio session and the crowd lapped up Kyle's infectious flow, calling for wheel up after wheel up. By the time Sharkey dropped Kyle's new track, the crowd were in a rapture of delight.

Watching from his corner, Sideeq smiled proudly as people jumped about, getting hype. Not only did it felt surreal for him to witness Kyle manifesting his dream, but he knew every time he heard Kyle shout out UDC, he knew his best friend was lining up their next move. Looking over the mass of dancing heads, Sideeq met eyes with Kyle, who while still rhyming gave him a wink and salute. He didn't notice Gobbler making his way through the crowd.

Neither did Danny, who had managed to make an impression on Paige. With two left feet, he did his best to hold her waist and bubble behind her. However, from the way Paige moved her hips and dropped down low when she was ready, it was obvious she had spent plenty of time dancing alongside her black friends. Every so often she teased Danny with a little twerk or bum flick in the middle of a skank, just to remind him it was a privilege to be grinding up on her. Drawing on a half smoked spliff, Danny put an arm across Paige's chest and whispered in her ear "Oi, you're effin' bangin', you know that, innit? You know that."

Feeling confident, he slipped the spliff into Paige's hand. As she went to take a drag on the zoot, he pecked her neck and wrapped his hand round her waist, thinking *go on son, that's the way, we're well in there*, when he heard, "Rahhh! Wha gwan Bieber? Is that you yeah?"

Instantly Danny froze and let go of Paige. Stepping back, he looked up to see Gobbler standing in front of him with a massive grin on his face. He recognised the smile from their last encounter and knew the bully was going to start some trouble.

"Watch my man, scrubsing it down," Gobbler said, turning to Hassan and Squingy, who followed behind him. All three laughed, mocking Danny. From the look on Danny's face, any onlookers could see there was no love lost between them.

"Yes, Bieber, what, you not gonna introduce me to your ting, nah?" Gobbler said, referring to Paige. Rubbing his hands together, he licked his lips, eyeing her with a lingering glare. His deviant grin made Paige uncomfortable and she looked towards Danny, whose whole demeanour had changed. Gone was the happy go lucky cheeky chap. Now he had a weary look, and his eyes shifted nervously between the three boys. It was clear he didn't know what to do, but his hatred for Gobbler made him find his mouth.

"Nah, I don't think so," Danny replied foolishly. He no longer feared provoking Gobbler. It wasn't as though they could kill his dog again.

"Say that again?"

"I said don't think I'm gonna do that." Danny spoke a little louder to be heard over the music.

"OK," Gobbler smiled, amused. He seemed to know exactly what was going to happen. It probably wasn't the first time someone he had robbed tried to find their voice on their next encounter. It was a formality Gobbler obviously in enjoyed. Sniggering, he played along. "No worries, say no more." Gobbler tapped Danny in his chest with his gloved hand. "I'mma give you that one, because I like you. But hear what I'm saying…" He tried to put his arm around Danny's shoulder. "I'm hearing you're the guy with the balloons. So what you saying about hooking me up? Or do we need to have a different conversation?"

"Yeah, yeah, sure, no problem," Danny said, wriggling out from underneath Gobbler's arm. "I'd love to mate, but I'm all out of canisters. Maybe next time, yeah?"

Maybe it was the drink, or maybe it was because he just didn't care any more, but Danny gave Gobbler a cheeky wink and patted him on the shoulder. It was his way of politely telling the bully to jog on.

Seeming tickled by Danny's bravado, Gobbler looked back at his two cronies. Squingy shook his head, and Hassan shrugged at Gobbler as if to say he thought Danny would have known better.

"Fine, have it your way, Bieber," Gobbler said, grabbing Danny's sweater. "Don't say I dint give you a chance."

Gobbler thrust Danny up against the wall with one hand, as those nearby by jostled to get out of the way. He was about snatch at Danny's man-bag when a huge arm came crashing down on his forearm.

The blow was powerful. Strong enough to break Gobbler's hold, and before he knew what was going on, another hand push him back. Gobbler tripped over his feet, stumbling back into Squingy and Hassan. The shove took him by surprise, and he was clearly shocked to see Siddeq step in front of him. Sideeq looked like a man mountain towering over Gobbler, and his athletic frame matched Gobbler's own muscular physique.

"Yo, what the hell you doing, blud?" Gobbler roared. "Are you friggin' crazy? Don't you ever put your hands on ME! I'll put you in an early grave!"

As Gobbler stood up straight, Hassan and Squingy jumped into action, barking like his two guards. "What fam! What! What!"

The music stopped and the crowd backed up, clearing some

space. Sideeq stood defiantly in front of Gobbler, with Danny sheepishly behind him.

"What d'you mean, what?" Sideeq eyed Hassan, who was pretending like he was going to pull something from his waist. "What you gonna do?"

"Oi don't run up your mouth ahk, coz you' already got drama," Hassan warned. "Gobz this is the same breh that was at the bus stop the other day."

Gobbler's eyes lit up as he registered who Sideeq was. "Ahh, Cyclops! You know you eff'd up now brudda? Y'know you're gonna catch a beating for talking to my ting? I was waiting for your little tangle eye."

"Your mum's got a tangle eye."

The crowd looked shocked at Sideeq's response, and some of the Gobbler's fellow Grove man and rival hoodlums looked on with interest.

Seeing Sideeq in the thick of the fray, Kyle dropped the mic and rushed into the crowd. Sharkey followed him, while one of the other DJs grabbed the mic and called for security. Kyle tried to push his way through, but Gobbler had already squared up to Sideeq.

"Oi blud, do you want me to knock you out or something?" Gobbler stepped forward, poking his first two fingers in near Sideeq's face. "Do you?"

"Do you what you're gonna do," Sideeq said. His face was like stone and showed no fear.

"What! Rudeboy, I'll take you outside and poke out your other eye."

There were a few sniggers from the crowd, and when Sieeq didn't reply Gobbler thought he had him on the back foot. Confident he stepped forward and tried grab Sideeq by the collar. "What! Come outside."

It was a mistake. He stepped into Sideeq's blind zone. Sensing danger, Sideeq flew into action. He slapped Gobbler's hand off him and hit him with a right hook. The punch caught Gobbler off guard and he staggered forward, trying to throw two blows of his own. They were limp. Sideeq side-stepped the first one and weaved away from the second, rolling his shoulder and ducking down. Flustered, Gobbler managed to grab hold of Sid, pulling his hood over his face. Gobbler was ready to unleash a combination of flurries, but it was too late. Sideeq had planted his foot and came up from underneath Gobbler with a huge uppercut. With all the force in his legs, he channelled his arm upwards. Following through, his fist rocked Gobbler's head back as it connected with his jaw. There was a symphony of *oohs* as Gobbler's eyes rolled back in his head and he went crashing to the floor.

His lifeless body hit the floor with a thud, causing the room to reverberate in a sonic boom of cackles as Sideeq knocked him out cold. The crowd went wild as he stood over Gobbler like Ali did Sonny Liston.

*

Adrenaline pumping, Sideeq looked down on the bully, who lay with his mouth open and one leg twisted underneath the other. He was willing Gobbler to get up so he could hit him again, not grasping the fact that troublemaker was finished. A multitude of feelings coursed through his veins, and in that instant the hood had found a new champion. He glared at Hassan and Squingy, who in their shock didn't know what to do. They left Gobbler on his back as the ghetto paparazzi swarmed both victor and defeated with their camera phones.

By now Sharkey and Kyle stood in front of Sideeq, who was being pulled to safety by Danny and Swank as a few more of the other road-men who were loosely affiliated to Gobbler started to step forward. Calmly, Sideeq fixed his jumper as Squingy spat a hundred and one death threats at him.

"Oi you're dead, fam. You know you're dead, right? You and your one eye. You're a dead man walking. You're not gonna see next week. You're over."

"Shut up and pick your bredrin up," Sharkey barked. "No one ain't touching him."

"Is that how you're moving yeah, Sharkz?" Hassan said, trying to wake Gobbler up.

"Blatant!" Sharkey said, proclaiming his allegiance. "That's my bredrin, and that's my bredrin," he said pointing at both Danny and Sideeq.

"Anyone who's got a problem with dem, gonna have a problem with me."

Sharkey's words boomed around the room and he looked at certain players, knowing his word was certified. There weren't many people who would go up against Sharkey, not on Gobbler's behalf.

Twitches and Benga finally arrived with Mya and Ashani.

Assessing the situation, Twitches looked at Hassan struggling with Gobbler in his semi-conscious state. Snatching a bottle of water from Ashani, he ordered Hassan to splash the drink in Gobbler's face. Dashed with water, Gobbler came around and asked, "Where am I?"

There were muffled laughs as he was hoisted to his feet and Twitches ordered Hassan and Squingy to carry their friend out.

As the music resumed, Kyle turned to his friend and asked, "Bruv what happened? Are you alright?"

CHAPTER 4.3

After the fight, Sideeq was too agitated to stay at the party. His night had been ruined and he sought the sanctuary of home. A part of him wanted to stay, but knew he would be on edge for the rest of the night. The idea of Gobbler returning didn't frighten him, but it wasn't something he need entertain. Sharkey agreed and offered to drive him home, but Sideeq insisted that they all stayed at the party.

"Stay here for what?" Kyle quizzed. He had no intentions of leaving Sideeq's side. "If you're not staying, I'm not staying."

"K, you don't need to do that. I'd rather you man just go back inside and jam."

"Nah man, that's long." Kyle refused to listen. "I'm coming with you. Wherever you go, I go," he said, pacing up and down. "Wherever you go, I go. That's the way it goes. We come together, we leave together."

To anyone who was watching the interaction it almost looked as though Kyle was giving Sideeq a good dressing down, and Sideeq noticed a few girls trying to eavesdrop. Sighing, he covered his mouth with both hands in a prayer-like manner and dropped his head.

"K, swear down bro, I don't need no more fuss tonight. I beg you don't embarrass me. I just wanna go home."

Before Kyle could say anything more, Sharkey put his hand on his shoulder and said, "Yo Wheelz, real talk bro, you need hear what family is saying and respect that."

Ten minutes later, the whole Ugly Dog Crew followed Sideeq outside and put him safely in an Uber. "Bell me tomorrow," Kyle said, making a phone sign with his hand. Nodding his head, Sideeq gave his signature smile, small and bashful.

There was a fretful look in his eye that troubled Kyle, and the two peered at each other. As the car pulled off, Kyle watched the white Toyota Prius till it disappeared round the corner. Something grave told he him he should be in that car. It was pain. A past pain that said he wasn't supposed to leave Sideeq.

Sitting in the back of the Uber, Sideeq looked at his phone. He had six missed calls from Nerissa and four text messages.

OMG Sid where RU????

Sid call me if U can speak..

SID PLZ CALL ME I'M WORRIED ABOUT U

Sid please call me. I need U to call me xxx

DD ARMSTRONG

Sideeq glared at the screen. He figured somehow Nerissa must have heard about the fight and was checking to see if he was OK. He knew he should call her back, but he couldn't. His mind was all over the place. He needed some time to think. To really digest what had happened.

Sideeq had never punched anyone in the face before. He'd never needed to. The majority of his fighting experience consisted of playground scraps. There was a big difference between putting someone in a headlock and rolling around on the floor to smashing your fist in someone's face.

Closing his eyes, he thought, *'What the hell did I do?'* And another voice inside him said, *'You did what needed to be done. Something you should have done a long time ago.'* The latter statement resonated with Sideeq. His mind roared with liberation. He told himself one eye or no eye, two ears or no ears, he was never going to be anyone's victim again.

Feeling hot, he cracked the window for some fresh air. The cool breeze gushed against his skin and he welcomed its chill. Trying to relax, he took a deep breath and listened to the Bhangra music playing lightly on the car radio. He didn't understand the singer's Punjabi lyrics, but found her delicate harmonies soothing. Her exotic tones were accompanied by a sarangi, and her extended words conjured images of an Indian summer. Letting his thoughts wander, Sideeq slowly started to relax. He would be home soon.

The journey didn't take too long, and Sideeq sat up as the cab entered into the estate. He directed the driver through the dark maze towards his block. As they approached, he noticed someone

241

in the distance sitting on the wall outside the intercom. At first he thought nothing of it. He assumed it was probably some crazy crackhead looking for somewhere to smoke. Then as they got closer, he recognized the figure shivering in the cold.

The car came to a halt and she stood up wearing a long dark green parka jacket. She squinted her eyes, trying to look beyond the headlights then, making out his frame, she shrilled out Sideeq's name and ran towards him. He was barely out the car when Nerissa threw her arms around him, squeezing tight. She crushed her body against his and he could feel that she was shaking. He returned the embrace.

"What you doing?" He pulled back to look her in the face.

"I'm sorry, don't be angry with me," Nerissa said. Tears began streaming down her face and she began blabbering at a hundred words a minute.

"I saw the fight. My friend posted it on Insta. I saw it, and I tried to call you, but you didn't answer, so I texted you and you still didn't answer. Then I got scared. I got scared and I didn't know what else to do. So I called my friend and she said she saw you going outside with Sharkey, but you didn't come back; and then she said that people were saying Hassan said he's going to get his gun, and when Gobbler wakes up they're coming back for you. And I wanted to warn you and make sure you were safe, but you wouldn't answer. So I, I, ordered an Uber and the man came and he, he, dropped me here and, and..." Nerissa became too flustered to speak, and Sideeq interjected.

"OK, OK, take your time. Take your time. Slow down. Breathe," he said, hugging her. He began stroking her hair trying to calm her down. Leaning in, he kissed her on the head. "It's fine, I'm here now. I'm here."

Angry, Nerissa pulled away. "No, it's not." She thumped him in the chest. "I was worried about you! I tried to call you! Why didn't call me back?"

Sideeq paused. He thought about lying, but said, "I don't know," shrugging his huge shoulders. He didn't know where to put his eyes and bowed his head, kicking at the floor. "I got a bit scared. I didn't feel safe at the party and needed to come home. I couldn't think about anything till I got here. I'm sorry."

Sideeq was embarrassed and couldn't meet Nerissa's eye. Instead he peered up at the balconies above. Wiping the tears from her face, Nerissa eventually smiled. Stepping forward, she reached out for his big hand. Taking it, she pulled him close and reared up on her tip-toes to kiss him. Pressing her lips against his, she leaned forward and slipped her tongue into his mouth. Sideeq cupped her face with hands and they began to kiss. After a moment, he moved his right hand down her neck and around her waist. Sideeq was about to start to caressing her when a gust of wind blew. Nerissa juddered, breaking their embrace, and they both laughed. Sideeq moved one of Nerissa curls out of her face and then ran his thumb over her moist lip.

"So what now? You coming upstairs or going back home?"

Apparently trying not to show how smitten she was with him Nerissa replied, "Do you want me too?" To which Sideeq just continued to smile.

Upstairs, Sideeq snuck Nerissa past his mum, who had fallen

asleep in front of the television. Creeping up the stairs, he never realised how creaky they actually were. Each one seemed to squeak or croak in its own special note, and the slower he went the louder they were. He cringed with every step. Laughing, Nerissa slapped him on the back and whispered, "Move. Your foot's too heavy." Pushing past him, she sprinted up the steps barely making a sound. Sideeq followed. He pointed to his room, whispering, "Go inside and chill. I'm just gonna get a blanket for my mum. You want anything from the kitchen?"

"No," Nerissa shook her head. "Just go and sort your mum out and come back fast."

She pulled Sideeq close and gave him a kiss.

Giving her a goofy grin, Sideeq snuck into his mum's room. He grabbed the duvet and a pillow and went back downstairs. Lifting gently, he slipped the pillow under his mum's head and threw the cover over her. She stirred slightly, changing positions and snuggling under the duvet. Picking up the remote, Sideeq switched off the television and went back upstairs.

When Sideeq returned to his room, he found Nerissa's in the bed. He looked at the small pile of clothes she had left on the floor. Biting her bottom lip she smiled at him seductively and said, "Take your clothes off."

Pulling the curtains, Sideeq stripped down to his boxer shorts. Feeling nervous, he got in the bed and slid beside her. Giggling, Nerissa tugged at his boxer shorts and asked, "Are you shy? Take these off, too."

Sideeq did as he was told. Stroking his ankle with her foot, Nerissa slipped her legs in between his moving closer. He knew she could feel he was aroused. She whispered, "Kiss me." Again Sideeq did as he was told, and the lovers kissed and caressed. Nerissa pulled him on top of her. His first time...

They enjoyed one other into the early morn. At one point Nerissa began to cry, and Sideeq stopped to ask, "What's wrong?"

"Nothing," Nerissa replied, but Sideeq insisted she told him. "Sid, promise you won't laugh."

"I promise," he whispered, softly holding her hand.

Nerissa sighed, laying her head on his chest, listening to his heartbeat.

"Sid, you're really special. No one has ever treated me like you have." Nerissa lifted up her head to look at him. "Sid, I think I love you. You don't have to say it back, but I think you're the one."

Nerissa laid her head back on his chest. She smiled in the dark as he replied, "I think I love you too."

For a moment the two fell silent, happy to be in each other's arms. Holding Sideeq tight, Nerissa kissed his chest. Taking his hand, she laced her fingers with his. "Sid, what d'you think your friends will say?"

"Nothing," Sideeq replied. "It might surprise them at first, but they'll be cool. They'll have to be."

Sitting up, Nerissa giggled. She climbed on top of Sideeq and kissed him slowly before trying to bite his lip. When he pulled away she laughed and whispered, "I think you're going to be the one to break my curse."

Part V

Trust, Love & Loyalty

CHAPTER 5.1

For every generation there is a classic fight between two warriors—a legendary clash between gladiators that the world will never forget. Bouts where heroes like David meet villains like Goliath, and demi-gods like Achilles face mortal generals like Hector. Whatever the stakes—power, revenge, love or state—these spectaculars are recorded in the fabric of religion, history, folklore and myth, weaving their place in life and art. A place, in modern times, where sportsmen become icons and everybody wants to be a part of the legend or have the chance to say 'I was there'.

And so with every generation there is an appetite to retell the tale—and never more so than in the age of social media. An age where memes, hashtags, retweets and reposts are the choice of the millennium bard and digital griot. An age, where influencers, followers and likes create the power to crown a champion or crucify a soul. In this realm where mob-fingers rule, a spontaneous moment of riding your bike into somebody working on their car, or getting caught in a compromising position with your co-worker on the steps outside the New Year's Eve party, can be turned into binary code and go viral. In a flash, your life can be trending and belong to anyone with an account.

The next morning, the fight between Sideeq and Gobbler seemed to be on half of West London's timeline and popping up in every group chat. By Sunday afternoon the fight had gone viral, and by the evening somebody had edited the different angles of footage into a highlight reel. The reel was scored with the *Rocky* theme music and a caption that read: *Wasteman gets KO'd by One Eyed Apollo*.

A petrol bomb of fuel was added to the fire when an image of Hassan holding a slumped Gobbler in his arms with his mouth open was turned into a meme. This time somebody had collated the picture of the two boys and it placed in juxtaposition to a picture of Forrest Gump holding his dying friend Bubba. The protruding jaws of both Gobbler and Bubba made the meme hilarious, and the lost looks on both Hassan and Forrest Gump's faces didn't make it any better. While the pair were totally ridiculed, Sideeq had become an overnight hood celebrity.

When everyone returned to college on Monday, there was a hum of excitement. The gossip mill was in full flow and those who were at the party eagerly told their account of the events. The courtyard was packed as everyone waited for Sideeq to arrive. There were those who speculated that he wouldn't turn up for fear of reprisal and those who even went as far as to say his time at Cardinal Manning was up; only a fool would come back to the college with Gobbler after them. Meanwhile on the other side, there were those who believed Sharkey's protection was enough and Gobbler would be more the fool to go against him. When Sideeq entered, the latter group smiled and welcomed him with a nod of respect or a random extended fist to bump. Even some of the girls greeted him with a casual, "Hi," or a smile. In the corridor, one slim, brown-skinned girl with long black hair pulled into a ponytail even approached him and said, "Hi, you're Sideeq, innit? Yeah you are. I'm Shereen." She spoke in a fast manner. "I saw your little video last night. Well done, babe, I'm so glad someone stood up to that bully. Good for you. We need more black boys like you that ain't afraid of all these little ediots and wannabe-roadmen. And you know what I like about you? You just keep yourself humble. Gwan wid your bad self, babe. Walk safe, yeah."

Before Sideeq could even reply, she leaned in and gave him a hug—then as quick as she appeared, she was gone. Oblivious to any threat, Sideeq found the attention humorous.

Kyle apparently did not share the same sentiment. At lunch time, he remained on guard and suggested they all stayed within the college to eat. Sharkey agreed, but outside, the atmosphere seemed light. In the absence of Gobbler, people went about their business free from being robbed or harassed. After college it was the same thing, and it wasn't until Tuesday lunch that a subdued Hassan showed his face. Humbled, he did his best to go under the radar, and Sharkey had to seek him out to have words. He warned Hassan, "You man need to take the L and call it dun, otherwise you're the first man I'm coming for."

Without Gobbler behind him, Hassan lacked any threat and his status was quickly diminished. By the time Thursday came around, no one had seen or heard anything from Gobbler and the hype surrounding the fight seemed short lived.

*

However, not even the recording session Kyle had booked could ease his concern. Standing in the sponge-padded booth with a pair of headphones on, Kyle blitzed the microphone with a flurry of lyrics. Through the glass, he could see Sharkey on the mixing desk twiddling away with the knobs. He tweaked the levels, giving Kyle a hand signal to keep going. Swank stood behind him, rocking her head to the beat. Screwing up her face, she gave a two-fingered gun salute every time he dropped a punchline, while Danny, who was supposed to be helping Sharkey engineer, sat with his head buried in his phone, smiling. Kyle saw Danny laugh out loud and pass his phone to Swank to see. When Swank started to laugh in hysterics, too, Kyle botched his lines.

"Yo! What's wrong with you lot?" Kyle shouted through the microphone. "I'm tryna lay my verse and you're jumping around putting me off."

"Sorry, mate." Danny hit the coms button. "Sorry, it's my fault, but you gotta come out and see this."

"Eff that man. Man ain't getting this studio time for free. You lot are playing. Man needs to record this ting and be out."

"You're right, but you might as well take a break," Sharkey said, stopping the music. "We can't finish the track until Sideeq comes with the vocalist for the hook, so you might as well chill."

"Nah, man, I wanna double up on my second verse again."

"Wheeler, your second verse is fine, don't overdo it. Come out and hear the track."

Sulking, Kyle exited the booth as Sharkey prepared to reload the track.

"Lemme see what you lot are laughing at."

Danny handed Kyle the phone. Someone had posted a Street Fighter II rendition of the fight on their Instagram account and it was getting a lot of traffic. The video showed a clip of Sideeq's head superimposed on Ryu's body, while Gobbler's head was fixed on the beast Blanka. In the sequence, Sideeq was seen destroying Gobbler with a fierce combo of blows before finishing him with a Dragon punch and achieving a perfect result.

Peeved Kyle handed back the phone. "Bruv, do think that's funny?"

"Yes," Danny replied. He had no intention of hiding the glee on his face. "That's why I'm reposting it right now."

"Bruv, that ain't even funny," Kyle snapped.

"Maybe not to you, but it's flipping hilarious to me."

"Hey K. C'mon, fam, you gotta admit it is bare jokes," Swank agreed. "Look how many likes it's got."

"That's what I'm saying." Danny continued to laugh. "But I'll tell you what the real jokes is—Sid killed all the big myth about Gobbler's little gunman glove."

"Rah, for real," Swank said. "I dint even think about that fam. That's nuts."

"Innit. I'm putting that in my caption right now." Danny started typing on his phone. *"What happened to Gobbler's other glove? Obviously not no gunman #MrOneGloveChickenChoker-chicken."*

"Bruv, are you taking this serious? You do know that when

you and everybody's finished bussin joke online, this breh is coming to try and clap back."

"Yeah, and he can get punch in the mouth again."

"By who? You? You couldn't punch your way out a wet paper bag."

"Yeah, and what?" Danny sat up in his chair. "At least I ain't walking around fretting about Gobbler. After what he did to Rizla, do you think I give two shits about what he tries to do? I don't. He's a nobody he can't rot in hell for all I care."

"Good, I'm glad you don't care. But *I* care. I care about my best friend who stepped up to back you. When the time comes, are you gonna do the same for him? Coz right about now you're just fuelling the fire."

The room felt silent as they all absorbed Kyle's words. They all understood why Danny relished Gobbler's demise, but there was a serious need to consider the roles they were playing in any repercussions.

Then before the argument could escalate any further, the studio buzzer went. Swank, who was closest to the intercom answered it. "Yo, who is it?"

"It's me." Sideeq's voice came through the speaker. "Buzz me up."

Swank buzzed him in.

A moment later, to everybody's surprise, he strolled in holding Nerissa's hand, apologising for his timekeeping.

"Yo, sorry I'm late, I had to go get Nerissa." He turned to Nerissa, who stood warily behind him. Looking around the room, she waved a shy hand at them and said, "Hi."

It was awkward. Everyone murmured a subdued hello except Kyle, who stood eyeing the couple in disbelief. His mind couldn't compute what he was seeing, and his eyes travelled from Sideeq's doting smile to Nerissa's nervy expression. If looks could kill, Kyle would have blown off her head. She stepped closer to Sideeq, apparently seeking refuge from Kyle's stare. She squeezed his hand. Sideeq smiled and proudly said, "Bro, I know what you're thinking, but before you say anything, just wait till to you hear her sing. I guarantee you, she'll murder the track."

"Really?" Kyle scoffed. "You know what I'm thinking?"

"Yeah, I do," Sideeq said confidently. "But when you hear her sing, you'll change your mind."

"Oh I will, will I?"

"Yeah."

"And you can guarantee that?"

"A hundred per cent."

"OK." Kyle nodded. Disgusted, he looked around the room to see if anyone else was thinking the same as him, and from the grimaces it was obvious they were. Swank took a seat, shaking her head, while Danny raised a dubious eyebrow. Sharkey, who remained indifferent, met Kyle's gaze and shrugged with an expression that said, 'It's your move, bro.'

Rubbing his chin, Kyle took a deep breath, thinking carefully about what he was going to say next.

"OK, well I'll tell you the truth. The only thing I got to say is I'm shocked. I really am," he said in a calm voice. It was clear he was building up to something.

"I'm so shocked I ain't even gonna beat about the bush. Coz I don't know what kinda ting you lot been smoking…" He waved his finger between Sideeq and Nerissa until it fell on just her. "Or what type of *juju* you try put on my bredrin, but he's got no business bringing you here. So I'mma tell you on da real, you gotta go. You gotta go now."

His words were sharp. Filled with disdain, they cut any niceties and it was clear that Kyle had no qualms in showing his dislike.

Looking at the others sniggering, the only reply Nerrissa seemed able to muster was, "Excuse me?"

"No, don't excuse yourself. Just leave," Kyle hissed like a viper. "Bounce. Find the front door, my G."

"Pardon?" Nerissa blushed. Had she been white, her cheeks would have been a rosy red.

"Are you deaf?" Kyle continued to sneer. "I ain't gonna tell you again, come out."

"Sid, are you just gonna let him speak to me like that?" Nerissa turned to Sideeq for support. Caught between the two, Sideeq looked bewildered. He began to stutter, but Kyle cut him off.

"Don't try and play us off against each other. This is my session, I decided who stays and who goes."

"No!" Nerissa shot back. "Why should I? I haven't done anything to you. What's your problem?"

"You're my problem."

"I'm your problem?" Nerissa mocked. "How? You've only spoken to me once in your whole life. How can I be your problem? You don't even know me."

"Rudegirl, I don't want to know you. I've heard enough about you to know. I don't want you in my session or around my brother."

"You what?" Nerissa's face twisted with scorn. Something triggered inside her and she stepped around Sideeq, taking the offence. "You think you know me because you've heard one or two stories about me? And you think that gives you any license to run up your mouth like any Miss Chatty Patty. That's a joke ting, because I'm sorry to tell you, you don't know shit about me."

"I know about you."

"Oh, you do, do you? Well c'mon then, tell me what you know. Tell me and I'll leave. Then you won't have no problem with me."

Fuming, Kyle twisted his mouth and fell silent. Nerissa had him on the spot and in his place as everyone waited for him to speak. He looked towards Swank, who had been silent all along. She had a wary look on her face. He wanted to divulge what she had told him, but knew he couldn't betray her trust. She had confided in him, and he wasn't going to put her business out there. He kissed his teeth.

"Don't worry what I know. I know enough to know you're full of drama and can't be trusted."

Subconsciously, Kyle looked towards Swank again to confirm his loyalty—only Nerissa followed his gaze. She turned, looking at Swank, and the penny dropped.

"This is you, innit?" she said with a scornful look.

"What you talking about, fam?" Swank frowned. "This ain't got nothing to do with me."

"Don't play dumb! This is you. I know it is." Nerissa pointed her finger. "I'm sick and tired of you putting your mouth on me, you lesbian. Everywhere I go you're always tryna cause some mix up, mix up and throw shade on my name. What's wrong with you?"

Swank shook her head in disbelief. "Me? How you gonna try put this on me?"

"It's true," Danny snarled at Nerissa. "The only one who looks like they're throwing shade is you."

"Please." Nerissa cut her eye. "Sid, this girl has got motive."

Sideeq turned to look at Swank, who continued to shake her head.

"You keep shaking your head, yeah, but why don't you tell them how you tried to move to me and I told you I don't eat crotches. Coz that's the real reason you're out here chatting my name."

Nerissa turned to Kyle. "I bet she didn't tell you that though, did she? Coz I guarantee she's the reason why you think you know me so well. Isn't it? It's her!"

"No," Kyle said unconvincingly. It was clear to see he was lying, and Nerissa began commanding the stage.

"Yes she did. Don't lie. Did she tell you that Gobbler was going to smash her face in and it was me that stopped him? No, I bet she didn't tell you that! Or that he tried to beat you up because of her? No! But I'm the bad person. Go on, Sabrina, tell them. Why don't you tell them everything, if you're gonna talk, talk. Coz you're a liar!"

"Fam, I not listening to this bull." Swank picked up her

jacket. "I'm outta here."

"Hold up, Swank don't go nowhere." Sharkey stopped her. "You're good here, sit down."

"Real talk," Kyle chimed back in. "It's my girl that's gotta to leave."

Nerissa glared at all of them with contempt. There was a wily fire in her eye. She seemed to revel in the bickering.

"Like I said," she closed in on Kyle, taunting him with a defiant grin. She knew he had been silenced and it was too late for him to stop her from having the last say. "I'm happy to go now, but please—" She stressed the word, cutting her eye at Swank— "I beg, let's not pretend the only reason isn't becoz you and this little lesbian haven't been sitting around chatting my name like two little schools girls. You're pathetic. Talking 'bout you know me. Who are you? You're nobody, just some dusty MC, and a dyke."

"Who you calling dusty, you jez?"

"You!" Nerissa roared in Kyle face. "Do think I'm scared of you, you tramp? You're nothing to me. None of you are." She addressed the whole room. "As far as I'm concerned you can all go to hell! Especially you." She pointed at Swank. "You better mind yourself, this ain't over." With that, she marched out of the studio.

Stunned at her outburst, everyone looked at each other, flabbergasted. Sideeq was about to follow her when Kyle grabbed his arm.

"Yo where you going?"

"Get off, me!" Sideeq snatched his arm away, furious. "Was

there any need for you to do all that?"

"All of what?" Kyle played dumb. "What I did I do?"

"You just tried to humiliate her."

"So?"

"So, what you trying to prove? That you know how to bad up girls? Oooh wow d'you feel like a big man now, yeah?"

"Ahh, c'mon, bruv." Kyle pulled a face in disgust. "Don't try an' switch dis on me. Don't even go there, bruv. Coz none this ain't about me, y'know. None of it."

"So who's it about?" Sideeq frowned. "Say something if you got something to say."

Kyle sniggered. He couldn't believe Sideeq was actually inviting him to speak his mind, but then again he couldn't actually believe Sid was so naïve as to be cavorting with Nerissa. Either way, he welcomed the forum.

"Bruvva, if I have to tell you then you really got your head in the clouds. Cah it come like you don't get it. You just had a fight with her man—"

"They're not together," Sideeq interjected.

"Fine, her ex then. Whatever you wan call him. But you just had beef with him. Fresh beef, y'know. And you lot think it's cool to just walk around together holding hands like its nothing. I mean like what kinda dippy ting is that?"

Kyle threw his hands in the air. Now the door was open, he couldn't help but rip into Sideeq, and stepped into his personal space.

"I mean, are you dumb?" he shouted in the taller boy's face. "Are you really that dumb or do I have point everything out to you?"

Taking advantage of Sideeq's blind spot, Kyle stepped to the side and poked his friend in the head. He darted in and out of Sideeq's striking range before he could react. Instinctively Sideeq pushed him, clenching his fist. He gritted his teeth, ready to throw a punch, but managed to physically restrain himself.

"Yo, Wheeler." Sharkey stepped in between them. "Ease that shit up, man. There's no need for none of that."

"Says who?" Kyle snapped.

"Says me," Sharkey warned. "Don't put your hand on the man and try disrespect him like that. Cah you wouldn't like if man did that to you."

"Fine!" Kyle roared. "Well why don't you speak up?" He pointed at Sharkey. "Or you, or you?" he bellowed at Swank and Danny.

By this point it was clear he was ready to argue with anyone, yelling at the top of his voice. "No! No one don't wanna say nothing, do they? But when something happens to him, it's me that's gotta go sit down with his mum. It's me that's gotta go sit up in the hospital. It's me that's gotta explain what happened. Me!" Kyle pounded on his chest. "Me, that's who! I don't want to be the one who has to do dat, because no one dint tell this idiot to stop messing around with dat girl. The girl is friggin' dangerous! Any fool can see she likes attention, and she don't care who she gets it from."

"Why don't you just sh-sh-shut up! SHUT UP!" Sideeq yelled at the top of his voice. "I- I-I'm sick and tired of you. You don't let anybody else breathe. Y-y-you just go on and on and on.

Y-y-you don't to stop talking. You just keep going, sucking all the life out the room. I-I-I can't breathe when you're around."

Furious, Sideeq rubbed the scar on the side of his face. He looked conflicted. Almost as though he didn't know whether to run through the door or carry on shouting. Chest heaving, he tried to compose himself and covered his face. He screamed into his huge hands, and the war cry shocked the room.

After a moment, Sideeq removed his hands, wiping his face. It was almost as though he had taken off a mask, and every muscle in his face become calm and controlled. Yet his stare spoke volumes. As he gazed down at his best friend with his weary dark brown eyes, his pupils become two pools of disappointment and Kyle was swimming in them.

"I'm tired of you," he said. "Tired of you always telling me what to do, or thinking we always gotta be joined at the hip. You treat me like I'm your flippin' sidekick, like you always know what's best for me, but you don't. I do! You're standing there talking about Nerissa craving attention, but from where I'm standing it comes like she's not only one."

"Me!" Kyle laughed. "Me?"

"Yeah, you," Sideeq replied accusingly. His face was alight with anger, and his fiery glare didn't move off Kyle. "Maybe that's the real reason you don't like Nerissa—coz you're frightened I won't have enough time to run behind you. C'mon, let's face it, what's the real reason we're friends? Because you need me to make you feel important."

"What?" Kyle laughed at the absurdity of Sideeq's accusation. "Bruv, do you know how dumb you sound right now?"

"No come on l-l-l-let's be real. S-s-s-peak the truth and shame the devil." Sideeq began to stammer. Kyle had pushed him to a tipping point and there were things he wanted to get off his chest. Slurring his words, he insisted on delving deeper.

"You need me s-s-so you can play Mr Big Man. Mr KJ Wheeler who's a-a-always looking out for his half blind and deaf bredrin. I know it and you know it. But if we get down to the hardcore truth, you need me s-s-so you can run away from guilt."

"Guilt?" Kyle stared at Sideeq. He knew where Sideeq was going, and was hurt that he would even take it there. "Bruv, what have I got to feel guilty about? All I've ever done is try look out for you."

"Look out for me?" Sideeq cackled in disbelief. "You're the same guy who ran off and left me to get stabbed in Bush market. Did you go to the hospital then? No! You left me there bleeding. Did you tell my mum that part? No! So don't talk about my mum now, and don't bother to stunt for these lot—" Sideeq pointed at the others "—about what you have to do for me. You don't have to do nothing for me. You don't have to look out for me; you don't have to feel guilty for me. In fact you don't even have to c-c-chat to me, coz me and you are dun."

Before Kyle could reply, Sideeq backed up and ran out of the door.

Dumbfounded, Kyle stood looking at the space Sideeq had just occupied. After a moment he turned to the others and asked, "Did you hear what he just said?"

From the expressions on their faces they did. But no one knew yet what to say.

CHAPTER 5.2

Sideeq's mind was racing as he burst out of the studio. The only thing he could think about was catching up with Nerissa. Running up the road he could feel the night air gushing against his face, but it did little to cool his temper. He was furious. No, he was *livid*, and there wasn't anything that was going to make him calm down. Not anything except her. He thought to himself, *Anyhow K, has ruined my chance with Nerissa I'm dun, dun, dun. That's it, our friendship over.*

As his legs pumped and arms swung in the air, Sideeq couldn't explain why he was so adamant. The more reasonable voice inside of him said, *Stop being, silly. How you gonna fall out with your best friend over gyal?*

But Sideeq didn't want to listen. It wasn't just over a girl to him, it was more than that. It was Kyle, his whole manner and attitude towards their entire friendship. It was one-sided, and that infuriated Sideeq.

All Kyle had to do was let Nerissa sing. That was all. Was that such a big thing? How many times had he done something he didn't want to do to appease Kyle? How many times? Countless. How else did he end up in the market that day? How else did he end up on the floor, blood pouring out the side of his face; deaf in one ear, blind in one eye? How? Because of Kyle. Because he followed and trusted him. Well, that was that, Sideeq figured. He wasn't doing neither anymore. If Kyle didn't want to accept Nerissa, they would have to go their own separate ways, because he wasn't prepared to lose her over Kyle.

As Sideeq ran to the top of the road, he wondered what the ramifications of that truly meant, and again a voice in his head said, *Are you crazy or are you dumb? You're being irrational.*

Sideeq didn't care. He was tired of being the only rational one in an irrational world. He had watched others do as they pleased while he lived his whole life inside in his head, over-thinking one precaution after another. It was his time now. And so like many young men, Sideeq began to chase what he thought was his future, without asking why he was running from his past.

When he reached the main road, he looked up and down the street, but Nerissa was nowhere in sight. Cursing, he took out his phone and called her number, but the automated response said her phone was switched off. Taking a second to think, Sideeq tried to figure out which way she might have gone. If Nerissa had turned off her phone, she obviously didn't want to speak. In that case he guessed she probably wouldn't go to the train station, knowing that would be the first place he would look to find her. That was, unless she managed to get a train straight away... Sideeq looked across the road, studying the red and blue London Underground motif. Its white lettering read 'Latimer Road'. Looking past it, he frowned at the stairs leading to the platform.

'No. Nerissa is a walker,' Sideeq told himself. 'If she was angry or upset, which she is, she's going to storm off somewhere rather than wait on the platform.'

Taking a gamble, he sprinted past a group of drinkers chatting outside the Station Bar and head towards the tall tower blocks of Edward Wood's estate. In the distance he could see the bus stop—and Nerissa's silhouette—ahead. He called out to her, but she ignored him. He called again, louder, until he was racing upon her.

"Nerissa, stop," he said, grabbing her shoulder, but she ripped it away.

"Why! What do you want?"

There was still venom in her voice, and Sideeq tried to work out whether the water in her eyes was from the cold air or crying. Panting, he stood blocking her way while trying to catch his breath. "Hold up, lemme talk to you for a minute."

"About what? I got nothing to say." Nerissa walked around him.

"Fine," Sideeq said, grabbing her arm. "But I got things to say too—"

"Don't touch me!" Nerissa snatched her arm away again. "Do I look like I care what you have to say? I said I don't want to talk to you. What part of that don't you get?"

"Nerissa, listen to me, I know you're angry, but hear me out—"

"No, Sideeq! No!" Nerissa cut him off. "You don't know the half of it."

She wiped the tears from her eyes. "Do know how hard it was for me to walk in there with you? Do you? I knew your friends wouldn't like me, I knew it, but I still went in there, trusting you. I trusted you and all you did was just stand there and let your friend cuss me out."

"I'm sorry, that weren't meant to happen. Everything happened so fast."

"But it happened, Sid, and you did nothing. Do you know how stupid I feel? How embarrassing that was for me? They were all laughing at me, Sideeq, and you just stood there. You didn't even say a word to defend me." Nerissa held up her forefinger symbolising the significance of her words. "Not one."

"I tried." Sideeq bowed his head in shame.

"When?"

"After you left."

"After! That's not good enough!" Nerissa yelled. "I don't want to be with someone who's gonna stand around and let his friends talk to me like that. I want to be with someone I know is gonna stick up for me and fight."

"I, I, I, did," Sideeq began to stutter. He was getting flustered and was rushing his words "I, I, I told Kyle that he was outta order and that me and him was dun."

"And what else?" Nerissa barked. She wanted to hear more. "What else?"

"What do you mean?" Sideeq replied with a lost expression.

It was the wrong answer. Nerissa gawked at him, waiting for an answer, but Sideeq fidegeted in front of her like a little boy not knowing what to say. Disappointed, Nerissa's eyes filled with water and she turned shaking her head. Sideeq stepped closer to comfort her, but Nerissa held up a hand.

"No, stay there," she said, trying to keep him at bay.

Freezing, Sideeq did as he was told. He stood dead in his spot like a Greek statue, thinking it was best to respect her wishes. But again, ironically, it was the wrong thing to do and irked Nerissa even more. Sideeq's silence clearly infuriated her, and she wanted to make him angry.

"This is a joke. I swear to God you going to make me have second thoughs about you. I thought you was a man," she said now. "But not even Gobbler would let his friends talk to me like that. Never."

The moment Nerissa said it, her face fell like she wished she could take it back. Sideeq's eyes flashed with hurt, then his gaze narrowed in disbelief. The scar on his face wrinkled with his frown. His mouth gaped open while his eyes searched hers. They sought the truth and relevance in what she said while still trying to deny the sentiment. His bottom lip quivered, looking for something to say.

"I'm sorry Sid, I didn't mean to say that."

"So why say it?" Sideeq retreated from her with his hand up for distance.

"I don't know, it just came out."

"Nothing just comes out of your mouth," Sideeq shot back.

"Well, I was angry."

"And you think I'm not?" Sideeq raged. "I just fell out with my best friend because of you. That's the reason why I'm here now and not back there. And the first thing you wanna tell me about is Gobbler?" he shouted at the top of his voice. "Gobbler?"

"Sid, don't shout at me."

"You just tried to compare me to Gobbler! Gobbler! And then tell me I'm not a man."

"OK, fine, but I didn't mean it. Can you just claim down and stop shouting?"

"No, I don't think you get it," Sideeq said, pacing up and down. He began clinching his fists, and pounded his right hand into his left until he let off a combination of body shots in air. He stopped sharply and spun to face Nerissa. He pointed his finger at her.

"Things come easy to people like you. People like you and Kyle, you can have or do anything you want."

"No, that's not true," Nerissa protested.

She watched as Sideeq marched three steps forward then four steps back, trying to compute everything.

"Yes it is. One day you love someone and the next day you've got second thoughts."

"Sid, that's not fair, I made a mistake…"

"Nothing's fair in my world!" Sideeq growled at her. "Nothing! Don't you get that?"

His tone startled her and Nerissa backed up. She took a seat by the bus stop.

Bubbling inside, Sideeq let aloud a roar of frustration. Fuelled with pure emotion, he was a ball of energy waiting to explode. Shaking his fists, he counted to ten and tried to simmer down. Taking a breath, he turned back to Nerissa with tension showing in his chiselled jaw.

"So am I the mistake?"

"Huh?" Nerissa responded. The question caught her off guard and she looked anywhere she could except at him. Waiting, Sideeq watched as she now nervously fidgeted. She looked up the road for any sign of her bus. He stepped in her way and said, "Answer me. I wanna know."

"No," Nerissa pushed him back "I don't want to. You're scaring me."

"Good." Sideeq punched the bus stop shelter above her head. "Because you been scaring me from the moment we met."

Nerissa flinched. For a moment she looked like she wasn't sure whether she should get up and run, but Sideeq was already backing away. He began to laugh to himself.

"Ahhh, you know what? Don't answer that question, I already know the answer. I don't even know why I've been out here playing like I didn't." He turned to face Nerissa. "Girls like you don't go for dudes like me, do they? No one does."

"Sid, don't say that," she said, becoming teary eyed.

"It's the truth, no one does. I've just been out here lying to myself. When you first started talking to me I thought, *wow, she amazing*, because you made me feel normal. I mean, s-s-so, so normal. Like you didn't even see my hearing aid or my scar. And I thought maybe this time, j-j-just maybe this time I could have something good. Like everyone else. But I can't, can I?"

Fighting back the tears, Nerissa looked at him, hesitating, then at last said, "I don't know."

Sideeq puffed up his cheeks and blew out the air. He tried to smile through the agony. Stepping forward, he held her hands,

"Talk to me. Don't you just want something good in your life?"

Nerissa seemed too frightened to answer. There was some truth in what Sideeq had said. "What if I can't have what I want?" Nerissa said. It was more a statement than a question. Looking up, she saw her bus approaching.

"Well, tell me what you want?"

"I can't, Sid. You won't understand."

"Then make me."

Nerissa began to cry again, watching the bus behind Sideeq draw ever nearer. Sideeq, who had his back to the road, was oblivious to its looming presence.

"Sid, stop. I don't want to come between you and your friends."

"Don't worry about them," Sideeq implored. "Just tell me what you want and I swear I'll do it. I'll do anything for you."

"I just want to be loved."

"OK, so let me love you."

Sideeq tried to kiss her, but Nerissa stopped him as the bus pulled up.

"Sid. I can't do this."

"Please, Nerissa." Sideeq begged. "Please just give me a chance. I love you."

"Sid, I can't do this with you now. I need time to think."

Pulling away from him Nerissa, ran on to the bus. Tapping her Oyster card on the fare reader, she dashed past the driver and made a beeline for the stairs.

The middleaged black man that drove the bus, with his bald head and greying beard, looked down the bus and then at

Sideeq. Seeming to recognise the despair in Sideeq's eyes, he held the entrance doors for a moment longer, minding his business. However, when he saw Sideeq look up for Nerissa on the top deck, he closed them again. The hydraulic brakes on the bus hissed as it pulled away, and left Sideeq standing on the kerb.

*

It was getting late and Nerissa still hadn't heard anything back since her last text. Feeling nauseous, she lay on her bed contemplating whether to switch off her phone. She figured at least that way she could say he took too long to reply and she had decided to go to bed. Realising that would just cause another argument, she waited. Getting up, she switched her Smart TV to YouTube, selecting an RnB mix. Picking up Lil Sid off her black dresser, she lay back down, cuddling the porcelain pooch. She stroked his head as though he were real, looking in his puppy-dog eyes.

"I know it was stupid, but what else was I supposed to do?" Nerissa whispered. Lil Sid looked at her, but offered no answer. As far as he was concerned they had already been through the pros and cons, and his expression stayed fixed. "You know and I know it won't work," Nerissa tried to reason. "He's too nice. He's too good for me, he deserves better. I can't make him choose between his friends and me. Even if he did choose me, he'll end up resenting me for it."

Again Lil Sid stared at her, and they both knew the truth. Nerissa was scared. Sideeq was offering everything she ever wanted. He would never bully her, or threaten her, or leave her locked in his hostel for hours, and he certainly wouldn't put his hands on her. No—Sideeq would be loving, loyal and reliable. He would literally do his utmost to make her happy and that frightened Nerissa, because she didn't trust herself. Love wasn't meant to be easy for someone like her, and she wondered how long it would be before she ruined it all. Before she grew tired or bored or pushed him too far. The women in her family were known for pushing men's buttons and she didn't trust that one day she wouldn't push his. Sideeq didn't deserve all the drama she came with.

Resting her head on her pillow, Nerissa began to cry. She hated Swank and Kyle for meddling in her business and found it easier to blame them for having to let Sideeq go. She told herself they would keep interfering. They would never let her and Sideeq be together in peace. If she didn't end it now she would only be delaying the inevitable. Then what would happen to her? It wasn't in Nerissa's nature to be on her own for too long. She knew she had to be with somebody, and if she couldn't have Sideeq perhaps she was better off with the devil she knew. Somebody who was predictable and revelled in palaver?

Sitting up, Nerissa read the text messages on her phone, trying to convince herself she had made the right choice.

Hey

Wat U want?

Can we talk?

No wat 4?

Bcz we need to

LOL I don't thinkso Ur dun out here

I'm serious

Talk den

I miss U

Ahh here we go wid ur dumb chat

I do!!

Cum off my line u waste girl

I swear I love U

U got jokes LMAO!!!

Fine screw you then

If U Luv me.. Prove it!

Cm see me n I will xx

Laying back down, Nerissa listened to her music. Her eyelids felt almost heavy as her heart and she began to slip into sleep. It was another twenty minutes before she awoke to the sound of Gobbler dashing pebbles at her window.

Part VI

Grey Skies & Concrete Cages

D. D. ARMSTRONG

CHAPTER 6.1

There's a saying that a good friend is one that knows all your stories, but a best friend is one that lived them with you. After Sideeq walked out of the studio, Kyle was furious. Like Sideeq, he was beginning to think it maybe *was* time for them to go their separate ways. For him, their story might as well be done, and he didn't care much to hear what the others had to say.

"Wheeler, you need to admit you were wrong," Sharkey stated. "You was pushing for an argument and you got one."

"So what? I don't care."

"What kinda attitude is that? That's supposed to be your best friend."

"He was. But obviously Mr Loverboy done lost his mind."

"K," Swank butted in. "Don't you think we should go after him, fam?"

"Go after who? If my man wants to get his head buss for that girl, that's his business. I'm not involved."

"Rah, mate that's cold," Danny said, crumbling his weed. He sprinkled the green into some rolling paper half-filled with tobacco as he prepared to wrap a joint.

"You proper just turned Mr Freeze on him. You can't say

279

that."

"I just did, and what?"

"And nothing," Danny said, picking up his joint and licking the sticky line on the paper. "Just, half an hour go you was saying we gotta look out for him, but I guess that's how the colliweed crumbles?"

"It true, K." Swank stood, biting her nails. "I feel like this all my fault. You lot can't not talk. We need to find Sid and sort this out, fam."

"I ain't sorting nothing." Kyle refused to listen. "I can't believe he said I made him go the market? What's he talking about? He's tryna blame me for tings that happened when we was 11 and 12. Eff that. That's dead! I ain't taking blame for that shit."

Knowing Kyle's anger was getting the better of him, Sharkey eventually offered to drop him home. He decided to take the scenic route so he could reason with Kyle. However, no matter what he said, Kyle kept returning to one thing. "All this is over that girl, y'know. You see how my man's going on? Over a girl, bruv."

"I do," Sharkey said pulling up, into the estate. "But if you think it's just over Nerissa, bro, you weren't listening."

"I was," Kyle insisted, but Sharkey put his hand across his chest cutting him off.

"Hold on, family, let me land," he said, turning down the car stereo so he had Kyle's full attention. "Coz you like to talk when you should be listening. And if there's one thing I know, a man can't talk and listen at the same time. So hear me out."

"Fine, say your piece then," Kyle said, screwing up his face.

Sharkey rolled his eyes. There were many things he liked about Kyle, but his pig-headedness wasn't one of them.

"Brother, you see the way you and Sid roll? That's a rare ting. But sometimes you—" he prodded Kyle in the chest "—have to understand lion and tiger can't live in the same jungle y'know, family. Both of dem got their own style of hunting. The tiger has got his stripes and the lion got his *pride*. But at the end of the day they each ha' fe recognise they're both big cats. You get what I'm tryna say?"

"I hear you," Kyle grunted. "But it's not the same."

"Alright cool, say no more," Sharkey said raising an eyebrow. He wasn't the type to argue and felt no need to stress his point. "Only you will know that. But remember this," he said, holding up his fist for Kyle to touch. "Pride comes before a fall, y'know, brother."

"Real talk." Kyle bumped Sharkey's fist. "But I'm not the only one being proud. So let's see who falls first. I guarantee it won't be me."

With that sentiment, Kyle got out the car and went upstairs. His anger had yet to simmer down, and he went straight to his bedroom. Dropping his bag, he was ready to flake out on his bed when he saw the large brown parcel waiting for him. Sniggering to himself, he flipped the parcel the middle finger and roared aloud.

"No, man, no," he whined, as though he had just lost a bet with God. He knew if the universe wanted to send him a message here, it was. Grabbing a pair of scissors, he carefully opened the parcel. As he examined the contents with a huge grin spreading on his face, he slowly began to realise how fickle his pride could be. He had to admit Sharkey was right, and he had to accept his time to fall. Sideeq deserved his own space in which to grow. His friend also deserved an honest apology. The type only a best friend has to make.

*

The next morning, Kyle was up nice and early. Warm puffs of air hissed out of the iron as he pushed the steam button. Gliding his hand carefully over the fabric, he pressed every crease out of all three of his UDC sample T-shirts with perfect precision. He had never taken so much pride in ironing any garment in his whole life. When he was done, he gently put each T-shirt on a clothes hanger, then hung them from the shelf above his bed. Jumping onto the bed, he cleared all the books and video games from the shelf, then strategically placed all of his sporting trophies in symmetrical order of height with the biggest in the middle and the smallest on the outsides. Underneath, he lay the remaining plastic sealed T-shirts in a colour-coordinated row: red, marl grey, navy, red and so on. Taking out his phone he took a few pictures, and by the time he put a filter on them, they looked like one of those locker room shrine-slash-hall of fame type ads you saw in the glossy sports magazines. Smiling, Kyle replaced the tees with two of the black hoodies hanging. He place them side-by-side, one showing the logo on the left side of the chest and the second showing the huge logo on the back. It was exactly like Sideeq had designed. He took another set of photos and prepped them to post on his Instagram later. Lastly, he placed the two of caps in between the trophies, once again displaying the front out and the other showing the embroidery of the Ugly Dog lettering on the back. He took his final set of pictures and packed his bag ready for college. Removing one of the hoodies from the hanger, he felt the heavy duty draw cords in the hood, and thick quality of the fabric. The jumpers had come out even better than he had imagined. He had to give credit to Sideeq.

He stroked his thumb on the red-and-blue vinyl-printed shield logo, with its white framing and silhouette of Rizla. The image of the old bull terrier was bittersweet, perhaps even ironic. Had Gobbler and his friend never taken the dog, he wouldn't be standing with the jumper in his hand, Danny would have never invested his money, and Sideeq would have never come up with the design and name. He didn't want to call it fate, but the irony wasn't lost on Kyle.

Putting on the black hoodie, he checked himself out in mirror and thought *long live Rizla*. The old dog was about to be immortalised as a fashion statement. Fixing the hood so it dropped neatly over the top of his rucksack, Kyle crowned his head with the black baseball cap. Curving the peak slightly, he nodded confidently at his reflection feeling *gangster,* and head for the door.

Strutting through the estate, he walked with a little bop as he made his way to Sideeq's house. He smiled at the old pair of Air Forces Ones dangling from the phone wire and again wondered what would happen to the other if one were to fall in the wind one day. Walking along, he tried to compose an apology but he was too excited. He couldn't wait to show Sideeq the samples. He figured they were the perfect peace offering. No matter how vex Sideeq was, the garments would be the first step in clearing the air. When he got to Sideeq's block, he bounced up the stairs and knocked on the door. He pictured Sideeq opening up with his hard face all sour, and prepared himself to apologise. However, when the door opened, Kyle was greeted by Siddeq's mum in her work uniform.

"Hello, stranger," she said with half a smile on her face. Freakishly, she had the same smile as her son, and it was easy to see where Sideeq got his placid nature from. "What you doing here?"

"I'm always here, mum, you're never in that's all," Kyle said giving Valerie a kiss on the cheek. "You're too busy running up and down like some young girl."

"Move from me." Valerie clipped Kyle round the back of the head. "You too cheeky."

"But you know me love you long time," Kyle said trying to cuddle Valerie. "Where's your big son?"

"How you mean?" Valerie frowned. "Sid left about half an hour ago son. He didn't call you?"

"No."

"Oh," Valerie said looking puzzled. "He said he was going college early. I thought he went to meet you."

"Nah, not even." Kyle scowled. He guessed Sideeq was still annoyed with him and probably left to get an earlier train. He sighed, realising he'd have to do some proper grovelling.

"Is everything alright?" Valerie asked. "Is something going

on with Sid?"

"Nah, nah, he's cool." Kyle tried to smile. He didn't want Valerie to know they'd had an argument.

"Are you sure?" Valerie gave him one of those *'fess-up'* looks that only a black mother could give. "I know he had a girl here the other night. Has it got anything to do with that?"

"Huh?" Kyle looked at Valerie, shocked.

"Yes." Valerie gave Kyle an accusing eye. "Don't play like you don't know what's going on. I hope you don't sneak girl past your mum as well."

"Nah, not even, mummy." Kyle smirked.

"Listen," Valerie gave her half-smile again. "Come from my door and go find your friend. You too dyam lie."

Laughing, Kyle gave Valerie a kiss before he ran off. "See you later, mum."

"Yes, see you later, son!"

Kyle burst down the stairs and out of the block. As he raced towards the station, he took out his phone and tried to call Sideeq.

CHAPTER 6.2

There are miserable days in every man's life, where he wishes he could run away from all its drama. When hope feels like a distant promise and he no longer has strength to call her name. The sweet voice that once spoke so loud in his mind now barely whispers with a murmur. From the dark corners, the low and ugly babble of confusion can be heard over the haunting whimpers of confidence, who lingers like a phantom. It's on days like these when we look up to the sky and envy the birds. Wondering why God saw fit to give them wings. And on days like these, our mind goes from being a dutiful servant—obedient, loving and loyal—to a tyrannical master, dangerous and cruel. We become slaves to our doubts and wrestle every dilemma, begging for the right choice to deliver us to freedom.

Sideeq was having one of these days. When he woke up, his mind felt numb. Exhausted from reliving and rehashing the events of last night, his brain handed over his central operating system to his body while it searched for the correct answer to his problem. Functioning on autopilot, he had an out-of-body experience. He could see and feel himself getting up, and getting ready for college. Washed and dressed, he packed his bag, he ate a bowl of cereal and said goodbye to his mum. When she asked, if he was alright, the mechanics in his brain selected an automated response and replied, "Yeah I'm cool."

It was only when he got to Wood Lane Station that he was aware that he wasn't in control. Something in his hardwiring malfunctioned. Instead of going up the stairs to the eastbound platform, which would have taken him towards Ladbroke Grove, his feet overshot their margin and took him to the westbound staircase. Standing on the opposite platform he looked along the tracks to see the train approaching. Powerless, he wondered whether his mind would recalibrate and correct its course. However, he found himself boarding the Hammersmith-bound train and assimilating with its commuters. Packed in and pressed against the mass of bodies, he looked at the phone in his hand. He registered Kyle's name flashing on the screen, and for the fourth time he declined the call. Not wanting to be disturbed, he switched his phone to airplane mode, assuming Kyle would get the message. Internally he still wasn't clear where he was going and followed his instincts. Slowly he stepped off the train at Goldhawk Road. Moving down the stairs, he exited the station and scanned the perimeter. Peering across the road, Sideeq looked up. His eyes locked onto the huge blue metal piping that held the large semicircle sign above the entrance. The hoarding, with it's colourful pictures of fish, fruit, textiles and produce, read *Welcome To Shepherd's Bush Market*.

It was here, looking at two middle-aged white men arranging the vast range of fruit and root vegetables at the Fletchers stall, that Sideeq's brain disengaged from autopilot. A green Ford transit van beeped its horn at him as he crossed to the other side of the road. There was something about the hand-written sign that read '4 Lemons for £1' that rebooted his mind. He stared at the sign for a moment, looking at the bruised fruit on display. Turning, he began to wander through the market, studying every little detail from the Sikh trader in his purple turban selling pots pans and other kitchen utensils on his stall, to the cheap plastic toy guns and robots that beeped at the stall adjacent. Further along, an old Asian woman with thick glasses and a long plaited pigtail sat scowling at the world as it passed by. Her stall was filled with cheap drapery, textile rolls, scarves and patterned dresses. From her fabric cubbyhole she stared at Sideeq with a miserable glare, not wanting or needing to attract his custom. Sideeq paid her no mind, smelling the spicy aroma and hot oils coming from a nearby food stall. He moved on, past the dread-locked Caribbean fishmonger to the passageway under the glass canopy and railway viaduct that hosted more stalls in the market network. The hanging meat and fresh cuts at the halal butcher's counter caught his eye, as the chubby butcher in his blood smeared white overcoat bantered with his morning customers. A train rattled thunderously above Sideeq's head as he reached his destination. Standing opposite a stall selling an array of hats, he stared at the vacant shop front that used to be Global Sport. Looking through the dusty window, he peered at the dark and empty store. Ironically, the vibrant urban fashion and sportswear shop which had once been a Mecca to young people in West London had completely disappeared, replaced by competitors who had copied their blueprint and located their businesses in prominent premises on the Uxbridge Road and Shepherd's Bush Roundabout. Unable to compete, the final blow came with the emergence of the Westfield Shopping Mall with its corporate sportswear and designer retailers, resigning Global Sports to its fate.

In its demise it now stood as an empty shell, a blank canvas for the next vendor to make their dreams of business come true. The white walls inside that use to be stocked with rows of brightly-coloured fitted hats and sneakers were bare, apart from the markings where the wall brackets had once been placed for shelving.

There was something eerie about seeing the neglected store sitting so lifeless and still. Its irrelevance hurt Sideeq, and he was transfixed by how hollow it appeared. His eyes wandered to the counter at the back querying what had happened to the fat-faced manager who loved blaring his music for the customers. Where would he be now? Had he found another store, or was he sitting behind a desk somewhere answering phones? Sideeq remembered how his face twisted up as he called to Nana, "Oi what you lot doing?"

In a flash, Sideeq was transported back to that fatal day, and he saw his younger self push Nana and run. Stepping back, he followed the visions of himself trailing behind Kyle, running through the market. Reliving the moment he'd felt overwhelmed. Sideeq's heart began to race as he traced his steps. He followed the sounds of his young voice shouting for help as he dashed past shoppers and market traders. Strangely, some of those same traders ignored him now, just as they did on that day.

It was surreal. It had been just over five years since Sideeq was attacked. In that whole time he had never returned to the market. Yet today, he found himself standing a few feet away from the same spot he had been stabbed. He looked at the grimy black-stained ground, remembering how hard the surface had felt when he crashed to the floor. The crushed stone embedded in asphalt had torn the skin on his hands and knees, and he had rolled onto his back in pain. Studying the cracks in the road, Sideeq wondered how much of his lost blood had trickled into its tiny crevasses and become a part of its DNA. The thought of his ordeal upset him, and his mouth quivered as a tear rolled down his cheek. *Now*, he thought. Now was the time, the only time and perfect time. Now was the time he wanted to know why. Spotting a coffee shop across the street, Sideeq wiped his face and crossed at the traffic lights. Ordering a hot chocolate, he took a seat at the back of the shop and settled at a table. Sifting through his backpack, he fished out the white envelope containing Nana's letter. For a second he thought about whether or not he really wanted to know what Nana had to say. He queried what significance it would have reading it now. What purpose could it really serve him? Nevertheless, Sideeq tore the envelope open and unfolded the letter. At first he sipped his hot chocolate, not actually reading the words but studying the letter's form. Nana's handwriting was a lot better than he imagined it would be, and there was a tidy manner and structure to the letter that he had not expected. Immediately, it angered Sideeq to see that he had written his prison number and address in the upper right corner as though he expected to receive some sort of reply. Sideeq cussed at the idea. Nana was lucky he was even reading it. Fuming, his eyes moved to next line, scanning the page.

Dear Sideeq,

What can I say? I don't really know how to start this letter, but I believe I must begin by thanking you for giving me this much of your time and reading.

I have tried to write this so many times and in so many ways—an apology to you. But in my heart I know anything I write seems trivial and minute in comparison to how much pain I may have caused you...

Chapter 6.3

By the time Kyle arrived at college, he had already called Sideeq's phone six times. From the last two calls, which had gone straight to voicemail, it was quite clear that Sideeq was still avoiding him. Nevertheless, Kyle headed to the common room in search of his best friend. Well actually, he thought, given that Sideeq had cancelled their friendship, that status was still pending. It sounded childish to him to have to think about whether someone was still your best friend or not, but then again, at times Sideeq did have a naive manner as to how he went about things. It often annoyed Kyle how in some aspects he felt like he had to spoon-feed his friend, and Sideeq could be a really broody bastard at times. Kyle rolled his eyes, wondering how long Sideeq would draw out their argument once he had apologised.

Entering the common room, Kyle gave his morning greetings to couple of the girls, stealing a hug and kiss, then said, "Yeah, yeah wha gwan?" pumping fist with one or two of the man dem.

He looked around the common room, half expecting to see Sideeq sulking in a corner with a hot chocolate, silently brewing for round two. However, to his surprise there was no Sideeq. Exiting the room, Kyle wondered whether Mr Loverboy had gone straight to his art room, or was skulking around somewhere else. He reasoned that the sooner they cleared the air, the better it would be all round, and went to wait outside.

When he reached the gates, Kyle saw Danny smoking his early-morning spliff. He was in the same spot they had met in on the first day of college, minus Rizla. It was still strange to see him without his trusted companion. Although he stood blowing smoke rings in the air like he didn't have a care in world, the impact of losing his best friend had affected Danny. There was a subtle change in his behaviour. He had an undertone of restless-ness and a simmering anger within him. Had one of the tutors came and asked him what he was smoking, Danny would have probably blown smoke in their face and said, "Lemon kush." On other days, though, he was plain old have-a-laugh Danny.

"Yes, yes, what's happening, Mush?" Danny said with a smile. "You calm down from last night, or what, geez?"

"I'm good," Kyle said, touching fists.

"Yeah, we'll see about that when Siddy lands," Danny teased. He was about to crack another joke, but stopped. Looking at Kyle's hat his eyes lit up, then trailed down to Kyle's sweater. "Oi! Oi!" Danny yelled. "Don't mess about!" He beamed. "You got the samples!" He tried to snatch the cap off Kyle's head.

"Move!" Kyle pushed him back.

"Oi, don't play with my life, where's mine?"

Taking off his backpack, Kyle rested the bag on the bonnet of a car and showed Danny the sample. In awe, Danny smiled and pick up two tees in his hand.

"Oh my days! Wait til Sid see this, he's gonna effin' love

them!"

Finishing his hot chocolate, Sideeq read over Nana's letter one last time. Staring at the white page, he studied the blue ink and grey lines with mixed emotions. The letter was relatively short. No more than a page and a half long, in comparison to what he wanted and deserved. However, Sideeq had counted the word 'sorry' sixteen times. At first it seemed as though Nana didn't know any other word. *Sorry* was littered everywhere like a full stop. Then roughly half way through the letter, the words *regret* and *remorse* began to appear. By the time Sideeq read the phrase 'all I can do is apologise profusely,' he started to wonder from whom and how much help Nana had received in composing the letter. Perhaps his legal team had assisted him, or maybe his prison tutor had given him a thesaurus and some pointers. Either way, there was not a gold star for effort, and with each sorry Sideeq began to hear Nana's distinct London-Ghanaian accent in the letter. Gradually his slanted handwriting came alive, with its elongated tails and exaggerated capitals. There was an intimacy yet complete formality within the letter; an unspoken respect in the words that enabled Sideeq to envision himself sitting alone face-to-face in a room with Nana; victim and attacker. The apprehension Sideeq had felt for so many weeks about reading the letter swiftly turned to anger. Then oddly, on his second reading, the anger simmered to disgust, and the disgust finally into an empty nothingness.

Here was the boy who had changed his whole life. Stolen his eye, crippled his ear and scarred his face, begging for his

forgiveness. Pleading for understanding and pity for the igno-
rance he once had. In passages he spoke about being haunted,
being punished, and repenting. He bought the name Allah into
his confessions and throughout he kept referring to not being
able to fully comprehend the impact his actions may have had
upon Sideeq. *Impact.* It was the only true word in all Nana's grovelling that actually resonated with Sideeq. The rest of the apology
sounded contrived and self-serving. An opportunity for Nana to
release his guilt before coming home.

Folding the letter, Sideeq placed it in its envelope. He
thought about tearing it up or burning it, but realised there was
no need. The letter had brought him a moment of clarity. He
asked himself one question: what had been the real impact of
his attack? Immediately, without any internal debate, he knew
the answer. *Fear.* For years he had been dealing with his physical
scars, conveniently dodging mirrors and hiding from his reflection—but what about his mental ones? How had he dealt with
the trauma that lay beneath the surface?

Standing up, Sideeq picked up his cup. Walking to the door,
he tossed it in the bin and stepped out onto the pavement. He
stared at the market across the road, realising he had never known
fear before that day. His introduction to it was so alarming that it
would later give birth and subliminally associate his every insecurity, doubt and anxiety with the physical pain he had endured. In
an instant he finally recognised that Nana's letter had also given
him a sense of freedom. Today, he no longer felt afraid. He didn't
need to hide away in his bedroom, or need Kyle to persuade him
to come outside and play. Nor did he need anyone to walk with

him to and from school every day. Standing opposite the market, Sideeq understood that whatever part of him he had lost that day, he was now here to reclaim it. If his life that been destroyed at the age of eleven, he was surely overdue a new one. One without fear. If not, who was the young man standing there now?

Sensing his own affirmation, he nodded his head, knowing what to do next. He already knew who and what he wanted for his new life. Pressing the button on the pelican crossing, he waited for the lights to change. As the flashing green man sounded and traffic stopped, he crossed over. He looked at the large poster outside the iron black gates of the Bush Theatre. Curiously, he studied the two black men on the poster wearing dusty denim dungarees and tatty cotton shirts. He had never seen black actors play the lead roles in Of Mice & Men. He liked the novelty, but wondered how that would affect the narrative of Crooks, the lone black stablebuck. Stepping inside, he approached the box office. Purchasing two tickets for the evening show, he asked the purple-haired attendant with tattoos and piercings, "Do you have a program?"

"Yeah, they're one pound," the woman said, then looked around conspiratorially. She smiled, putting a finger to her lips, and then gave Sideeq a program for free. Grinning, Sideeq mouthed thank you and disappeared. On the train he flipped through the programme, feeling assured that a maiden trip to the theatre would win Nerissa round.

*

Nerissa sat in her performing arts class, watching in awe as Monni—a short, slim, dark skinned girl with a gold open-faced crown round her front tooth—delivered her latest monologue of *Sharlene the Ghetto Queen*. Using quotes from Shakespeare in a modern setting, she scrunched up her face and appropriated the most exaggerated South London accent to bring her character to life.

"He said to be or not to be, that is the question? I said, pardon? Do you think you're funny? Furthermore, I can't even lie, when he said it I thought, *nah he is taking the P? Is he?* Like, I was actually trying to talk to him and he wants to start spouting Shakespeare. Like, am I dumb? Who does that? I mean, you tell me, which roadman do you know just randomly throws Shakespeare into a conversation, in between cutting up their work and their girlfriend telling them they're pregnant?

"I'm telling you, swear down, no lie, that's what he said. If I could have reached down the phone I would have shot him a straight box. No, two. He was blatantly trying to play games. I'm like rah, rudeboy, are you wasting my free minutes on Shakespeare? No, no, I don't think you are. Because you know full well I did not call to hear no Shakespeare. Hear him. 'Listen, listen, stop getting all irate, you're moving like you wanna call a plague on both our houses.' A plague! I told this fool he better mind I don't call my brothers and make dem run up in his mum's yard. They won't give him a scratch. Ask for him. He will be a grave man tomorrow!"

Sitting as still as possible, Nerissa tried not to laugh along with the rest of her class, but Monni's comedic timing was hilarious, and with each laugh Nerissa felt a sharp twinge from the bruises around her lower back and abdomen. Cringing with discomfort, she masked the pain when something caught her eye. Looking past Monni, she saw Sideeq peering in through the circular window in the classroom door. Realising he had caught her attention, he waved her over. Checking to see if anyone else had noticed him, Nerissa shook her head. Titling his head Sideeq frowned, raising an eyebrow, and continued to beckon her out. When Nerissa didn't move, he stepped inside. Not knowing what he would do next, Nerissa stood up as Monni finished her monologue. Clapping, she slipped away and pushed Sideeq outside so they could speak.

"Sid, what are you doing? You can't just walk into my class like that."

"Sorry, but I had to," Sideeq apologised.

He studied her for a second as she stood with her arms crossed. She had let out her curly locks, which dropped just passed her shoulders, and she matched a purple jumper and black jeans with the purple and green paisley patterned scarf around her neck and a purple pair of Airmax 90's. As always, she wore minimal make up with a touch of lip gloss.

"Look, Riss I don't mean to put it on you, but I had to speak to you."

"Sid, please." Nerissa dropped her gaze. "I don't wanna do this today."

"So you're not gonna hear me out?" Sideeq asked. He waited for Nerissa's reply. When she bit her lip and shrugged her shoulders, he continued. "Listen, I thought about everything that happened last night. I played everything over in my mind and you were right. I should have stuck up for you and made it clear to my friends that I'm in love with you."

His words made Nerissa look up. For a spilt second, her eyes lit up as she looked into his, then she remembered her stance. Yet that was enough for Sideeq to know it wasn't over, and he carried on speaking.

"So I'm here to apologise and let you know that if you give me another chance, that will never happen again."

Again Nerissa pleaded with him, "Sid, I told you I don't wanna do this today." She patted the corner of her eyes with the palm of her hand. She could feel herself getting teary-eyed and didn't want to ruin her make up. "Can't you just forget about me and move on?"

"No," Sideeq said, smiling. "That's not how it goes."

Puffing out her cheeks in an attempt not to cry, Nerissa said, "Sid, please just leave it. It'll be better for everyone if we just end things here. I don't want you getting hurt."

Sideeq laughed, pulling Nerissa close. Wrapping his arms around her, he hugged her, kissing the top of her curly locks.

"Listen, you could never hurt me. No one can, so I'm not taking no for an answer. Do you understand?"

Nerissa nodded her head. She buried her face in his chest. Sideeq seem to notice her flinch as he stroked her back with his big paws.

"Sid, there's something I need to tell you."

"Tell me later," Sideeq said, wiping her face. He kissed Nerissa on the cheek. "I got a surprise for you after college. We can talk more then."

"What is it?" Nerissa asked.

"Don't worry." Sideeq smiled. "Trust me, you'll like it."

Pecking her on the cheek one last time, he left Nerissa to go back inside, and set off to his class.

CHAPTER 6.4

After apologizing to Mr Ghodstinat for being late to his lesson, Sideeq slipped into his seat. Taking out his brushes, he settled in at his desk. At her own desk, Swank ignored him. Busying herself, she pretended to be too engrossed in the collage she was making to notice his presence. She didn't know what to say after the events of last night and kept her head down, avoiding eye contact. Instead, she sifted through a pile of magazine cuttings, carefully selecting the right images and colour tones to create her collage. She tested each cutting against those she had already torn and glued onto her black spray-painted 40x20 inch canvas, then snipped away at each new piece accordingly before stick it into position. Using large lettering, Swank had screen-printed the word 'mapenzi' (which was Swahili for love) in white acrylic. Then halfway down the lettering she had drawn two figures locked in an embrace, passionately kissing. After almost two weeks' worth of work, the collage was finally starting to take shape. Peering over, Sideeq studied the detail in the two figures kissing. Initially when Swank had drawn the outline, he had assumed it was a man and a woman. Now with the small cutting intricately placed it was clearly two black women in kente cloth; a full-blown declaration of her sexuality and coming out piece.

Acknowledging the statement in her art, Sideeq broke the awkward silence. "Looks, good."

"What?" Swank looked up, double-checking he was speaking to her.

"I said, it looks good. It's coming together nice."

Swank took a brief moment to look at her progress, then thanked him. Sideeq responded with a nod, letting Swank know she was welcome. With the ice broken, Swank decided to clear the air. "We cool?"

"Yeah, calm," Sideeq said, baring her no animosity over last night's events. Instead he asked, "Is that your final module piece, or are you planning on doing another one?"

The remainder of the morning passed quickly as the two began to share ideas and discuss concepts for their module pieces. When the pips for lunch break beeped, Swank jumped up like a jack-in-the-box.

"Yo, my belly is ripping, I need to munch," she said, grabbing her backpack. She looked at Sideeq, who had barely moved. "What you doing you, coming downstairs?"

"Nah." Sideeq shook his head. "I'm gonna just chill."

Immediately, Swank read the situation and decided not to push the subject. "Cool," she said. "You want me to bring sutting back?"

"Nah."

"Alright, say no more, fam. I'm gone." Swank bumped fists with Sideeq and headed downstairs. The class quickly emptied, and Mr Ghodstinat left the art room in Sideeq's judiciary as usual. Forever the lone watchman, Sideeq took a break from his artwork to indulge in his favourite pastime. Peering down on the courtyard, he watched small flocks of students pour out of the building and disappear about their lunch time routines. Beyond the gate he spied Kyle waiting for Danny by Sharkey's car. When Swank arrived, they all seemed to discuss something. Kyle looked disappointed, and just before he got into the BMW, he looked up towards the window. Shielding his eyes from the sun, Kyle stared directly at the room as though he knew Sideeq would be watching. Eventually he got in on the passager side, and the car pulled off.

Stewing, Sideeq began to contemplate what he was going to do about his situation with Kyle when something caught his eye. Getting up, he walked round the table to get a better look. On the far side of the street he saw Nerissa, who was being followed by Hassan. Pulling her arm, he managed to block her way. Nerissa snatched her arm away. She tried to walk around him, but every time she did, he kept stepping in her way, offering her his phone. Stepping back, Nerissa fixed up her face and crossed her arms. She looked agitated. Furious, Sideeq was getting ready to run down stairs, but his instinct told him to wait. He wanted see how the situation would play out.

Again Hassan offered her the phone and she refused. The two were at loggerheads. Then, to Hassan's surprise, Nerissa snatched the phone out of his hand. He stood there with a big grin on his face as Nerissa spoke to whoever was on the phone. Sideeq was in no doubt that it had to be Gobbler. After a short while, Nerissa came off the phone. She slammed it back in Hassan's hand.

Barging past him, she stormed off. Hassan, who continued the call, walked off in the opposite direction, laughing. Immediately, Sideeq took out his phone to call Nerissa, but then he paused. He knew what she was like when she was upset. Any mention of him seeing what happened and not doing anything about it might go against this favour. Alternatively, Nerissa may also be accusing him of spying on her. Sideeq refrained from calling. He had no intention of getting in Nerissa's bad books again. He'd just decided it was better to send a text message when his own text alert sounded.

FFS!!!! ☹

I friggin H8 WestLDN ppl

Why what's goin on?

Nothing

U sure?

Yh it's nothing new. Where RU?

Upstairs. Art room. Just me here

U comin thru? ☺

No

Oh ok den ☹☹☹

Sorry not in the mood. What
U doin last period?

Why?

Who wants to kno, U or Lil
Sid?

Me. Can we go Westfield?

I need to go chill out

Cool I'll meet U by the gates
LP

Thanks xxx

☺ x ☺ x

Sideeq put away his phone. He smiled to himself. It seemed things
were working out better than he planned. Westfield was literally
two roads away from Bush Theatre. A trip to the shopping mall
would be ideal. He could kill some time window shopping and
let Nerissa vent, then take her for something to eat before the

show. Looking out of the window, he began to plan the best way to surprise Nerissa with the theatre tickets.

*

Sideeq looked at his watch. It was almost 3 o'clock in the afternoon. As last period approached, there was a lethargic energy in the class. Most of the other students either silently pottered away at their artwork listening to music on their earphones, or nattered away in trivial chit chat. Not far from the door, Mr Ghodstinat was in the middle of a debate with a Filipino boy named Ray about the influence of graffiti and street art on pop culture. Somehow their discussion had lead them to compare Wu-Tang Clan's producer, RZA, to street artist Jean Michel Basquait. Sideeq thought it would be the perfect time for him to slip out of class. Clearing his desk, he began to wash out his paintbrushes and put away his artwork.

"Where you goin?" Swank asked.

"Nowhere," Sideeq said, packing his backpack.

He took a moment to think, then realising he had nothing to hide anymore. "Actually, I'm going Westfields with Nerissa, then I'm gonna take her to Bush theatre to see a play."

Sideeq flashed Swank a glimpse of the theatre programme before shoving it in his backpack.

"OK, OK," Swank teased. "The lighty lover is on a romance ting, yeah?"

"Whatever," Sideeq smirked. "I beg you just cover for me if Mr G asks where I've gone."

"Course, fam," Swank agreed, looking over at Mr Ghodstinat. "But I don't think it will make a difference by the time he notices," she said as the teacher waved his hands in the air, animatedly performing Busta Rhymes' verse from *What's the Scenario*.

"Bless, I owe you one." Sideeq laughed. He slapped hands and hugged Swank, then quietly slipped out of the room.

Outside, he met Nerissa by the gates. From the frown on her face he could tell she was still agitated. He wondered what had her so riled up. Considering her earlier interaction with Hassan, he told himself if he took an educated guess. He would put any money on Gobbler.

"What's happening?" he said, leaning in for a hug and a kiss.

"Nothing," Nerissa said, flinching as he hugged her. She treated the hug like a formality. Her embrace lacked sincerity, and Sideeq asked, "What's wrong?"

"Nothing," Nerissa said, looking up and down the road. "I just wanna get out of here."

"Cool, whatever you wan' do," Sideeq said, following her eyes.

It was obvious she was checking so see who was about. Apart from a few smokers at the bottom of the street and Pat the security guard reading his paper in his Portacabin behind them, the road was deserted.

"I'm ready to bounce if you are?" Sideeq said. He began to walk to the top of the road and head towards Ladbroke Grove station when Nerissa said,

"No, not that way. I don't wanna take the train. Can we just walk? You're not in a rush, are you?"

"Nah," Sideeq replied. "I told you, I'm cool for whatever."

Nerissa smiled politely, and the two headed down the road walking side by side. As they reached the junction of St Mark's Road, Nerissa slipped her arm between his, linking arms.

*

By late afternoon, Kyle's jovial spirit had slowly disappeared. Sitting in the back of his class, he scribbled an acronym in block capitals.

U
GOTTA
LOVE
YOURSELF

DEN
OTHERS
GONE
SEE

He was still in his feelings about Sideeq shunning them for lunch. Although the others told him not to take it to heart and that it was better to give Sideeq some time before they cleared the air, Kyle couldn't help but feel disappointed. His ego had been bruised and his excitement to show Sideeq the samples had been subdued. However, Swank had reminded him while they were at the chip shop that it wasn't out of the ordinary for Sideeq to stay upstairs for lunch. The art room had long been his sanctuary and he had missed lunch many times before.

"OK, yeah, you man did have an argument, but Sid is cool. Chat to him later and say your piece then, innit," Swank advised. "Trust me, fam, it's minor. You man are boys."

Feeling restless, Kyle was studying the acronym again when Sharkey came back from the toilets. Kyle eyed him as he stepped in the room. With one look, he knew something was wrong. For the first time ever, Kyle saw a crack in Sharkey's cool exterior. There was anger in his eyes—something had disturbed him. His face was as hard and tight as wood, and he appeared to be trying to figure something out in his head. "Yo family, I beg you call Sideeq," he said.

Frowning, Kyle looked at him. "Why, what's going on?"

"I don't know," Sharkey said, grabbing his bag. "Just call Sideeq."

Bewildered, Kyle looked to Danny to see if he understood what was going on, but did as Sharkey told him. "It's just ringing out."

"What class is he in?"

"He's supposed to be upstairs in art. Why?"

"Come," Sharkey ordered.

The three of them rushed out of the room. Racing towards the art block, Sharkey handed his phone to Kyle. "Watch that."

Kyle pressed play on a video clip to find someone had sent Sharkey a discrete screen recording of Gobbler on Facetime. He appeared on screen with his wide jaw and ugly face in mid conversation, recklessly ranting while the unknown caller remained anonymous. They had been smart enough to place their phone facing up to the celling so their face couldn't be seen. Only their voice could be heard in the background, goading and laughing along.

"Eff Sharkey!" Gobbler declared. "Do you think I give a fuck about him and his uncles? He's a pussy. As far as I'm concerned, if he wants to get involved he can get it, too. I'll shoot up their whole station."

The unknown caller laughed and said, "With what, my G? You ain't no gunman. Everyone dun seen the blind and deaf yoot punch you up man, behave."

"Oi blud, are you tryna take me for some dickhead? Don't try mock me."

"Oi Gobz, calm down, my G. I ain't even mocking you. I'm just saying the whole hood dun seen Hass and Squingy drag you out the shoobs sparko, cuz. Your jaw was all hanging, G! So why you gassin' now?"

"GAS'! Me! Blud do I look I gas'? Does that look like gas?"

Gobbler pulled out a black nine millimetre Jericho 941 handgun. The gun looked like it had seen better days. Its faded paintwork was beginning to wear thin, showing the grey stainless steel metal beneath. However, it took nothing away from the threat of the weapon.

"Ahhh OK, OK." The unknown caller sounded impressed. "That you, yeah?"

"Yep. Tell me if I'm gassin now?" Gobbler laughed.

"Nah, nah, I see you bruv with the baby eag', say no more, my G."

"That's right. I've been waiting to bust my artillery. Watch later." Gobbler pointed the gun at the screen. "See when I squeeze this ting, man dem's gonna learn about the baby eagle."

"Rah, what you sayin? You goin after the blind yout, G?"

"I ain't saying nothing, just watch the news, innit. I guarantee you by 5 o'clock there's gonna be bare forensic man in Edward Woods. Bare. Man like you better leave your grub at home."

"Nah bruv, you're gassin'."

"Blud, I already told you what it is. I rep LG, Powis Square, 10-11 out here!"

The video cut off with Gobbler cackling into the camera. Kyle didn't know what to say. The moment he had seen the gun his heart stopped. A cold sweat hit him and he was overwhelmed with terror. He knew Gobbler was stupid enough to use it. He handed the phone back to Sharkey and asked, "What you gonna do?"

"I don't know," Sharkey replied, handing the phone to Danny.

When they reached the art room, Sharkey called Swank outside.

"Where's Sid?"

"He dipped out."

"When? How long ago?"

"About ten minutes. Why, what's wrong?"

"Did he say where he's going?"

Swank hesitated, not wanting to be in the middle of another argument. "Why?"

"Just tell us!" Kyle snapped. "We ain't got time for no 21 questions."

Swank frowned and coiled back. Then Sharkey pushed the

matter.

"Swank! If you know where he is just say."

"Tell them!" Danny joined in.

"He said he was going Westfields, then to some theatre play with Nerissa."

The sound of her name rendered Kyle powerless. Instantly his mouth went dry and his stomach started to churn. Was his mind playing tricks on him? Yet the bewildered expression on Swank's face told it all. He half-hoped perhaps she had got it wrong. Better yet, he hoped that she was clowning around and Sideeq had just stepped out the class to go toilet. Yet the bewildered expression on Swank's face told it all.

"Yo, what's wrong?" she asked again.

Kyle felt like he was going to throw up, but he knew there was no time for that. Lost, he looked at Sharkey for direction. Like a telepath, Sharkey read his mind.

"Wheeler, don't panic. We'll find him," he said, grabbing Kyle by the shoulder. "Try his phone again."

Kyle called again as Sharkey and Danny filled Swank in. The ringing boomed in his ear as he watched Swank dart inside the classroom, grabbing her belongings. She burst back out of the room with Mr Ghodstinat calling behind, but the quartet took off.

Thumping in his chest, Kyle's heart chased every ring as he willed Sideeq to pick up. Rushing out of the building, the gang sprinted to Sharkey's car. He hit the central locking and they all bundled in. Turning the key, Sharkey fired up the engine. He did a three point turn and spun the car around.

"Where we going?" Danny asked.

"Westfields."

"No, don't go Westfields," Kyle said. His intuition whispered that Sideeq would never make it there. Fearing the worst, he said, "Go Woods. Gobbler said there would be bare forensic in Edward Woods."

Sharkey glanced into the rear view mirror. Meeting eyes with Kyle, he pressed down on the accelerator, shifting gears.

CHAPTER 6.5

After Kyle's second call, Sideeq switched his phone on silent mode. Heading towards Westfields, he strolled alongside Nerissa with his hands in his pockets. Initially he had tried to hold her hand, but when she pulled it away he decided to let her be. Instead he tried to entice her with some small talk every couple of metres, but Nerissa kept shutting him down with short and closed-ending answers. Luckily Sideeq didn't take it personally. He could see she had her guard up, and he wasn't about to let that phase him. He had been looking forward to spending time with her all day and couldn't wait to surprise her. He had a vision of the two of them sitting in the audience at Bush Theatre, watching the all-black *Of Mice & Men*. He pictured Nerissa in the dim lights, doing that goofy thing she did. The one where she would stare at him dreamily when she thought he wasn't looking. Then he would turn to her and say 'what?' She would giggle and say 'nothing' before scooping into a small tub of ice cream. He tried to calculate whether he still had enough money to buy both food at Westfields and ice cream and beverages at the theatre. Nevertheless, he figured somehow he would make it work. He had got this far already.

Passing the bright red Embassy Café on Latimer Road, the couple turned into Mortimer Square and cut through Hunt Close. At the top of the quiet back street, beyond the grey railings, Sideeq could see the little green mounds in the middle of the Norland open space—the communal area that served the Edward Woods Estate and surrounding streets, which sat between Poytner, Mortimer and Stebbing House tower blocks. It was too small to be called a park, but with its football pitch and playground it was big enough for the residents to appreciate. From here you could see the big red lettering of the Westfield shopping mall logo on the other side of the West Cross dual carriageway which lead to Shepherd's Bush roundabout.

Strolling through the communal area, Sideeq smiled at a young Somali boy who had a blue toy gun in his hand. He couldn't have been any older than three, and his curiosity got the better of him. He stopped and stared at Sideeq. His young eyes studied the scar on Sideeq face. He smiled, pointing his gun and shouted, "Pee-ow, pee-ow!"

His mother, who wore a hijab, trailed behind him pulling a shopping trolley. With her free hand she gave the boy a light clip around the head and said in a heavy Somali accent, "Fuad, don't do that. That's naughty."

Rubbing his head with a cheeky grin, the little boy smiled. Closing one eye like a marksman, he pointed his gun one last time at Sideeq before he ran off, shouting "pee-ow, pee-ow" at a bunch of pigeons.

"Oh my goshhhh," Nerissa said, coming alive. "Look at his red wellies." She pointed to his Spiderman Wellington boots.

"They're so cute."

"Is it?" Sideeq grinned. "I use to have the same pair when I was young. Do you think I'm cute?"

Nerissa smiled. "I don't know. I'd have to see you in some red wellies first."

"If I can pull off a hearing aid, I can pull off red wellies, easy" Sideeq said, brimming with confidence. He nudged Nerissa playfully. For a minute, she seemed to forget she was in a sour mood.

"You're so dumb." Nerissa pushed him back.

"Is that a smile?" Sideeq asked realising he had temporarily broken the spell of misery cast upon her. He figured now was probably the best time to surprise her. Otherwise he would have to follow her grumpy arse around the Westfield for the next couple hours, pretending he didn't mind window shopping. He didn't relish the task. Following Nerissa, he exited the communal green area.

"Mind where you're going," he said, pulling her back on to the kerb as a white Ford transit van pulled out in front of them. "How you gonna try get yourself run over before I get to give your surprise?"

Nerissa frowned at him. "What surprise?" she said.

"The one I mentioned earlier." Sideeq smiled. He could see she had totally forgotten. He was about tell her when two school boys in black blazers and burgundy-and-sky-blue striped ties walked past them. The first one, who was about fourteen with a small uncombed afro and kicked out Wallaby shoes, eyeballed them. The look irritated Sideeq, but he easily dismissed it. However, there was something familiar about the boy's face.

Sideeq couldn't put his finger on it. He watched the boy as he leered at Nerissa, checking her out. Speaking on the phone, the boy brazenly smiled in Sideeq's face and kept on staring. Sideeq shook his head and ignored him. The boy was obviously looking for trouble. Laughing, he nudged at his friend to look. The thin, brown skin boy who carried a football under his arm did the complete opposite to the first and nervously lowered his gaze when he met eyes with Sideeq. As they walked pass the entrance for Poytner House, Sideeq carried on speaking.

"Yeah, like I was saying; I'm gonna be on the level with you."

He stopped Nerissa by the by a block of low rise sheltered housing that separated the two sides of Edwards Woods. It was built with a walk way that you had to pass under to get the other side.

"I know I totally eff'd up yesterday. So I decided to speak with Lil Sid."

"You did, did you?" Nerissa dropped her head. "What did he say?"

"Well, obviously he told me that I messed up," Sideeq joked. "But he also told me that you were a good girl, and that all you ever really wanted is for someone to love and protect you."

"Sid, stop," Nerissa said. Her voice started to crack as she began to cry. "Can we do this at Westfield, please? Let's just get to Westfields."

"No, I'm doin' this here." Sideeq cupped her face in his big hands. With his thumbs he wiped the tears from her cheeks. Reaching in his inside pocket, he fished out the two theatre tickets and put them in her hands. Nerissa gasped at the sight of them. Her eyes whizzed across the words printed on the tickets, and her legs seemed to go weak.

"Why did you do this?"

"What d'you mean?" Sideeq laughed.

"I mean, why now?"

"Because…" Sideeq grinned. He couldn't stop smiling—her reaction was even better than he had anticipated. "I love you. I wanna be the first person to take you to the theatre, the only person who sits next to you at a movie premiere, and the last person you fall in love with."

Crying, Nerissa looked him in the face and said, "No. You need to run."

Baffled, Sideeq frowned—then turned to see a hooded man walking towards him. His face was half-covered with a black bandanna, but Sideeq could tell from the man's black gloves and stature that it was Gobbler. He was flanked by two other boys who Sideeq didn't recognise.

Pushing Sideeq, Nerissa urged him to run in the opposite direction, but he wouldn't move. He simply smirked with his signature half-curve smile and said, "I'm done running."

Either way it wouldn't have made a difference, as Hassan and Squingy approached from behind him. They were accompanied by the young school boy with the uncombed afro. It was at this point Sideeq realised why the boy had looked so familiar. He face was a lot thinner, but the abnormal jaw was still there. Sideeq thought it must have been a family trait because there was no denying the boy's resemblance to Gobbler. He grinned at Sideeq, sniggering like a hyena with its mouth open as the gang slowly started to surround their prey.

"Wha gwan now, pussy?" Gobbler said, stepping forward. He started reaching into the waistband of his denim jeans. "I dun warned you, didn't I? Did you think you could violate man and get away with it?"

Before he could pull out the handgun, Nerissa rushed towards him. She flung herself at Gobbler, pleading.

"Gobbler, no! Please, no!" she begged shamelessly, pulling at his hood. "He's not worth it, please!"

"Move." Gobbler shoved her out the way. One of his goons tried to hold her back, but Nerissa swung frantically at the boy, fighting him off. She chased behind Gobbler.

"No, Gobbler. Please. You don't have to do this. Just let him go. I'll do anything you want please. I'm begging you."

Brandishing the gun, Gobbler swung his heavy hand and backhanded her with the pistol. "MOVE!" he yelled, slapping her across the face.

The blow made Nerissa spin and fall to floor with a burst lip. One of the boys laughed, and the sight of Nerissa being dropped triggered Sideeq into action. Without fear, he charged straight at Gobbler. Panicking, Gobbler tried to cock the weapon, but it was too late. Sideeq landed a swooping right hand. It knocked Gobbler into one of the boys, and Sideeq followed through with a sweet left.

It was like the party all over again, only this time, Gobbler's gang swarmed in to defend him. The third boy punched Sideeq in the side of the head, knocking off his hearing aid. Sideeq stretched out his long leg and booted the boy in the stomach. He was still intent on getting hold of Gobbler, who clambered to get off the floor. He pointed the gun at Sideeq, squeezing the trigger.

For a split second, Sideeq though he was a dead man—but to everyone's surprise, the gun jammed. Gobbler squeezed again and again, but got nothing. Lucky for him, Hassan fly-kicked Sideeq in the back. The power of the kick sent Sideeq flying forward. Losing his balance, he stumbled a few feet before someone hit him in his side. The first blow felt like a punch, but by the third and fourth he couldn't tell the difference. He crashed to floor, feeling something sharp in his back. It definitely wasn't a punch. It pierced his skin making him gasp as he took another shot to the ribs. Suddenly he couldn't breathe, and rolled onto his back.

The gang pounced on him like savages, violently stomping away with no mercy. They rained down blows on Sideeq in a frenzied attack, pushing and shoving each other trying to land a strike wherever they could. By the time Squingy stabbed Sideeq above his collar bone, his whole defence was destroyed. He lay on the ground struggling to breathe as he absorbed every kick. Their muffled voices echoed in his burst eardrums, and above them all he could hear was Nerissa screaming. She yelled for help, wailing for them to stop. When they didn't, her wailing just became a constant scream that rang in his ears. Suddenly the kicking stopped and he received a last boot to the face. He gathered it was from Gobbler, but he wondered which of them spat on him.

Lying on the concrete path, Sideeq felt the rubber grip handle of the knife lodged in his side. His top was soaking wet, and blood leaked from each of his wounds. Shivering, he tried to focus on breathing, but with every breath he could feel the

blood pouring into his lungs. It caused him to cough, and drop-
lets spurted from his mouth.

He looked up, confused. He had no idea when Nerissa's
screams had morphed into Kyle's, but he was certain they were
Kyle's now. He reached out his hand to the figure that stood
above him.

*

Crying, Kyle dropped to his knees. As Sharkey roared into the
estate, he hadn't even waited for the car to stop. He jumped
straight out, racing to where Gobbler and his gang jostled around
Sideeq in a huddle. Tripping over his own feet, Kyle had dropped
his backpack. Running towards the walkway he began screaming
and yelling, which brought more attention. Immediately Gobbler
and his friends had begun to run. They scattered like roaches,
fleeing toward the other side of the estate. There were at least five
of them, and two boys in school uniform running behind the
pack. He watched their black blazers darting between two parked
cars as they raced off. On the other side of the street, Kyle saw
Nerissa run in the opposite direction.

Shaking, he reached down and grabbed hold of Sideeq's
blood-stained hand.

"HELP!" Kyle screamed, crumpling to the ground and
cradling Sideeq's head in his lap. "Somebody help." Tears
streamed down Kyle's face as Sideeq put both their hands on the
grip of the knife.

"Out," he said in a gargled whisper. He urged Kyle to pull the blade from his side. "Take it out"

"No!" Danny yelled, holding Kyle's backpack. "He'll bleed out faster."

"What do I do?" Kyle looked towards Sharkey. "What do I do?"

"Talk to him," Sharkey said softly, approaching with Swank. He was already on his phone, calling the emergency services. "Keep him talking til the ambulance gets here."

"Did you hear that, Sid?" Kyle began to rock gently back and forth with Sideeq's head in the crook of his arm. "The ambulance is on its way, bro. So you gotta hang in there for me, bro. Just hang in."

Smiling, Sideeq squeezed Kyle's hand. Extending a finger, he pointed to the UDC emblem on Kyle's jumper.

"Ahh you see that, yeah?" Kyle looked down, wiping blood from Sideeq's mouth. "They came last night, a whole box of them. Hats, tee, jumpers, everything." He signalled to Danny to pass him the samples. Quickly, Danny pulled out Sideeq's hoodie and cap.

"Look, look." Kyle showed the Sideeq the samples. "What did I say? What did I tell you?" He balanced the cap on Sideeq head. "I told you we was gonna have our clothing line, didn't I? Three months, that's what I said."

Coughing up blood, Sideeq gripped the jumper, trying to smile. He pulled Kyle closer, struggling to breathing.

"See that there, bro?" Kyle held Sideeq's hand. "That's all you, that's your design. Just like you said, just like in the lyrics."

"Ah huh," Sideeq groaned. He started panting fast.

"You remember?" Kyle tried to stop him from panicking. "Tell me how it went." Softly, he began to recite Sideeq's lyrics. "*Gonna have a label, gonna have cash, gonna have wife with a big phat gash, gonna do clothing, gonna do art, gonna do music that comes from the heart. Gonna be big, you're gonna know my name, gonna know my dream coz I ain't the same. I'm a hardcore G. Bare man can look like but could never be.*"

When Kyle finished the lyric, he could hear the sound of sirens blaring in the distance. But it was too late. Sideeq had already slipped away.

Looking down, he kissed Sideeq's limp hand. It was still clutching his UDC top, staining Rizla's white silhouette with his blood. Tenderly, Kyle lay the jumper across Sideeq's chest. Crying, his own chest heaved up and down as he tried to hold back the tears.

Whispering to God, he closed Sideeq's eyes and waited.

EPILOGUE

Kyle's eye was drawn to the framed nautical map of Barbados that hung on the wall behind Mansfield's head. Throughout his interview, he had used the golden brown chart to settle his nerves. From where he sat, he couldn't read the minute compass markings or the thin guiding longitude and latitude lines, but they reminded him of the interview techniques his former tutor, Mr Tulloch, had once taught him in an employability workshop.

"When your interviewer asks you a question, don't rush to answer. Take your time. Try to apply the STAR method, and speak with confidence," Mr Tulloch had advised.

At the time, Kyle had thought that was easy for his teacher to say. Mr Tulloch always spoke with a sharp assurance. The tall, dark skinned man with a goatee beard and long dreadlocks pulled back into a ponytail bared a slight resemblance to the rapper Snoop Dogg. This might have added to Kyle's idea of him having been by far the coolest of the teachers at his school. His teaching style was so unorthodox at times it felt like he was freestyling his way through lessons. At the front of the class, he would casually sit on the corner of his desk as if it was a wall on some street corner. With one foot swinging, he would teach like he was one of the older heads holding court. Simply passing on some jewels of wisdom and sharing opinions amongst friends. It's what made his class memorable, and easy for Kyle to recall years later.

"If you get nervous in an interview, try not to fidget. Instead, try being subtle. Look around the room and find something directly behind your interviewer's head to focus and settle your sight on. This way it will give the impression you are always looking and speaking directly to them."

Another technique Mr Tulloch had taught Kyle, knowing that his student didn't respond well to being questioned, was, "Learn to read the room. Work out what it can tell you about the person or persons interviewing you. Do they have a family picture on their desk? Do they drink out of a favourite sports mug? Is their office very clinical and corporate? Reading the room may help you feel more comfortable in telling the interviewer about yourself. You can conjure up a mental image of the person you are speaking to or want to speak to. But most importantly, you need to remember this—it is your attitude, not your aptitude, that will determine your altitude. If you walk in there believing you are the ideal candidate, the interviewer will see that. However, if you walk in believing something else, they will see that, too."

Mr Tulloch's words had resonated with Kyle. With every interview he had honed the skill of reading the room, and today he continued to settle his nerves by finding the map behind Mansfield's head. At first he had wondered what significance the Caribbean island held to the barrister, then when he saw two red Mount Gay Rum baseball caps encased in a glass display case. Beneath them, there was a picture of Mansfield in his forties. He stood on a yacht in the second row of a regatta crew. Each man wore an identical red Mount Gay winners caps and held a bottle of champagne in their hand. It was this that had given Kyle the confidence to tell his story. He imagined that Mansfield was not only a leader, but a man who knew the value of friends.

When Kyle finished speaking, he looked across the table to the old white man who sat before him. Removing his glasses, Mansfield closed his eyes and bowed his head. Sighing, he pinched the bridge of his nose and remained silent. Kyle could see he was visibly touched, perhaps even fatigued. Throughout, he had listened attentively to Kyle's blow-for-blow account, never once stopping to interrupt or ask questions. The barrister had just sat silently and listened. From time to time he would play with the signet ring on his little finger, or wring his hands, groaning with frustration. Occasionally, he scowled and Kyle pondered how many cases had he heard and made the same facial gestures. At which point did he become desensitised, or was criminal law like a safari to him where each case gave him a chance to explore the underworld of the big game hunters and urban beasts?

Sitting up, Mansfield reached for his cooler. Pouring out some water, he topped up his glass then offered to pour for Kyle. Graciously, Kyle declined.

"Well, Mr Jones, I don't really know what to say."

"There's nothing to say," Kyle replied in a matter of fact manner. "It is what it is."

"Hmm," Mansfield murmured. "Perhaps," he said noticing Kyle's blunt lack of emotion. "Nevertheless, it a very tragic story and I empathise with your loss."

Watching Kyle, Mansfield took a sip of his water. "I guess this experience had very profound effect on you. Would you say this single event became your inspiration to study law?"

For a split second Kyle sniggered, forgetting he was being interviewed.

"I don't know whether I would use the word *inspiration*. I'd prefer to use catalyst, sir."

Mansfield raised an eyebrow. "Interesting." He sat back in his chair. "Would you care to elaborate?"

Kyle didn't, and he shifted in his seat. He hadn't expected to divulge so much in this interview. Asking him to elaborate now was like opening a Pandora's box of hurt and pain. He wanted to tell Mansfield about how incensed he felt when the police refused to let him go in the ambulance with Sideeq. Or the rage that consumed him as they took him into custody, locking him in a cell to await questioning even when they knew he wasn't one of the perpetrators. He could also elaborate on the amount of time they spent quizzing him again and again, giving Gobbler and his friends time to dispose of evidence and blood-stained clothing. Better yet, perhaps he should elaborate on the shame he felt when he first saw Valerie and she asked him what happened. He could detail the way she held him to her bosom, stroking his head to comfort him as he turned into a snivelling wreck. All the while knowing he should be the one comforting her. How about the fear he had of being labelled a snitch when her legal team told him that he would need to give evidence in court. Or the disgust he had for himself for actually thinking, *how would going to court affect his music career?*

Yes he could elaborate on the self-loathing he hid giving the eulogy at Sideeq's funeral. He could describe the weight of Sideeq's coffin as they carried it to his burial site, or the dark brown soil that dirtied his shoes. He couldn't forget the whiff of its damp smell as he helped shovel earth into the grave. Nor the guilt he felt every time somebody hugged him and said how brave he was. *Not brave enough to swallow his own pride,* he would tell himself. If he had perhaps tried to apologise to Sid earlier that fatal day, he might have been able to save his friend. He bet Mansfield didn't want to hear that. How he had blamed himself for not looking out enough for Sideeq. How it led to a slow depression that cloaked him in a morose darkness for months. One where on most days he refused to get out his bed, then on the days he did, he sat in his room staring at the walls. Had it not been for his friends Sharkey, Danny and Swank lifting him out of despair, he may not have found out what it meant to be an Ugly Dog. He may have never contacted Sanusi from Art Meets Culture. Who then, with Mr Ghodstinat's help, assisted him to curate a solo exhibition in Sideeq's honour.

Dressing the entire gallery in Sideeq's artwork, they created a sports-shop inspired instillation. Inside it, they displayed each of Sideeq's customise painted trainers. With the support of the 2AM girls and Reload FM, the three-day exhibition was sold out. With hoards of teenagers coming to pay their respect, it didn't take long for the exhibition to go viral. Images of people posing by Sideeq's artwork were tagged online with hashtag #RIPDeafEye1.

By the third night the gallery was filled to capacity. People of all ages mingled both inside and out as Sharkey and Touch

One played music. Inside the gallery there was a small of range of U.D.C. tops and baseball caps available for sale. Danny and Swank also took orders for two limited edition Deafeye 1 T-Shirt designs.

For many this was their first art exhibition, and they cheered as two pairs of Sideeq's custom trainers were auctioned to the highest bidder. Amazingly, the auction was cut short when Mr Ghodstinat got a call from an anonymous buyer who bought the rest of the customised collection. The closing night was one of healing. All the proceeds raised were given to Valerie to help pay the cost of Sideeq's funeral. Taking the microphone, she gave a passionate speech thanking everyone for attending.

"I can't express how much this means to me. To see my son's art hanging on the walls of this gallery makes me so, so proud. This was one of Sideeq's biggest dreams, and I know he is with his brother and the Lord now, smiling down on us."

Tearfully, Valerie challenged *'you youngsters'* as she called them. "You need to find a way to stop the violence. Stop the stabbings. Stop senselessly killing one another. Cah when you take someone's life…" She pounded on her chest. "It's not just that one person you murder. You murder a mother's hope, you murder somebody's dream, you murder a family's future, and sometimes you murder yourself. Cah if the police don't get you, karma and guilt will."

Valerie went on to say that she believed each one of them had the power to change the narrative of young black men. "Justice is coming for those who murdered my son, but don't let his death be in vain. If you want to show your respect, learn from it. Ask yourself, what will your legacy be?"

Emotions were high and tears were in free flow as the audience applauded Valerie. Finally, she invited them all to join her and Sideeq's friends on a vigil after the exhibition. Embracing Kyle, she kissed him lovingly before handing over the mic.

Kyle tried to hold it together. His hand shook as he opened with a short speech using his UGLY DOGS acronym (*U Gotta Love Yourself Den Others Gone See*) then he signalled for Sharkey to play the music. The crowd fell quiet as he performed a tribute to his best friend. The eerie song, with its ballad-like instrumental, was a heartfelt dialogue between Kyle and his lost friend. It detailed some of their boyhood conversations about girls, video games and art. Opening up, he apologised for the fight they had the night before he died, and baring his heartache on the track, Kyle had said his last goodbye. Hauntingly, he finished the song using its title and expressing that 'Uglydogs Don't Cry'.

Sitting in his chair now, Kyle wondered whether Mansfield wanted him to elaborate on that. Or how those who went on to attend the vigil gathered to light candles at the spot Sideeq died.

Looking at the nautical map behind Mansfield's head, Kyle refocused his thoughts. Assuming a poker face of professionalism, he smiled, thinking about his answer.

"Well, Mr Mansfield," he began, shifting in his chair. "My journey into law is no different from that of any explorer at sea." He grinned, using Mr Tulloch's advice. "Yes, I had plotted a course and set sail, but like any captain that finds new land, do you credit the storm for your discovery, or do accept your ability to adapt?"

Surprised, Mansfield raised another eyebrow. He tried not to smile, but Kyle already knew his analogy had caught Mansfield's attention. Speaking in a soft and inviting manner, he continued.

"The events of my friend's death were definitely a catalyst, like any storm. After completing my A-levels, I had no intention of studying music at university. In fact, if I tell the truth I had lost all passion for music. However, a combination of my experiences within and around the judicial system pushed me towards law. During the trial, I didn't like how I was treated and I didn't like what I saw."

Kyle remembered taking the witness stand in the first trial. Giving evidence, he had been asked to point out the assailant he saw running away. Raising his finger, he pointed towards the dock where Gobbler and his friends glared at him. When their hour-long mean mugging and slitting his throat signs had no affect, they had joked amongst themselves, coughing and heckling under their breath.

Only one boy sat quietly throughout. An outcast, he sat between two guards separated from the other boys. He was the youngest on trial, and it showed. He looked frightened and barely raised his head. Kyle couldn't forget him. He remembered he was the last to run. He recalled Gobbler's younger brother actually dragging the boy by the collar.

The boy had stirred a strange feeling in Kyle. The more he stared at the ground, the more Kyle had felt sorry for him. Once or twice they had even met eyes. Had he not seen the boy running on the day, Kyle would never had believed he had anything to do with Sideeq's murder. However, the image of the two school boys running in their blazers haunted Kyle. It was like a reoccurring nightmare he couldn't escape. Every time he looked down from the public galley he wanted to ask the boy: what were you doing there? Why did you run?

Slowly, the question become internal and he asked himself, "Why did he run?"

He envisioned himself and Sideeq, sprinting through Shepherd's Bush market in their blazers, and it dawned on him. The boy, along with Gobbler's younger brother, echoed a dark reflection of Sideeq and himself. Doppelgangers. The idea disturbed him and he came to the conclusion that when you're a young black boy from the hood, you're either running away from your environment or you're chasing it. There was no middle ground.

"Throughout the trial, Mr Mansfield, many stereotypes were thrown around about me and my friends." Kyle chuckled, shaking his head. "There were more thrown at the defendants. But for the most part, sir, I truly believe that neither the judge, the prosecutor nor the defence team really saw much difference between any of us. To me it seemed like they saw the whole case as something that black boys do. Argue fight and then kill one another over some dumb sh—" Kyle was about to swear, and remembered where he was. Sitting up he stroked the length of his tie. "That's what made me study law. I realised people from my community didn't need another MC. We have plenty of those. And they don't need me reinforcing the idea that the only 'way out'—" Kyle held up his hands and made quotation marks in the air "—is through sports, drugs and entertainment. And they certainly didn't need me to pick up a knife or a gun to go retaliate. So in the end, I realised young men from my community need to change our narratives and steer our way to new land. I want to be an example of that change, and a part of the new narrative."

"Hmmm," Mansfield nodded his head. Impressed, he sat back, seeming in awe of Kyle's delivery. "Well, young man. I will have to tell you this. You have an amazing sense of oratory. One that I could see doing very well at this firm."

Kyle smiled. However, Mansfield returned it with a wary eye.

"Yes," he said, reaching for Kyle's essay. Putting on his glasses, he flicked through the file again. "I also notice you have a shrewd ability to pander to your audience." Swivelling in his chair Mansfield look back at the nautical map and red caps. "The sailing references were a nice touch, but try not to look at your orientations so much."

Kyle gave him another cheeky grin. After another ten minutes, the interview was over. Shaking Mansfield's hand, Kyle said his obligatory pleasantries and thanked the QC for his time. Laying it on thick, he stressed he looked forward to earning the opportunity of working together at some point and would await their call.

Rising to his feet, Mansfield pushed out his bottom lip, pouting like a trout and pinching the waistband on his trousers. "Yes, yes," he said, patting Kyle on the back. "Let's see what life has in store. You certainly impressed me today."

Smiling, he walked Kyle to the door, then stopped as though he had just remembered something. "Ah yes. I have one last question for you before you leave, Mr Jones."

Kyle smiled, gesturing for him to ask.

"What happened to the young lady involved in the case? You never said."

Kyle took a moment. He thought about Nerissa. Her legal team had been savvy enough to get her a separate trial, but that did her no favours. She was almost seven months pregnant when she took the stand, squeezing her belly into a grey pant suit. Weeping, she testified that she knew nothing of the planned attack, yet when questioned admitted she had seen Gobbler the night before. When the prosecution asked if had they been intimate, she said no. To this, the Crown responded by asking her about her texts. He wanted know how she intended to prove she 'loved Gobbler'. Bowing her head, Nerissa replied, "I can't remember", to which even her own barrister fixed her wig and grimaced. When accused of luring Sideeq to be ambushed, Nerissa refuted the claim. Her legal team argued that unbeknown to their client, Gobbler had put a tracking app on her phone. However, after seeing evidence of Gobbler's Facetime call, stating Edwards Woods as the location for the attack, the jury were unconvinced. They deliberated for five hours and returned with a guilty verdict. Feeling a sense of indifference, Kyle had watched Nerissa hysterically pleading her innocence and love for Sideeq. He had the exact same feeling now as he turned to Mansfield.

"What always happens to girls like that," Kyle said. His face was a cold and set like stone. "She became irrelevant."

*

Heading towards the lift, Kyle saw the guy in the black hooded top and gilet still waiting in the lobby. Again, they glanced at each other. However, this time the man nodded his head and tapped his chest with his fist. Recognizing the universal black nod, which let every black person know the other had seen them, Kyle winked. Smiling, he returned the sign of mutual respect and kept it moving.

Leaving Mansfield and Thompson, Kyle decided to walk to the closest Hammersmith & City line station. He could have taken the Central line back to White City, but he was in no rush and decided to take the long way home. He was in a reflective mood as he bounced down the stairs to the platform. He thought the interview, as strange as it was, went well. Knowing he had put his best foot forward, he was eager to hear the outcome.

Boarding the first train, he took the end seat by the glass screen. Fixing his overcoat, he fished out his earphones and mobile. Turning his phone to 1Xtra, he played the last download of One Touch's late night show. Smiling, he listened as the DJ interviewed Trapman Bird, one of the latest artists in Sharkey's management stable. The chemistry between Sharkey and One Touch was still evident, and it reminded him of his first time on radio. Loosening his tie, Kyle closed his eyes. He chuckled to himself as they played Trapman's latest single. Immediately he recognised Danny's production, with its booming electronic baseline and ska sample. It was nice to hear they were still working together. The last time he had seen Danny, he had been driving a black Peugeot van with a huge logo plastered on this side that read 'THE BIG DOG WALKING Co.' Kyle laughed at the originality of the name and Danny told him, "Oi listen, mate, we do exactly what's on the tin—or the van, in this case."

Danny asked after Swank, and Kyle told him she was working out in Brazil. She had landed a job teaching art at an outreach centre in Rio that work with favela kids. Thinking about Swank, Kyle went onto her Instagram page. As the train weaved its way through the city's dark underground tunnels, he scrolled down her page, browsing. Looking at all the pictures, he couldn't help feeling envious. Swank looked like she was living the life, surrounded by beautiful women, street food and art.

He stopped to study a collection of pictures in one post. It showed Swank with a bunch of kids, painting on old pairs of shoes. Staring at the screen, Kyle swiped left to reveal the second still. It showed all the shoes hanging from an electrical line high, above the corrugated rooftops. Each was elaborately decorated and bared a name: Rufio, Dadinho, Eleuza, Bené… and Sideeq. Underneath the picture the post the read,

It's been six years now and I still miss your smile. You had the most beautiful soul. Rest in eternal peace my beloved friend. Nuff love Sid aka @Deafeye1 #UDC4life #UGLYDOGS-DONTCRY!!!

It reminded him of the night of the vigil. After the exhibition, Swank had done the same thing—throwing up customised shoes over the phone wires with the words *Justice 4 Sideeq* and *RIP DE1* painted on them. Those who were there cheered, posting the images of the dangling trainers on social media. A reporter who attended the night did a piece in the Evening Standard on Sideeq's death. The trainers, along with his art, became a symbol of youth violence and tragedy. Ever since then, on the anniversary of his death a small following of his fans threw up trainers all over the world. It also amazed Kyle, and warmed his heart, to know that there were people out there who knew Sideeq's story. He considered his friend, in life and death, a true artist.

Exiting the city tunnels, Kyle's westbound train journeyed further down the Hammersmith & City line. As it travelled past the burnt-out skeleton of Grenfell Tower, he peered up from his phone.

Gazing at the large green heart-shaped emblem on the building's protective wrap, he thought, *'Wow, another one of West London's famous tragedies.'*

Watching the green heart slowly disappear, Kyle wondered how many dreams had died on that fatal night, and couldn't help but think of the one he had once shared with Sideeq. Approaching his stop, he stood up, realising that dream was now gone. Saddened, he looked around the carriage when suddenly he noticed a young teenage girl chatting away on her phone.

Stepping off the train he smiled at the design on her Ugly Dog hoodie.

Acknowledgements

First and foremost I would like to thank Allah the most merciful and beneficial for whom nothing is impossible. I would also like to thank Valerie Brandes, for bestowing me with such a massive opportunity. It is truly an honour to be selected as one of the Twenty in 2020 writers. I hope I've done you justice. Big shout out to Jazz, Mags and the whole Jacaranda team for their patience and diligence in bringing this project to life. You are all amazing! Also special thanks to my editor Sareeta Domingo. A super nod to Chris, Annie and all the staff at London Library for creating such a creative haven for writers. As always nuff love to my writing brother Courttia Newland, for I stand on your shoulders.

Salute to my Godbrother Leon who kicked me out of the 'Man Dem group chat' till I finished my work. Big up my brothers Lapo Reg, Beth and Dizzman for the support. To Lynsey at TeamYellow. Rona & John at Platform 10. Shout out to Craig and Topps at Castletown Arts. Big G O'Flaherty and Big Des! To the Spit Gang and all the heads at Baker Street. To my big sis Belinda Goodin who let me camp out in her office. Thank you for inviting me back year after year to work with the boys on your Black Excellence scheme. Their need to see themselves in British literature inspired me to write this book. Special thanks to my London Irish sis Ms Roisin Fleming. I'm very proud of your journey over the last year. To my boy Triggs come home soon. To my entire family Mum, Hill, Uncle T, Marky, Troy, Steve, Minny, Thai, TJ, Lott, Liss, Caleb, Romy, Miami… wait wait wait I'm not going through the whole list. To everyone I didn't mention you know what it is. Lastly and not least to my Super Son Ni, love you fella.

About the Author

DD Armstrong is a British author, playwright and international educator who earned a MA in Stage & Screenwriting after winning a scholarship from Regents University. He is also a script consultant who has worked at the BBC Writersroom and his portfolio includes consulting for a number of British feature films including *The Intent* and *Adulthood*.

The creator of *The Beyond Words Anthology & Educational Courses* DD is known for tackling tough and contemporary issues in his writing and work. He also teaches self-development through creative writing to both young people and prisoners in the UK and the United States.